Left in His Closet

Left in His Closet

Mary A. Krome

TATE PUBLISHING & *Enterprises*

Published by Tate Publishing & Enterprises, LLC
127 E. Trade Center Terrace | Mustang, Oklahoma 73064 USA
1.888.361.9473 | www.tatepublishing.com

Tate Publishing is committed to excellence in the publishing industry. The company reflects the philosophy established by the founders, based on Psalm 68:11,
"The Lord gave the word and great was the company of those who published it."

Book design copyright © 2010 by Tate Publishing, LLC. All rights reserved.
Cover design by Blake Brasor and Mary Krome
Interior design by Stephanie Woloszyn

Published in the United States of America

ISBN: 978-1-61566-153-4
1. Fiction / General   2. Fiction / Gay
10.01.05

To Theresa

"When the dust settles and the pages of history are written, it will not be the angry defenders of intolerance who have made the difference. The reward will go to those who dared to step outside the safety of their privacy in order to expose and rout the prevailing prejudices."

—*John Shelby Spong, Episcopal Bishop*

Coping

2009

Witness

I see Soledad at the funeral twelve years after they were murdered. Her deliberate and graceful movement toward the body of the man lying in the coffin hypnotizes me, exposing me to the commanding presence of the woman who used to be my brother's wife. I smile at the tall, lean figure donned in a simple, stylish black dress, thrilled that she is able to be with us tonight, the way she used to be. Yet, concealed within the warm eyes smiling back at me is something else, something that only someone who knew her so long ago would be able to see. The thick glaze of her smile has been scraped away by murder, a massacre that outlives the three billion seconds since I last saw her.

· · · · ·

The motive was a mystery as thick as the damp air that hung over her. We were at her cousin's wedding reception. My brother, Bob, sat at the head table with nothing in front of him but dirty dishes as Soledad gracefully glided her way through the crowd, ignoring his eyes boring through her back. Her edginess was shrouded with a tongue of silk and lace as she moved from table to table, chatting with her relatives. But its sharpness lay in waiting, beneath the stiffness of her courteous words, ready to articulately slash their way through anyone attempting to expose her pain. That's how she made it through that dreadful night when their life unraveled into a yarn right in front of my eyes, the second I defended my brother.

It all began when Soledad approached the table where Barb and I were sitting with my brother. Before she could sit down, Bob fired a few sharp words at her. I couldn't make out what he said, but I knew from his tone that something was amiss. Soledad's eyes shifted back and forth between Barb and me as she cupped the palm of her hand around her mouth and whispered back what seemed to be a warning. Bob folded his arms across his chest and touted her with the shifting of his eyes back and forth between Barb and me.

Soledad was smart. She didn't take the bait. "Later," I heard her mumble as she scanned the darkened ballroom. The chairs were empty, except for those around the table next to us where a handful of her relatives remained nursing their drinks. She curved her lips into a half smile and asked my sister where she got the flowers in her hair.

Barb told Soledad, "I was walking back to the table when I was knocked into the wall by a flying bouquet attached to someone's arm. The woman didn't hurt me," my sister reassured her, "but she felt so bad she offered me the bouquet. When I wouldn't take it, she insisted on decorating my hair with these flowers."

Soledad's smile snapped into a sneer as Bob's hand brushed across her back and came to rest on her left shoulder. She moved to the edge of the chair so quickly that my brother's hand fell onto the back of the chair. I had never seen her do anything like this before. Bob's response was equally unusual. He put his weight on the back legs of the chair and shrugged at me smugly.

"Don't look at him as if I don't have a right to be upset," Soledad sprayed in his ear. The tone of her whisper sharpened to a rasp as my brother fired a haughty glare at her. "I've put up with your nonsense for the entire day," she seethed. "Now you have the nerve to sit here and pretend to be something you're not. But you're not fooling me. I know how disgusting, mean, vile—"

"Hey, hey, hey," I interrupted. "This is my brother you're talking about."

Soledad swung her head toward me but held her rebuttal back as laughter rang from the table next to us. She gave me a firm but polite warning, "You don't know anything about this so please, Kenny, stay out of it."

Barb, in her usual overly helpful way, jumped in to defend my brother.

"Don't start in on me too, Miss Barbie doll," Soledad snapped at my sister.

That's when I lost it. Pressing my palms firmly into the center of the table, I shot out of the chair. "Don't you dare talk to my sister like that," I screamed in her face.

Before I realized what I did, I heard the legs of the chairs at the table next to us scratch the floor in unison. What followed was the thunderous slap of an army of shiny shoes marching toward me. The buttons of my shirt were gathered around my neck, and I was hoisted from the ground by one of Soledad's cousins. A circle of her relatives formed around us as he suggested firmly and politely that I leave.

Bob described the events of the day as Barb and I drove him home. He told us they had a fight when Soledad came home from a business trip. He blamed himself for it, but he wouldn't tell us what he had done. The certainty of his words, "There's nothing anyone can do about it," hung in the night air like dew.

I wasn't mad anymore. I was scared. I knew I had witnessed something I didn't understand. All I knew was that it was the beginning of the end of their relationship. It was portrayed in the electric shock of Soledad's persona and in what belied my brother's story. I knew my brother had led her to the edge, offering her the frayed end of the fabric of everything that held them together. As soon as I stood up to defend him, I gave her the opportunity to pull it. And she did. What followed, I am sorry to say, was the unraveling of a sacred treasure, a marriage that all of us believed to be indestructible.

• • • • •

That was the last time I saw Soledad. Her erect pose at the coffin tonight doesn't reveal anything about our altercation that night, but the coldness still swimming in her sapphire eyes reflects her surrender long ago to something beyond her own endurance. She has lost the battle for the dignity of an existence that no one seems to care about except her. And yet tonight, she has no choice but to fling it out of my brother's closet and onto the funeral parlor floor. Something in her bones pushes her toward me. There isn't anything left for me to say except, "I'm sorry."

My Life Is a Movie

My daughter won't forget about her first husband even though she has been remarried for the last five years. Her obsession has less to do with love than circumstance. You see, Nita's ex-husband left her for, you know, someone other than a woman.

The thought of it still makes me shiver. I don't understand how anyone would prefer to be that way when my daughter has everything any man would ever want. She's a beautiful young lady who works full time at the college bookstore so she can get her degree at one of the best universities in the country. She has all A's, except in the two courses she took the year she divorced Jim. She burns the midnight oil so she won't deprive our grandson of a good dinner, a nightly bedtime story, and a Saturday afternoon at the park. I used to worry about all the boys who wanted to go out with her in high school. Now I worry more about her not getting enough from the two husbands in her life.

Nita still talks about Jim, the first one, but I cannot stand to hear the name of the man whose life in the closet stripped my daughter of her honor. Her mother is more patient than I am. She encourages our daughter to get on with her life. After all, what does Nita gain by dwelling on something she can't change?

Nita left our house a few minutes ago in a huff because she thinks we don't care to know what she went through when Jim divorced her. She claims we are being insensitive to how much his lifestyle has bled into her life. But she's wrong. We know she hasn't been the same since it happened. We just don't know what to do.

· · · · ·

Nita arrived at our house earlier tonight for the dinner Ana prepares every Friday for our children. Eric, her second husband, didn't come, as usual. I was on my way down the back stairs when I heard

Ana scolding Nita about the critique she wrote for her film class on the circumstances of her divorce. I stopped at the top of the stairs as I heard Nita protest loudly. "It's not as if I'm going on a talk show, Mom. It's only a critique about the treatment of spouses of men who come out of the closet. Take *Birdcage* for example—"

"I haven't seen it," Ana interrupted her.

"Well I have," Nita told her mother. "The mother is portrayed as an uncaring, professional woman who only had sex so a gay man could have her child."

"Comedies are not supposed to be taken literally," Ana explained to our daughter.

"It's not only *Birdcage*," Nita snapped back. "Most movies about coming out don't deal with the spouse. That's why they get it wrong. Characterizing the two wives in *Brokeback Mountain* as frumpy and sexually aggressive oversimplifies the relationship these women have had with their husbands. In this one," she held up the DVD case of *In and Out*, "a woman has a tirade at a bar when she finds out her fiancé is gay. No one who has been through what I have would react the way she does to the news that the man she has been sleeping with prefers to have sex with men."

Ana must have heard my footstep creaking on the landing above the kitchen because she whispered sharply, "Hush Nita, your father will hear you."

"You can stand at the top of the stairs for as long as you want, Dad," Nita shouted up the stairs to me. "It won't change the fact that it happened to your daughter."

"It happened five years ago, honey. Let it go," Ana told Nita. I heard her shoes click across the tile and the cutting board slide out from the counter. "I don't have time to talk about this now, honey. Your sister will be here any minute."

"She's always late," Nita muttered. The sound of a knife chopping and the smell of onions wafted up the stairs as our daughter continued her critique. "Most of these movies fail to capture the impact on spouses because they look at the experience from the outside in, instead of from the inside out. You see, Mom, the betrayal that knocked me off my feet isn't any less real because we are more politically correct about it. As a matter of fact, the political correctness that has made it easier for Jim has made it harder for me."

The dicing of the onion stopped. "I know it's been hard for you, honey," Ana admitted. "Thank God it's over now. Why don't you help me set the table?"

"Don't patronize me, Mom!" Nita exclaimed. "Most people think I'm not supposed to be skittish about men like Jim because of their homosexual preferences. This is a good thing in general, but when it's your husband, it's too close for me not to be skittish."

I could feel rage toward Jim rising from my gut. I walked back into the bedroom and sat on the edge of the bed, flipping through the channels until my feelings settled back into place. On my way down to the kitchen, I stopped again at the top of the stairs. I couldn't make out the conversation, but I could hear the ruffling of pages slapping against each other followed by our daughter's voice shouting, "I thought you and Dad would be more interested in this."

"Your father won't read this," Ana scolded.

"But you will," Nita pleaded.

"It's for an audience, a special group of people with a unique problem," Ana whispered harshly.

"You don't have to whisper."

"Why are you dwelling on this, honey?" Ana asked our daughter.

"Because no one else will," Nita barked. Her voice softened when she added, "Come on, Mom. You always read my papers."

I heard the garbage pail swing open to Ana's words, "Throw it away, honey. It's the only way to get past this."

The tension between Ana and Nita crept up the back stairs at the same time laughter from the living room rang up the front stairs. "Your son is out there watching television with your brother," Ana reminded Nita. "Do you want him to know about his father?"

"I'm not talking about his father. I'm writing about my life," she corrected.

I heard Ana whisper, "Do you want José to know?"

"Of course I don't, Mom. He's too young to know he has a gay parent."

"Did I hear you say you are gay?" Ned asked Nita as he walked into the kitchen.

"Don't be silly," Ana barked at him. "Where's José?"

"He's watching television. Hi, Mom," Nikki said. "Who's gay?"

"Nita is," Ned chuckled.

"I can't wait for Dad to hear this one," Nikki laughed loudly.

Nikki's raspy laugh ringing through the kitchen was silenced by Nita's growl. "That's not funny."

"Why didn't you tell me?" Ned teased her.

"Stop it!" Nita shouted.

"Leave it alone," Ana warned our son.

"I don't want *it* to be left alone," Nita exclaimed. "I want you to hear me."

"I've been listening, honey," Ana defended herself.

"You haven't heard a single word I've said," Nita snapped back. "All you do is shut me up, make fun of me, or hide from me," her voice traveled up the stairs to me. I saw her arm reach for two coats on the hooks at the bottom of the stairs. "I've had it with all of you."

"Nita, don't leave," Nikki's voice traveled into the living room with the sound of Nita's footsteps.

"I didn't mean it," Ned added.

"You never do," Nita scowled.

Ana's voice could be heard echoing up the front stairs. "What does Eric say about this?"

"We don't talk about it," Nita muttered.

"It's a good rule to follow," Ana insisted.

"For whom?" Nita snapped back. "Come on, José. We're going home."

LEFT IN HIS CLOSET

I heard José plead with his mother to stay, but Nita wouldn't listen. Ana tried to reason with her, but Nita was too mad to listen. My heart rushed down the stairs, but my feet were stuck like glue to the carpet. I stood at the top of the stairs as helpless as a mannequin as our daughter stormed out the front door with our grandson.

"Why did you have to set your sister off?" Ana scolded Ned.

"Don't blame me, Mom!" Ned exclaimed. "No one has ever told me Jim was gay."

Give It a Rest

I love my mother, but I hate what she does. She is Dr. Judy Clark, Distinguished Professor of Social Sciences and director of the Out of the Closet Research Center. She has written numerous books about the impact on the families of gays and lesbians who have come out of the closet.

I do not support what she does because of what it had done to us. I don't like that Mom has publicly admitted my sister and I have a gay parent. I don't like that our family life was shattered when my parents divorced in 1985, or that we didn't discover the real reason for their divorce until five years ago. Worst of all, I don't like how it has affected my mother.

When I heard about the latest development in our family saga yesterday, I called my sister in Boston. We drove down to the Drake Hotel in Chicago after her flight arrived at O'Hare. We entered the lobby as my mother was returning from the conference center after exposing our life to a bunch of academics at her annual research colloquium.

"Well, well, look who's here," my mother exclaimed as she gave Kim a hug. "You haven't given me a hug like that in a long time, honey," she noticed as I squeezed her tightly. "What's up?"

"We came here to—" I started to explain to Mom when Kim interrupted, giving me a look of caution, "to surprise you."

"Did your sister have to twist your arm to get you here?" Mom teased me.

"Actually, it was Jerry's idea," Kim explained.

"We wanted to spend the weekend with you, Mom. You know, just the three of us out on the town, the way we used to," I suggested.

"We haven't done Chicago together for a long time," Kim added.

Her smile was enough to know that she liked the idea, but she said it anyway. "That's a great idea." She looks at her watch and says, "Oh dear, it's after four and I was on my way to meet Paul. Let's have dinner tonight. Since I'm free all day tomorrow, we can—what did you say—do Chicago together."

I took her hand and said, "We need to talk to you, Mom."

"What's wrong, Jerry?"

"Everyone's fine," Kim reassured Mom. "It's—" she began as the voice of a woman bellowed at our mother, "It ain't right!"

I positioned myself between my mother and this woman. "I won't hurt your mother," the woman tried to reassure me. "I want to know why she wants people to know that this sin runs in your family."

"Please go away," I told her.

Mom touched my arm and said to the woman, "We can talk on the way to the elevator."

I relaxed a bit when she seemed appreciative of my mother's time. "Being homosexual," she began, "isn't any different than being mentally challenged. We don't encourage those who catch on to things slower than I do to stay that way just because they can't help it. We work with them to improve their mental capacity so they can be more effective in the things they do. It's the same for homosexuality," she continued. "Maybe people who are gay can't help being that way, but we shouldn't encourage them to stay that way. We should work with them to direct their interest toward sexual activities between men and women."

She held my attention until she said, "You'd do a lot more good, Dr. Clark, if you focused on your sinful behavior instead of on other people." The woman's words, "Only a lesbian would tell people it is okay for their loved ones to be gay," echoed through the lobby as the elevator door closed between us.

I was livid as the elevator began to rise. "This has gone too far," I told Mom.

"Relax, Jerry," she replied. "The only reason that woman said what she did is because someone in her family is gay."

"How do you know?" I demanded.

"Experience," she fired back.

"Why are you defending her?" I barked.

"She needs me," Mom insisted.

Kim stepped in, as usual, to soften my words. "What Jerry means is we want to know how you keep going when people hate you for exposing a reality of our world that they don't believe in."

Mom glared at me as she replied, "I wouldn't be much of a person if I let one angry woman stop me from doing what needs to be done."

"It's getting out of hand," I insisted.

"It's just getting started," she corrected me. "That woman isn't any different than anyone else who comes here to make sense of what has happened to them. She's probably reacting to the discovery of someone in her family being gay. Now she's in the same psychic wilderness you were in when you found out, without a roadmap to guide her through it."

"I know why you do it, Mom," I told her, "but I don't like what it's done to you."

She crinkled her brow at me. "Do you really want me to tell these people I can't help them anymore?"

"It's for your own good," I replied.

"If you came here to scold me, you can turn around right now and go back home," she barked. "I won't have my son handling me."

"Stop it, both of you!" Kim scolded. "Let's not forget why we're here."

"Why are you here?" Mom glared at me.

I turned my eyes to the floor as the elevator door opened. Mom held her head high with her usual stoic pride as she marched passed me out of the elevator and down the hallway.

"We want to talk to you, Mom," Kim insisted.

Mom's huffy voice traveled over her shoulder toward us. "Well I don't!" We followed the imprint of her long heavy stride in the carpet towards her room.

"Don't do this, Mom," I begged as she inserted the key card into the lock and opened the door.

She turned to glare at me. "I didn't do anything. You did," she said sharply before closing the door to her room behind us.

"You better stop picking on her about her work," Kim whispered sharply to me as we stood in the hallway outside mom's room and knocked on the door.

"I wasn't picking on her," I sputtered. "I was—"

"You were picking on her," Kim insisted. "It's about time you start thinking about what she needs from us."

The door opened to mom's sharp words, "You two better stop bickering." I could see Paul sitting on the couch in her suite. She blocked the doorway to keep us out as the tone of her voice softened. "What do you want to talk about?"

I knew she was mad because she refused to look at me until I said, "I ran into Jeffrey yesterday and he told me everything."

It's Never What It's Not

"Most of the people at your party were gay," Soledad reminds Judy.

"Some of them were," Judy corrects.

"Maybe not, but you write about them," Soledad replies.

"I write books about families of gays," Judy explains. "If you write enough books, you get to know a lot of gay people. Sometimes we become friends. Sometimes we don't."

"Aren't you worried about what people will think of you?" Soledad asks.

"Don't be so homophobic."

"I'm not homophobic," Soledad disagrees, "just shy. Shy people like me don't discriminate. We're afraid of everyone." Soledad looks at Judy sourly as she tastes the wine. "Don't drink it," she warns. "It's vinegar." She takes the wine glass out of Judy's hand and tosses the wine down the drain. "I'll be right back," she says and disappears down the back stairs.

Judy slides off the stool at the kitchen counter and strolls around the room, examining all the interesting objects Soledad has collected. An eclectic collection of paintings from various unknown artists is hanging on the walls. Crystal and porcelain are neatly placed in clusters on the fireplace mantle. Unusual paperweights are sitting on top of stacks of news articles on her desk.

Judy is examining a pewter bear with a fish in its mouth when Soledad reappears with a bottle of wine. "Where did you get this?" she asks.

"That paperweight came from Alaska," she explains.

"I didn't know you've been to Alaska."

"It was during my wilderness years," Soledad explains. "Bears line the riverbeds on the Kenai Peninsula, waiting for the salmon to return from their long trek down the Aleutian Islands to Japan. They come back to spawn and die."

"You have so many interesting things from interesting places."

"These things keep my friends alive."

"Alive?" Judy inquires.

"Sure," Soledad replies.

Judy returns to the stool and opens the lid of an appliance on the counter. "That crepe maker was a gift from the couple who lived next door to me in Paris. Every time I use it, I am reminded of the day he made crepes after his wife and I returned from the Montmartre market." She follows Judy's eyes to the wall behind her. "That cuckoo clock is from a photographer I worked with in the Swiss Alps. He set it fifteen minutes fast when he gave it to me because I was always fifteen minutes late for our assignments. And this," she holds up the corkscrew and says, "is from a special night in Platja d'Aro."

"You have way too many friends for someone who claims to be shy." Judy laughs.

"If you travel enough, you meet a lot of interesting people. Sometimes they become my friends. Sometimes they don't," Soledad repeats Judy's earlier words.

"Where did you get this?" Judy asks of the painting on the wall next to her.

"An artist friend, Kenny, painted it for me when my uncle died. It's an oil of Beaver Tail in Jamestown, Rhode Island, where she used to live."

Judy walks over to examine the painting as Soledad uncorks the wine. "Something isn't right."

"You have a good eye," Soledad notices. "My friend knew I liked sailboats, but he didn't know enough about sailing to realize that the boat wouldn't be able to get that close to the rocky tip of the island."

Judy moves to the painting above the fireplace. "I like this one. The woman is very—"

"—mysterious," Soledad finishes as she hands Judy a glass of wine. They stand together in front of the fireplace as Soledad explains, "She's a special creation of a very dear friend I met in Platja d'Aro. And this is my favorite wine from Catalonia." She clicks her glass against Judy's and adds, "Cheers."

Judy tastes the wine. "Wow. This is good stuff."

"The French may be serious about making wine, but the Spaniards are serious about drinking it."

"Would you like to order the wine for my next book party?"

"Sure." Soledad laughs. "Do you always have parties for your books?"

"Only since my father died," Judy explains. "It's a tradition he started. He said he did it for me, but he really wanted to brag about me to his friends. Now I host my own parties. It's as if he is right here with me, egging me on."

"That's sweet." Soledad holds a hand over her heart. "He must have been ahead of his time to be so supportive of gay books."

"He died before I wrote my first book for families of gay people," Judy corrects Soledad again. "He would be very proud of any book I wrote, regardless of the topic."

"Why do you write about gay people?"

Judy sighs. "My book is about—"

"I know what your book is about," Soledad interrupts as they walk back to the kitchen counter. "I want to know why you write them."

Judy eyes Soledad, not sure if she can handle what she is asking to know. "You see." Judy pauses. "A long time ago …" She pauses again. "I was married."

"Why did you stay with him?" Soledad asks curtly.

"Things were different back then." Judy watches Soledad dicing up the chicken. "That looks good. Can I help?"

"I don't think so. I've tasted your cooking." Soledad laughs as she drains the noodles. "What time do you have to be back to work?"

"I have to meet with Nita, my research assistant, at two. We're driving down to the Drake this afternoon for my research colloquium. What about the repair man?"

"He said he'd be here sometime this afternoon, but I don't know when he'll show up. You know how vague they are." Soledad turns on the faucet and washes her hands. "Don't worry. I'll get you back to work on time. All I have to do is mix everything together with my homemade pesto."

"My father used to make pesto. Now I buy it in the store."

"Commercially made pesto is usually mixed with walnuts instead of pine nuts and parsley instead of fresh basil. It keeps the cost down." Soledad opens the freezer and hands a jar to Judy as she brags, "This is the way it is supposed to be made."

"What would I do without a friend like you?"

"Starve to death." Soledad laughs.

"You make it look so easy," Judy replies.

"All I do is follow two simple rules," Soledad explains. "Keep it fresh and don't skimp on the ingredients." She places a scoop of chicken pesto salad in the center of the cooked spinach and arranges fresh sliced tomatoes in a circle around it. She finishes it off with a few sprigs of freshly clipped cilantro. After setting the plate on the placemat in front of Judy, she sits across from her at the counter.

"When do you leave for Providence?" Judy asks.

"Monday," Soledad replies flatly.

"You don't sound very excited," Judy notices. "What's the story?"

"It's nothing. The *Tribune* agreed to do the series I pitched about the preparedness of Chicago metro hospitals for catastrophic events. I was planning to approach it the way I did my September 11 interviews, but the paper wanted to include a parallel, locally-oriented tragedy like *The Station* fire. *The Station* is that nightclub where over a hundred people died when a pyrotechnics show ignited the insulation in the building."

"Weren't you living in Providence at the time?"

"I was in Boston," Soledad corrects. "The fire happened in 2003, right after I returned from Europe and before I moved here. Since I wrote several pieces for *The Globe* about the fire, *The Tribune* wants me to interview the nurses and doctors at Rhode Island Hospital where the victims were taken. It's a decent story." Soledad wrinkles her nose. "I'm just not a fan of Rhode Island."

"At least you'll get to see all the people you used to know."

"I don't have anything in common with anyone who lives there anymore," Soledad mutters while stabbing a piece of chicken with her fork. "When does Jerry open his practice at Boston General Hospital?"

"Next month. It'll be good for him to live near his sister, especially now." Judy sighs and feigns a smile. "I'm really going to miss him."

"I know, Jude." Soledad pats her hand. "You're tight with your kids, especially Jerry."

"It wasn't always like that," Judy explains. "Remember how tense our relationship was when you first moved here."

"I've watched you get closer and closer through the years."

"We have. It's a mother's prerogative to forget the tough times," Judy chuckles. "I'm lucky to have had Jerry living so close to me all these years. Now it's time for him to get close to his sister."

"How is Kim?" Soledad asks.

"She's great, Sole." Judy's eyes light up as she continues. "She loves practicing law, but I knew she hit the glass ceiling when she asked me last month for a copy of a book I wrote in 1971 about women's equality in the workplace. A couple of weeks ago, she told me that it helped her make a career decision. She doesn't feel she can go any further at the law firm and wants more time with my grandchildren. Her husband was just promoted to partner, so the time seems right for her to start her own practice."

"It must be nice to have a doctor and a lawyer in the family. Those of us who aren't so lucky to have successful kids have to pay dearly for their services."

Judy laughs. "At least you have one base covered with Jay."

"If it works out," Soledad interjects.

"What do you mean if?"

Soledad shrugs.

Judy swivels the stool toward Soledad. "Aren't you interested?"

"I am. I think I am. I mean I was." Soledad shakes her head. "He's awfully needy."

"You think Jay, a partner at a prestigious Chicago law firm, is needy!" Judy exclaims.

"I do."

"Why?"

Soledad sets her glass down. "He calls so often that I can't get anything done. When I don't respond, he stops by after work. It's been so bad recently that I won't answer the door."

"Wouldn't it be easier to tell him you don't want him to call as often as he does?"

"If I do that, he'll stop by more often," Soledad predicts.

"What do you expect him to do when you don't take his calls?"

"Give up."

"Why?"

Soledad gives Judy another indifferent shrug as she gets up to rinse the dishes. She opens the dishwasher and begins to stack the dishes in rows by size and type.

"What's with you?" Judy scolds. She picks up the corkscrew and points it at Soledad. "You have all these trinkets from men all over the world, yet you can't find a single one in the Chicago metropolitan area who is good enough for you."

Soledad snatches the corkscrew from Judy's hand. "Who are you to lecture me on relationships when the only ones you have are with your gay research subjects?"

"My research subjects are not gay."

Soledad puts her hand on her hip and crinkles her face at Judy. "You don't believe me, do you?" Judy exclaims.

Soledad folds her hands across her chest and shakes her head no.

"You'd believe me if you came with me to the Drake Hotel tomorrow."

"What for?"

"For an education," Judy retorts. "Paul will be there."

"Is Paul a research subject?"

"Paul and I have known each other for a long time," Judy explains. "I met him when he was visiting Northwestern back in 1980."

"Were you dating him?" Soledad asks.

"I was married at the time." Judy leans over the counter and sighs. "I lost touch with him after he went back to UCLA." She stops to finish the last few drops in the wine glass. "I told you this story before."

"No," Soledad replies.

"Our path crossed five years ago when a grad student asked me to participate in a study on internet dating subcultures. She wanted to demonstrate that electronic dating subcultures could develop and act as screening mechanisms. I fit the profile of someone who, for professional reasons, had a preference for anonymity and didn't want to post my photograph on the website," Judy explains.

"You dated as part of a study," Soledad comments with a snort.

"Paul was the only one I dated," Judy defends her actions. "Every time I got an e-mail from someone who liked my profile, I explained what we were doing and provided them with a survey link. I ignored the emails from those who were interested in dating, except Paul. After a few months, I caved in to his persistence. There was something familiar about him. When we finally exchanged pictures, I was surprised to see Paul's face on the screen in front of me, the visiting professor I met a long time ago and Chair of Psychiatry at The University of Chicago Medical Center. When we met for dinner, he offered to facilitate a session at my conference in Grand Cayman, and the rest is history . . . ," Judy's voice fades into memory.

"What have you been doing with him?" Soledad asks.

Judy sighs before returning to her story. "Our relationship was a bit rocky at first because of all the things that were going on with my kids. Paul and I have come to an understanding since then and are as comfortable with each other as an old married couple."

"Old married couples live together," Soledad reminds Judy. "Why don't you?"

"It's a long story," Judy mutters as she racks her brain for a reason that will appease Soledad. "I don't think it's a good idea for a professor to benefit from the research of a graduate student."

"So he is a research subject."

"No. He didn't complete the survey," Judy explains.

"What are you doing with him now?"

"I'm going to see him tonight." Judy gives Soledad an inquisitive look. "What's with the twenty questions?"

"It's the journalist in me," Soledad snaps back as she scrubs the pan in the sink.

Judy glares across the counter at Soledad. "Why don't you tell me what you really want to know?"

"Okay, I will," Soledad exclaims. "How long are you going to string Paul along in the interest of your research?" She places the frying pan in the dish drainer next to the sink and warns, "You better tell him the truth, Jude, before it's too late."

The Hearth god

Soledad closes the door behind Judy and dials her voicemail. This is the first time she has listened to any of the messages Jay left for her over the last two weeks. The first two were invitations to dinner. In the third message, he was wondering if he had upset her. By the fifth, he was worried about her. The last one ended with, "All I want to know is whether or not you are okay."

She speed dials his number. The rhythmic tapping of her finger nails on the desk keeps her from hanging up the phone. On the last ring before going to voicemail, Jay answers. She hangs up.

She doesn't know what to say about her two week silence. She can't use bad news as an excuse because he is a friend of Judy and Paul. He knows she's an orphan, so a family emergency is out of the question. She hasn't been to yoga class or ridden her bike by the lake because she doesn't want to run into him. She even missed her poetry class last night because he might show up. What can she do to get away from him? He knows way too much about her.

A look of relief washes over her face as she realizes that, without a reason, he must know it's over. Her relief quickly shifts to panic as caller ID on her cell phone displays Jay's name. Her thumb is suspended above the answer button until the call to goes to voicemail. She waits for the message beep before calling voicemail. "I see you tried to call," Jay's voice says. "I hope you are okay. Please, Soledad, call me back right away."

She tosses the phone down and mutters, "Why doesn't he give up?" The steady buzzing of the doorbell down the hallway sends her heart into palpitations. She peeks out the window at a ladder leaning against a man wearing paint clothes.

She pushes the entry button and shouts down the stairs, "I'm on the third floor, unit six."

"Where's the elevator?" the voice of the workman travels up the stairway.

"It's a walkup," she shouts down to him. She waits on the landing, listening to his heavy breathing as his footsteps trudge up the stairs. "You're almost there," she encourages him as he comes into view on the last riser.

"These vintage buildings have their charm," he pants, "but they're not very practical."

"You get used to it."

"Not a fat old man like me." He chuckles through a few more pants before stating his purpose. "I'm Fred. The condo manager said there's a leak in the roof above your unit."

After inspecting the stain on the ceiling, Fred tells her, "It looks like you caught it early. I'll have to replace this corner patch, probably the crown molding too. It's too bad. Whoever put it up knew what they were doing."

"You're looking at her," Soledad tells him.

"Well I'll be darned. It's a mighty fine piece of work."

"Thanks. I remodeled the whole room," she tells him. "I took the wall out that separated the kitchen and dining room, added this countertop with a large cook top, double oven, and oversized refrigerator. It was expensive, but I actually use it. I love to cook and bake. I make ..." she rambles on.

"Did your husband make the cabinets?"

"I'm not married."

"A charming lady with all this talent not married?" Fred asks as he examines her work.

Soledad recites a rhyme. "I once had a husband who was a carpenter and taught me the tricks of his trade, but when I wasn't there, he had an affair and left me for our male electrician."

Fred studies Soledad before responding with a chuckle, "Stop teasing an old man."

"You're on to me, Fred," she concedes. "I'm a journalist who likes to tell stories."

"They're not anywhere near as good as your woodwork," he teases back.

"What if it is true?" she challenges him. "Would you believe me?"

"You're too funny." He attaches a form to a clipboard. "Okay, Soledad the storyteller carpenter, you need to sign this form."

After Fred climbs up to the roof, Soledad replays Jay's messages. Halfway through the fifth one, she snaps her phone shut. She looks through the window at the early December dusting of snow, wishing she were anywhere but in Evanston. There is so much more to do in New England than in the Midwest at this time of the year. Maybe she'll skip the funeral and go hiking in the Whites. Maybe she'll stay home, but then she'll have to deal with Jay.

She shakes these thoughts out of her head and positions herself in front of the computer. The rhythmic tapping of Fred's hammer keeps her focused on the image she conjures up on the computer screen of a father and son remodeling a house on the East Side of Providence. She can't grieve for someone she hasn't seen for twelve years. The screen goes blank as Fred calls out, "Excuse me, Soledad," through the back door.

"The door is open," Soledad calls back. "Come on in."

"I patched up the hole in the roof," Fred pants, "but it's only temporary. I'll have to come back." He takes an appointment book out of his back pocket and flips through the pages. "Let's see. Will you be home Monday?"

"I'll be out of town next week. What about tomorrow?"

"I don't work on Saturday…" his voice fades off. "I'll tell you what. I'll come by at seven a.m. if you're up."

"Ouch," Soledad grimaces.

"I'll bring an extra cup of coffee for you," Fred offers.

"Better yet, I'll brew one for you," Soledad suggests.

"That's a deal." Fred smiles at her. "Do you mind if I leave the ladder in the hallway?"

"Sure," she agrees. "Did you park out back?"

"Yep," he replies as he leans the ladder on the wall in the hallway next to her door.

"This staircase will take you out the back to your truck."

As Soledad leans her back against the door she closes behind Fred, the cuckoo clock reminds her it is three thirty p.m. She picks up the business card sitting on the mantle and dials Jay's work number. *He won't pick up because has meetings on Friday afternoons.* "Don't worry about me, Jay," she tells his voicemail. "I'm fine. I'm really sorry I haven't called, but I've been really busy. I'll be in Providence most of next week and will call you when I get back. I don't know what to say except I'm sorry for not getting back to you sooner," she stammers. "We'll talk when I get back. Have a great week."

She hangs up the phone and wraps her arms around herself, mimicking the hug Jay gave her the last time she saw him. Soledad didn't mind when Jay stayed that night, but he was a different person the next morning. She saw it as soon as she opened her eyes. She remembers reaching for the covers and pulling them all the way up to her neck, embarrassed by the ten-pound thickness that has built around her waist during menopause. She remembers how uncomfortable she felt when she leapt out of bed and rushed into the closet. She came out wearing a long terrycloth robe and rested her knee on the edge of the bed, admiring the outline of Jay's lean body beneath the sheets before planting a quick kiss on his lips. "Take your time in the bathroom," she told him. "I'll make some coffee."

Her footsteps down the hallway were slow and controlled, but the only thing she remembers, even now two weeks later, is the way her heart raced down the stairs that morning. How can she tell Jay she doesn't want to be with him? How can she tell him she still wants him around?

Soledad tosses Jay's business card on her desk, longing to melt into the past where she doesn't feel the onus of people around her. She doesn't want Jay's expectations. She's tired of listening to Judy complain about the way she dismisses men. All she wants right now is to be alone. The stereo is calling her.

She feeds it her favorite CD and stretches her arms in opposite directions across her chest until her fingers meet at the small of her back. Her torso sways back and forth as the music begins its journey through her ears.

> She ebbs and flows eternally
> For his return to never come,
> A snore holding their time in place
> Without leaving a footprint behind.

> His devilish twinkle dances toward dawn
> And melts her down to her longing,
> Piercing through the dampened sand
> Where their love is shaken to life.

> Hunger lifts them from their grave
> In rhythmic dance from dusk to dawn,
> Caressing again for the first time
> The beat of her heart in innocence.

Squatting by the hearth, Soledad ignites the newspaper beneath the wood. The flame building around the logs slowly removes the chill in her heart. She hovers over it, waiting for the promise of the red hot flame to take her to another place, another time, to the arms of the man who used to love her. She repeats his words over and over in the same way he whispered them to her at the altar where they were married over a quarter of a century ago. A lone teardrop splatters on her toe.

She uses the poker to position the wood beyond the twelve years since she came face to face with the man who murdered her marriage. She pokes at the wood until it is positioned in a time when their love was vibrantly alive. The poker's steady searching through the burning news kindles in her heart a yearning. Warmth fills the air around her. The heat shoots through her veins and leads her to the dark corner of her heart where their murdered life is buried. She watches them rise up together between the logs, flame to flame, to dance the dance that outlives the crime. She sinks back into the sofa as their roaring blaze unites and divides over and over again, the way it did during the fourteen years they were together.

She opens a small box and unwraps five pieces of broken glass. Light shoots through each piece like a prism as she holds it up to the fire. She glues the pieces together until the gondola they shared on their honeymoon is sitting on the coffee table in front of her.

When she closes her eyes, he is sitting across from her. The waiter ignites a candle on the courtyard table where they shared their first meal as husband and wife before taking a moonlight ride through the Venetian canals. The flame brings her face to the same glow she wore when they were in Switzerland and the lodge fire took away the chill hovering over the Jungfrau and Eiger. The crackling roar through the air leaves a blazing red trail oozing down the mountain toward the thundering Hawaiian surf. Their bare feet kick up the hot sand as they twirl around each other for as long as she can hang on to him.

She opens the fireplace screen and places another log in the hearth. The fire around her rushes toward him once again and draws him back into his place in their dance. She holds the flame in her eyes while they sleep on a chilled porch in the White Mountains during a rain storm. Their laughter accelerates the pace of their dance down a ski slope in the Green Mountains. He falls. His flame was last seen rising like steam from her skin as her exhausted body ran from the hot tub into a cold pool of water.

Her gentle tapping of the poker on the charred wood heightens to a swift beat as Soledad tries to revive their dance. But it's too late. The music floating with them through the air is silenced as their feet step back into the grave she maintains for them in her heart. Their ashes, still warm enough to burn through her, remind her of what he left in her bones and what he took out of them.

When she walks across the room to her desk and sits down in front of the computer screen, she sees a flicker of their dance reflecting from the hearth. Her fingers hang over the keyboard as she waits for the warmth to leave their bodies. She brings her hands together, briskly rubbing away the numbness the same way Jay did the night they walked back to her condo after seeing *Casablanca* with Judy and Paul.

"Betrayal is the worst thing that can happen to anyone," Soledad remembers telling Jay, "because it wounds your spirit. It shatters your faith in what you believe is real and breaks you in two. That's what happened to Bogey. He was split in two by his inability to reconcile Ilsa's love for him and her reckless abandonment of it. So he leaves Richard, the principled man, in Paris and becomes Rick, the bitter man."

"How were you wounded?"

"I'm an independent spirit, not a wounded one."

"What's the difference, Sole? Either way, you end up playing chess alone."

Soledad rubs her cheek, remembering how much Jay's words that night felt like a slap across the face. It wasn't long before the random movement of her fingers across the keyboard turned into a coherent pattern of words.

> The shadow of their long lost love,
> Brought to life whenever she pleases,
> Grows darker as time slithers by,
> Giving her nothing to carry.
> She wears him like a diamond leach
> And resonates thunder through the ears
> Of all the men who want her near,
> Stay away from me.

Her fingers stop moving. "Bob," Soledad whispers. His name sounds like a profane oath. She covers her ears and turns to the closet where their life is buried in the fourteen boxes neatly stacked on the floor, away from all who wish them dead. She grins and sneers, loving and loathing the memory. Her eyes fall on the last box, the one with pictures from her cousin's wedding. She wants to forget all over again, if only for a little while longer.

She grabs the suitcase and carries it into her bedroom. As she opens it, the words spoken to her on the phone last night by her ex-brother-in-law, Kenny, are released from the empty container. *Bob wants you to come to the funeral.* When she looks through her closet for something to wear and can't find anything to fit the occasion, she snaps the empty suitcase shut and returns it to the closet.

She walks back to the fireplace. The ashes lying in the hearth, pulling her back into the dance are stilled by Kenny's words, *He won't be alone.* She uses the poker to stir up their remains and fans them alive with Jay's card. The last act of kindness is a tiny flame bursting out of their dance, greedily devouring Jay's name and number.

It's Too Late

"Don't," is the only word Judy can get past her throat. She looks out at the couples passing by the restaurant window while Paul's eyes follow the rhythmic motion of her fingertip brushing back and forth across his knuckles.

The waiter's mantra, "Are you interested in dessert?" breaks their silence.

"No thanks," they reply in unison.

"I'll have a cognac," Paul adds.

Judy nods when the waiter asks, "Do you want one too?"

She waits for the busboy to clear their plates away before saying, "Paul, there's something…"

Paul gently lifts her chin until their eyes meet. "I promise to make you happy for the rest of your life."

"For the rest of my life," Judy murmurs.

"Yeah, Jude, I want to be with you forever."

Judy forces a smile at the waiter when he returns with the cognac. She swirls it around the glass and smells its warm aroma. "What movie do you want to see tonight?"

"Screw the movie," Paul retorts.

She sets down the snifter. "Marriage at our age doesn't make sense. I'm too old for more children, and commingling our assets only complicates things."

"That's a copout," Paul interrupts.

"I want my children to have my—

"—I don't want your things, Jude. I want you."

Judy gives him a sharp look. "Do you want to hear what I have to say?"

"I thought you were done," Paul says softly.

"We are done," Judy mutters under her breath and turns her

attention back to the nervous habit of folding the cocktail napkin around the bottom of her glass.

He puts his hand on hers and says, "It's not like you to be so coy, Jude."

"I want to tell you something, Paul, but I don't know how to say it." Judy sighs. "We've been good together, but," she inhales a long breath and expels, "it's too late for us."

"What do you mean by *too late?* We have been so good together since we reconnected. Grand Cayman was a dream come true. Granted, it was a little rough at the beginning, but we've settled into a wonderful relationship as predictable as that of an old married couple. What happened to change all that?"

"Hurricane Ivan hit the island a few months after the conference."

"I don't care about the hurricane that has hit your life. I love you. I let you get away a long time ago because you convinced me it was what you needed, but I won't let you go this time."

"You want the magic—"

"I want you," Paul jumps in.

"—and I need to be practical," Judy insists. "We will never be able to repeat the magic of all those wonderful nights we spent together twenty-five years ago ..." her voice fades off into memory.

Paul picks up on the memory where Judy left off, "eating Chinese food while ..." He stops. "I forgot that you don't like it when I bring up sex."

"Or marriage," Judy adds.

"We don't have to get married, Jude."

"Yesterday, maybe we could've, but not today."

"Did something happen today?"

"Something happens every day, Paul, but that's not the point. I'm not good for you anymore," Judy states firmly.

"Why don't you let me be the judge of that?" Paul shoos the waiter away with the wave of his hand and repeats his question. "What happened today?"

She brushes his face with the back of her hand. "I have enjoyed every minute with you even though I knew…" she wanders off into her own thoughts. "I don't think we should see each other anymore."

"You can't get rid of me that easily," Paul insists.

"You're going to have to let me go." These words somehow make her come alive again. "I know everything is fine now, but let's not forget the less than perfect conditions in which we met."

"Have a little faith in us, Jude. We take care of each other in different ways than we have in the past and we'll take care of each other differently in the future." He leans across the table and whispers. "Are you afraid you won't be able to take care of me?"

"I can't do this anymore," Judy replies with her head turned toward the table.

Paul takes a few deep breaths. "I can see we won't get anywhere with this tonight, so let's forget about it and go to the movie. Things have a way of looking better in the morning."

"Things won't get better," Judy whispers sharply.

"Relax, Jude," Paul says calmly. "I take back what I said."

"You can't take it back," Judy replies.

He holds out his hand to her. "Come on, Jude, let's go."

She looks around the restaurant and whispers, "People can hear us."

"Then let's go," Paul whispers back sarcastically.

Judy leaps up, searching for something to grab onto that will keep her grounded. She is barely able to mutter the words, "I didn't want you to get hurt by this."

Her first few steps are forced, but soon she is maneuvering her way around the tables and out the door. She rushes through the lobby to the garage elevator bank, steps in the elevator, and pushes the P2 button. Paul is entering the elevator bank as the door closes. When the elevator door reopens, she hits the remote, leaps into Paul's car, and throws the transmission into drive. As she exits the garage, she sees Paul in the rearview mirror, searching for her.

It isn't long before she pulls into an empty space near the yacht club at Belmont Harbor. She follows the path of light across Lake Michigan to the rising moon on the eastern horizon in much the same way she and Paul watched the sunset along the Caribbean Sea after a reef dive off the shore of Grand Cayman. She can still see its light reflecting in Paul's dark blue eyes when he said, "You're beautiful, Jude."

"Not with all these wrinkles."

"I don't see any wrinkles."

"Right here," Judy pointed to the corners of her eyes. "And here."

"It's your wisdom." Paul touched her face. "It can't help but reveal itself on your skin."

"I used to wonder what it would be like to be with you and not have a husband."

"You're free now," Paul reminded her.

"I'm still afraid of what will happen."

"You worry too much, Jude."

Judy lays her head on the steering wheel, knowing she doesn't have any choice but to worry. She tried to tell him the truth that night five years ago as they watched the sunset, but he brushed it away as quickly as he did the strands of hair slapping across her face in the wind.

As the wind whistles through the cracked window of Paul's car, she recalls her amazement at his interest in her. "You still want to see me, even now, twenty five years after you found out the reason for my—"

"—for your divorce," Paul interjected. "It doesn't bother me."

"Really?"

"Yes, really," Paul replied. "Does mine?"

"No, but the circumstances of my divorce are very different than yours," Judy protested.

"So what," Paul shrugged. "We are lucky to have found each other again."

As she sits in driver's seat, mesmerized by the moonlit path across Lake Michigan, she remembers the hope that floated back to her across the Caribbean Sea on the dive trip that evening. "We *were* lucky," she shouts a reminder of hope, now trapped in the movement of the wind through the slightly cracked car window. Opening and closing it silences the howling squall that is taking her away from the man she loves.

As she closes her eyes to the moonlight flickering across the water, rage bubbles up out of the fog in her mind. Her fists tightly wrap around the steering wheel until her knuckles turn white as she screams over and over, "Why did you ruin it for me?" while thrusting her body back and forth between the steering wheel and the seat. Then she lays her head down on the steering wheel and sobs.

I Want to Go Home

"Something's missing from the story," Nita insists as Eric turns the DVD player off. "Anyone who has invested that much of herself into him wouldn't have left him for an affair. I know I wouldn't."

"That's good to know, babe," Eric chuckles, lifting her into his arms.

Nita's lips brush against his as she whispers, "I have to write this critique."

"Go ahead," Eric pouts, "abandon your husband for a film about *The Way We Were*. What about the way we are? I'll show you the way we can be when ..."

Nita tosses her hair back with a laugh and waves the assignment sheet at him. "This can't wait. It's due tomorrow," she reminds him.

"It can wait," Eric insists, planting his lips firmly on hers.

She wiggles away from his grasp. "This is important. It's due in," she looks at her watch, "yikes, less than twelve hours."

"Why did you wait until Sunday night to do this?"

"I was at Dr. Clark's research colloquium this weekend. Remember?" she replies.

"Do I detect a bit of sarcasm in your voice?"

Nita ignores Eric's question. She turns the DVD player on and sits on the couch with her laptop. Eric stands behind her as she types, "Several critical scenes appear to be missing; 1) Hubble's producer confronting him with the accusation that Katie is a Communist subversive, 2) Hubble trying to convince Katie to rat on—"

"Why do you think so poorly of Hubble?" Eric asks. He brushes his hands across her back and starts to massage her neck.

"It won't work, Eric," Nita says without taking her eyes off the computer screen.

"Come on, babe; tell me what's wrong with Hubble?"

"He's a fraud," Nita says as she continues typing.

Eric reaches around her shoulders and grabs her breast. "Don't you want me, babe?" he whispers in her ear.

"Stop," Nita warns. She pushes him away and turns back to the computer.

"Oh, all right," Eric mutters, "but let's do this quickly. He has an affair. She leaves him. The only thing new about the story is that she doesn't come back." He takes her hand and tries to lift her from the couch. "Now we can go to bed."

Nita pushes him away. "If you really want to be with me tonight, you'll let me get this done. Do something else for a while, Eric," she suggests. "I'll find you when I'm finished."

Eric retreats to the chair across the room. After ten minutes of tapping his foot to the rhythm of Nita's keystrokes, he is back on his feet, hovering over her shoulder, reading the words that appear on the computer screen. He is silent until her keystrokes form a sentence with which he doesn't agree. "What do you mean, babe, when you say that their identities are at odds throughout the movie?"

She eyes him cautiously before saying, "They are good together as long as one of them lives the other person's life. He lives her life in New York until Beakman Place gets in the way. She lives his in Malibu until the witch hunt starts. Without the missing scenes, it looks as if the affair is the reason she left."

Eric sits down next to her and says, "You're so sexy when you're on fire."

"Forget it," she mutters and goes back to writing her paper.

"It's his fault," Eric concedes, "if that's what you want to hear." He stretches his legs across the couch and nudges Nita off of it.

"What are you doing?" she barks as she picks herself up off of the floor.

He clasps his hands around the back of his neck and touts her. "He leaves Katie for his old girlfriend."

The eye-to-eye combat begins as she glares at him. "It's not about the other woman," Nita argues. "It's what she represents; a return to his old life. If the director had left in the missing scenes, the reason would be more obvious."

Eric is charged up by her response. "If the scenes were as critical as my wife seems to think they are," he insists, "the director would have left them in."

Nita takes the bait as she sits down at the end of the couch. "That doesn't change the fact that Hubble can't help being a coward," she points out. "He has principles, but he's afraid to live by them. He's so threatened by her principles—principles he himself believes in—that he sells her out. He's not happy with fighting for anything she believes in. All he wants out of her is fun and games."

"Katie doesn't know how to have fun. That's why he breaks up with her in New York. He changes his mind because of the sex."

"He changes his mind because she agrees to live the life he wants in Malibu," Nita interjects.

"Uh uh." Eric points at her as he spits out his words. "He changes his mind because he loves her."

"He doesn't love her," Nita argues, "unless it's convenient for him, when there's something in it for him. He doesn't want her around when her principles interfere with his cushy lifestyle."

"She's the problem, babe. She's more important to him than his principles and her principles are more important to her than he is. Their relationship falls apart because of her politics."

"Their relationship falls apart because he doesn't like her politics," Nita corrects Eric. "He is more concerned with how her principles might spoil things for him than in loving her as she is—politics and all."

"I get it!" Eric exclaims. "I'm going to have to agree with you if I want to sleep with you tonight."

"You're just as bad as Hubble," Nita barks. "He loves her for the sex she gives him, but he doesn't love her for who she is."

"She's the one who doesn't love him," Eric insists. "That's why she leaves when he cheats on her."

"It's not the affair," Nita protests. "It's what the affair represents, a return to his old life."

"Why won't my wife listen to me? I'm the one with three degrees," Eric reminds her in his typical roundabout way, "and she's still in a four-year rolling undergraduate program."

"That's a mean thing to say to me!" she shouts. "You know damn well I've had to work full time since my divorce in order to take care of José."

"You could be finished if you would let me take care of you."

"The price is too high," Nita mutters as she walks toward the kitchen.

"You are too stupid to let me help," Eric mutters back.

Nita turns around sharply. "What did you say?"

"You heard me."

"Do you enjoy hurting me?" Nita asks with fire in her eyes.

"I'm looking out for your interests!" Eric exclaims. "I'm telling my wife that there are no missing scenes in the movie. I'm telling her that Douglas will give her a big fat F if she turns in this critique."

"No he won't," Nita insists.

"Because you're sleeping with him," Eric accuses.

"Stop it," she snaps at him.

"If Douglas were here instead of me, you'd be all over him."

"It's not about Douglas!" she screams in his face. "I happen to like this class. I want to learn this stuff. And I don't want you getting in my way."

"I knew it! You are having an affair with Douglas."

"It's not Douglas," she mutters.

"Then who is it," Eric sneers. "Judy Clark, your lesbian advisor?"

"Pfft!" She waves him away. "Believe whatever you want to believe. I'm out of here."

Nita gallops up the stairs with Eric following close behind. When she reaches the top, he grabs her waist and twists her around to face him. She wrestles free from his grip and slams the guest room door in his face.

She leans her back against the locked door and sinks to the floor as the pleading begins. "I'm sorry, babe. I didn't mean to hurt my girl. Come with me to bed." She knows Eric will tire of his pleading in about fifteen minutes. They have been through this too many times before.

The sound of the shower door sliding shut lifts Nita from the floor. As she sits down on the bed, her eyes fall on their wedding picture. She used to love the yearning in Eric's eyes and the way his shoulders broadened and his stomach tightened when he noticed her looking at him. But all she sees now is the way his stomach folds over his belt and his flabby arms wobble. The fatty folds of his cheeks falling around his mouth are as long and deep as those of the cowardly lion in the *Wizard of Oz*. A thought crosses her mind that has not entered it before. He is way too old for her.

She blinks several times, hoping to destroy the image before returning to the picture. The tanned creases around his eyes and the leathery skin she used to refer to as ruggedly attractive only serve to solidify the aging image of Eric. She recalls how the neck wrinkles in the picture change shape when his chin bobs up and down with his jabbering jaw.

She catches her own reflection in the mirror. What happened to the bride in the picture? How did she end up with such a boring man? Eric has a simple mind with lots of rules about what lies within one standard deviation of the mean, but he doesn't have a clue how to react to anything outside of these statistical bounds; something she would expect from a computer science expert who develops algorithms for a living.

Nita shakes these thoughts out of her head as she turns off the light so Eric will think she has fallen asleep. She lays quietly in the dark, working through the film critique in her head. When the grandfather clock strikes twelve, she slowly opens the door and tiptoes down the stairs to get her computer. The power cord isn't

where she left it. Eric must have hidden it again. She rummages
through the big drawer on the left side of his desk until she finds it.
The outlet prongs are stuck beneath Eric's papers. She turns on the
desk lamp and moves a stack of journal articles in the drawer to the
top of the desk. That's when she sees it.

As she is flipping through the document, Eric comes up behind
her and slides his arms around her waist. "Come to bed, babe," he
whispers in her ear.

Nita turns around sharply. "How could you do this to me?"

He looks at Nita holding a paper in one hand and a power
cord in the other. "What did I do to the power cord?" Eric inquires
innocently.

"Why did you do this?" she repeats, waving the paper in his face.

"Oh that," Eric replies nonchalantly. "I was protecting my girl."

"From speaking my mind," Nita snarls at him.

"Why speak it when you don't have anything to say?"

"Stop it!" Nita screams.

"You're going to wake up your son," Eric reminds her.

"He's with my parents."

"You mean to tell me he hasn't been here all night, and you
didn't want to sleep—"

"No, I don't want to sleep with you, Eric," she finishes his
thought. "All I want to do is get out of here."

"You're not going anywhere."

"Yes, I am." She takes a deep breath to calm her temper. "I can't
do this anymore, Eric," she says calmly. "I'm leaving you for good."

He grabs her by the arm as she tries to leave through the
garage.

She pulls her arm from his grip. "Don't come any closer," she
warns. "My father is a police officer."

He steps back. "It's because of him, isn't it?"

"Him?" Nita repeats.

"You're seeing Douglas," Eric accuses.

"Let's not make my leaving another thing to fight about."

"Don't go," Eric pleads as reality of what she says sinks in. When Nita doesn't answer, he asks, "Why do you want to leave, babe?"

"Because I hate being with you!" Nita exclaims. She looks at him, unaffected by the rage building in his eyes. "I'd do just about anything to turn the clock back to the day we were married so I could say no to you."

"You … you … you're mean," Eric stammers.

"I don't know any other way to get through to you that all I want is to get away from you." She turns toward the door and mutters, "What's the point when all we do is fight?"

"I love you, Nita."

Nita turns back toward Eric. "I think this is the first time you've addressed me by my real name."

"No, it isn't."

"Please, Eric, let me escape from my mistake."

His eyes fall to the carpet as he plops in the chair and nods.

• • • • •

Thirty minutes later, Nita finds herself sitting in her car in her parent's driveway. She wants to tell them what has happened to her since Jim left. She wants them to know what has been drawn out of her since she found out the truth about Jim. She wants to tell them about the consuming regret that hovers over her since she married Eric.

When looking up at the window into the darkness of their bedroom, she imagines the light in her parent's bedroom going on as she unlocks the back door. She stands in the dark kitchen and hears her father footsteps creaking down the back stairs. When he sees her tearstained face, he takes her by the hand and leads her up the stairs into her mother's arms. A worried crease builds on his forehead as he waits at the kitchen table for her to take the hot bath her mother has drawn for her. She drinks the hot cocoa her mother has made and tells them she has left Eric for good. Her father picks up the phone and calls a lawyer. Her mother suggests she move back home until she gets back on her feet.

She reaches for the car door handle and stops, knowing that this is nothing more than a fantasy. She recalls the last time she went to her parents for advice when her first marriage to Jim was in trouble. She can still see her father peer over the top of the newspaper as she stood in their kitchen with her hands wrapped around a mug of her mother's freshly brewed coffee. She recalls his advice as he put down the paper. *Marriage is a sacred thing. It shouldn't be taken lightly. Don't you think it would be best to go home and talk to Jim about saving your marriage?*

"Some things can't be worked out," she mumbles to the darkness inside her parent's bedroom window. She melts into the seat of the car and mutters, "They're my parents. They have to help me." She swings the door open and leaps out of the car before she loses her nerve.

Halfway up the walkway, she stops. How can she tell her father that her second marriage is on the rocks? How can she watch her mother try to hide the worried look in her eyes as her father scolds her for the way her life has turned out? She doesn't need to hear how messed up her life is. She already knows. What she really wants to know is how it got that way.

Her feet trot back to the car and she slides in behind the wheel. She doesn't really blame her parents. She didn't think about the kind of man Eric was before she married him a few months after they met. She was vulnerable to his strong ego, a fortress that blinded her of all that she wanted to forget and shielded her from the entrances to all the places where temptation laid. Her future was in his desire, in the way it ended up imprisoning her and replacing her youthful vitality with a calming numb. Eric was nothing more than a diversion from Jim's betrayal, holding her in place for as long as she needed to heal.

As she turns the key in the ignition, she thinks she hears the engine purring her father's mantra. *Save your marriage. Save your marriage.* She covers her ears, but the cacophony intensifies. To silence the advice spinning in her head, she shifts the car into reverse and backs out of the driveway. Tears well up in her eyes as her car idles in the middle of the street, uncertain of which direction she will turn.

The Debate

Summer, 2004
Five Years Earlier

Never Been Kissed

"Marriage is a sacrament," Father Patrick tells Nita. "Since it is a sacred covenant that two people make before God, marriage vows must be exchanged by the couple knowingly, willingly, and honestly. If intent isn't there, the vows don't mean anything. If the vows don't mean anything, the marriage never existed."

Nita looks out the window of Father Patrick's office at the church playground. She spots José in a crowd of boys on the monkey bars. He looks happier than he did an hour ago when she made another excuse for Jim canceling his evening with Jose. She was able to temper José's disappointment by reminding him that her father was taking him to his first Cubs game tonight. His smile was replaced by a frown as he asked, "What if Grandpa gets sick the way Daddy did?"

When she looks back at Father Patrick, her eyes take a few seconds to adjust to the light in the room. "If I understand you correctly," Nita begins, "I have to provide evidence that my ex-husband didn't mean the vows you heard him say to me five years ago at the altar in this church. But if I can't, our marriage will still be legitimate in the eyes of God, even though he is gay."

"That's what the annulment process is intended to determine. If your husband is a homosexual as you say he is, he probably couldn't or didn't want to enter into a marriage covenant with you."

"You mean he lied to me," Nita corrects Father Patrick.

"It's not always a conscious choice, Nita. He may not have been able to adequately evaluate his marital obligations beforehand or fulfill them afterward."

"It's also possible that he didn't intend to remain faithful when he married me."

"There are many legitimate reasons that would fit your situation."

"If he's the one who didn't enter into a covenant with me, why is it necessary for me to do anything about this?"

"The Catholic Church doesn't recognize your divorce, Nita. Divorce means the covenant is broken, and breaking a sacred covenant is a sin. Luke 16:18 says, 'Everyone who divorces his wife and marries another commits adultery, and the one who marries a woman divorced from her husband commits adultery.' This means that if you remarry without getting an annulment, you and whoever you decide to marry will be committing adultery."

"Wouldn't it be easier to tell the truth? The covenant was made and broken. I didn't break it," Nita protests. "My ex-husband did."

"A sacred covenant can't be broken if it wasn't entered into knowingly, willingly, and honestly by both parties," Father Patrick repeats. "If Jim didn't intend to make a covenant, there is no covenant."

"Wait a minute. Are you telling me that the Catholic Church is letting him off the hook for lying to me in front of God, while I and someone I haven't met will be considered adulterers if we try to enter into a legitimate marriage covenant?"

"You will not be committing adultery unless you remarry without an annulment," Father Patrick explains.

"I didn't do anything wrong," Nita protests.

"If the ecclesiastical tribunal says a covenant didn't exist, which they probably will under these circumstances, you will be free to marry whoever you want." Father Patrick rummages through his drawer as he recites to Nita, "I will need your baptismal certificate, marriage license, and divorce decree. I, as your advocate, will write a report explaining why you should be granted an annulment. You will need to give me a detailed account of what happened and the names of witnesses that can support it. Your family and friends will be a big help here."

"Do they have to know?"

Father Patrick looks over the top of his glasses at Nita. "Not if you don't want them to know, but then they can't be witnesses." He hands her a packet of information. "Everything you need to know is here. I will be notifying your husband. He doesn't have to respond or agree to the annulment in order to get it."

"Ex-husband," Nita corrects.

"The church still considers you to be married to Jim until you get an annulment."

"I don't want to annul my marriage, Father Patrick. I only want an opportunity to remarry in my church sometime in the future."

"Do you have someone in mind?"

Nita bows her head and replies, "Not exactly."

"An annulment isn't important unless you want to get married again, but I urge you to start the process because it'll take about sixteen months and cost around five hundred dollars."

"Maybe I should just get married in a different Christian denomination."

Father Patrick leans across the desk and says, "I'd encourage you to talk to your parents about this. I'm sure they'd approve of an annulment."

"Excuse me, Father Patrick. I'm having trouble with this. This is my church. You married us and baptized our son. Now I'm being told that the only way I have a future in my church is to pay five hundred dollars to prove my ex-husband didn't marry me for the right reasons."

"That's where the statements of friends and relatives will help."

"I'm not going to ask anyone to lie for him. I want to tell the truth. Our marriage did exist, and my ex-husband broke the covenant."

"We're not asking anyone to lie," Father Patrick protests.

Nita's words, "Then what do you call it?" drown out the rest of his response.

When she has his attention, she continues. "If I tell the truth, the Catholic Church won't allow me to get married again and be a participating member of this Christian community. And if I marry anyway, the church I've gone to and worked at all my life will label my new husband and me adulterers. So the only way I can prevent myself from being an adulteress is if I commit another sin and bear false witness to the Church about my marriage." She gives Father

Patrick a puzzled look. "Are you suggesting that lying is less of a sin than adultery?"

He looks down at the paper on his desk and speaks softly. "It's only a formality, a requirement of the Church, not a reflection of anything you've done. There is no other way."

"I see." Nita gathers the packet of information in front of her and stands up. "I will take this under consideration. Thank you for your time, Father Patrick."

"Come back and see me after you talk to your parents," he suggests while shaking her hand. "By the way, I saw your father at the September 11 memorial service yesterday. I can't believe it's been three years since that dreadful day. He told me you were in Grand Cayman. Did you get stuck on the island by Hurricane Ivan?"

"No, I didn't," Nita replies politely as she steps back from him and slides through his office door. So much has changed in the two months since she left the island that she prefers to keep to herself.

The echo of her shoes clicking down the hallway stops outside the office of the religious education director. She takes a pen and paper out of her purse and scribbles a note, resigning from her Sunday school teaching position. She slips it under the door. Her heels click farther down the hallway and into the church office where she crosses her name off the Epistle reading schedule. She marches across the parking lot to the parish school and withdraws José from preschool.

As she leaves the building, Nita looks up beyond the steeple at the gray clouds thickening in the sky. Rain is inevitable. José will be disappointed. He jumps off the swing on the church playground and rushes to her. "Mommy, where's Grandpa?" he asks.

"He's with Grandma, honey." She gathers him in her arms and takes him to her mother's for dinner.

The Corpse Dies

"He isn't dead," Theo snaps at Soledad. "You're married."

"Of course I'm not married. I told you that the man I married doesn't exist anymore." Soledad propels the rocker on the patio into long swinging motions back and forth as her eyes sweep the hillside down to the Mediterranean Sea. She picks up the newspaper and flips it open. "Look at this, Theo. It says, excuse my translation, *Michail Gorbachev, former President of the Russian Federation, Mr. Martti Ahtisaari, former President of Finland, and Mr. Rafic Hariri, Lebanese Prime Minister, will be speaking at the World Urban Forum in Barcelona tomorrow.*"

Theo ignores the information she gives him. "Help me understand how someone who no longer exists can have dinner with that woman you were with at the bar on Platja de la Barceloneta."

Soledad continues to report the news. *"Grand Cayman was hit by a level five—"* Theo pulls the paper out of her hands and tosses it on the patio floor. Soledad studies his mood before suggesting, "Why don't you tell me what you want to hear?"

"I want the truth."

She looks at him over the top of her glasses. "What truth do you want?"

He grabs the chair to stop her rocking and barks, "Stop talking in circles and tell me who you are."

"You know who I am, Theo. I'm Soledad, an investigative reporter who lost my husband seven years ago."

He paces the length of the deck a few times before leaning on the railing in front of her with his arms folded across his chest. "I don't really know you, Soledad," he declares. "You've been coming to Barcelona one week a month for the last two years, and I still don't know what you do with the other three. I love that you're so comfortable here with me. I love showing you what I painted while you were away. And I'm fascinated by the beauty that comes out of your heart when you sit here and write your songs. But we live in my world, and I've never seen yours. I'm not even sure where you live."

"You know my work takes me all over Europe. It has ever since I wrote that series on economic development in Eastern Europe after the collapse of communism. It's been a great ride, but I wouldn't call any of the shoebox apartments I've lived in over the last five years a home. It's hard to invite someone to a place that isn't a home."

"Where is home, Sole?"

"Well, let's see. I live in Paris now. Last year, I was in Prague. Before that, it was Berlin, Moscow, Warsaw, and Budapest. I guess I haven't had a home since Bob..." she pauses, "well, you know."

"No, I don't know," Theo says softly. "What happened?"

Soledad takes a long, deep breath and smiles at him. "Home is a feeling. Sitting here with you in your courtyard in Montjuïc, looking out over Barcelona at the Mediterranean Sea, is the closest thing I have to home right now."

"What really happened to Bob?" Theo asks.

She buries her head in the newspaper and mutters, "You're blocking my view."

"Where have you been since I last saw you?"

"I traveled to Alaska last month after meetings in Boston and Chicago."

"Why didn't you ask me to go with you?"

"I didn't think you would be able to go."

"I would have if I had known where you were going."

"I didn't think I had to tell you," Soledad snaps.

"Did you see your husband when you were in Boston?"

Soledad sighs. "We're back to this again. I told you, Theo," she recites, "I was married for seven years to a wonderful man who no longer exists."

Theo shakes his head in disgust. "I can see we're not going to get anywhere with this right now. I have to meet someone at the

café down the street. I'll be back by seven. I expect you to be prepared to tell me the truth."

Soledad waits for the door to close behind him before dashing
into the house. The chair on the porch is slowing its rocking movement as she grabs her large suitcase from the closet and heaves it
onto the bed. She mumbles angrily as she flies through the room,
sweeping everything she brought with her into it. When the slamming of the dresser drawers ceases, she leans her forehead against
the wall and shouts, "I can't get away from his problem no matter
where I go!"

Her feet stomp down on the carpet pile as she returns to the
deck. After taking in a few breaths of the summer sea air, she steps
back into the house and follows the imprint of her path back into
the bedroom. Her weight is thrust on the overstuffed suitcase until
the clasp closes. Her fist tightens around the handle as she yanks it
off the bed and drags it to the door.

As she is sitting on the couch waiting for Theo to return, her
eyes fall on the painting above the fireplace. She remembers when
Theo painted it. He said she was his inspiration. He said it was her.

The idea came to him when they met at a creative expression
conference in Platja d'Aro. Soledad was standing in front of a large
window in the lobby, looking out at the Mediterranean Sea when
Theo came up to her and began painting her with his mind. "I see a
woman mesmerized by the sea," he said. "I can't see her face because
her back is to me, but I know she wants to be free."

"How do you paint freedom?" Soledad asked without taking
her eyes off the sea.

"It's in the hot sand covering her bare feet, in the wind blowing
her dress toward me, in the red scarf falling loosely from her neck,
and in the wide-brimmed hat that keeps me away."

Her eyes follow the sound of his voice and fall on a tall, dark
man eagerly smiling at her. "I'm impressed," she exclaimed.

"Why don't you try it?" Theo suggested. He brushed the palm
of his hand over her eyes and whispered, "Don't look at the sea.
Feel it."

She closed her eyes and began, "I see the woman, but her feet aren't buried in the sand. She is sitting on a bench, constrained by a long wool dress and boots laced up to her knees. Her elbow is propped up on her knee. One hand is clenched in a tight fist so she can hold up her weary head, and the other is reaching across the back of the bench where her hat and umbrella lie. No one can sit down. Her eyes hold too many secrets."

"Feel the contrast," Soledad whispers the words Theo said to her that day. She takes the painting off the wall and sets it next to her suitcase. She wanders through the house like a blind person, brushing her hand across the furniture, artwork, lamps, books, pillows, photos—everything in the house. She stops at a glass gondola sitting on the desk where she works. She watches the afternoon light shoot through it and dance across the wall next to the desk.

She picks it up, fondles it, and sets it back down on the desk. She takes a small box out of the drawer and flattens the creases out of the crumpled tissue it contains. The delicate glass gondola is carefully wrapped in tissue and returned to the box.

· · · · ·

When Theo returns, he steps around the painting leaning against her suitcase in the hallway and rushes to the deck. He skids to a halt at the door when he sees Soledad sleeping in the rocker. Her song journal is lying on top of the book she was reading, propped open to an entry with a five-year-old date. The original title was crossed off and replaced so many times that he can't decipher it. He checks to make sure she is still sleeping before reading it.

> She stares inside his open closet
> At their life once filling its emptiness,
> As a phoenix is born from his own corpse
> And his false image dies.

Her disquieted heart beats feebly
For the fatality left in her bones,
While his phoenix rises to life
And snatches their years away.

Her wailing is quieted by deafened ears
That slash through her bones with lies,
As they seek to reconcile the unfathomable
And end up exterminating her pride.

She yearns for belief in his heartfelt lie
To wear long after the phoenix flies,
But there is no honor in being alive
Unless in his closet they still reside.

"Now you know," Soledad whispers with her eyes still closed.

"I hope you don't mind that I read it," Theo tells her.

"You don't have to see me anymore if you don't want to," she murmurs.

"Don't say that, Sole." Theo says softly. He pulls up a chair in front of the rocker. "I like what you've shown me of yourself, and I want to see more. You've told me so many wonderful things about your life with Bob. I also want to know what happened to you when Bob came out."

"I'd rather talk about what happened when we were married."

"Look at me," Theo says softly. He waits for her to open her eyes to him. "I want to know you, Sole, but I can't unless you open up to me. I want to know everything that happened at the beginning, in the middle, and at end of your marriage."

"You couldn't leave it alone, could you Theo?" Soledad mutters as she swings herself out of the rocker and goes into the house.

Theo leaps up and follows her down the hallway. "I didn't know why you told me he was dead. That's all."

"Would it have been better if I had lied about our life together?" Soledad asks.

"There's no reason to be ashamed of what he did to you, Sole."

"Don't lecture me on shame, Theo," she warns as she picks up the painting. "It floats through the room every time I mentioned his name. It's in the questions, the disbelieving looks, the changes of subject, and the constant reassurance from men that they are not gay. It'll even change you."

"No it won't," Theo protests.

"You'll never look at my marriage the way you did when you knew Bob was dead."

"I can't bring him back to life, Sole."

"You just did, Theo."

"What I mean is I can't bring him back to you."

"I don't want him back. I want you to leave him in the grave where he belongs."

"Tell me what happened," Theo pleads.

Soledad sets down the painting and folds her arms across her chest. "Okay. I'll tell you." She sighs. "You say he isn't dead, but he is to me. I don't expect you to believe me, but Bob was a good husband in every sense of the word. I know our marriage wasn't flawed. Neither is Bob. The gay man he has become, Robert, isn't the man I married. The man I married is dead."

"I believe you." Theo gently squeezes her arms. When he sees the surprised look in her eyes, he adds, "Yes, Sole, I believe you. I don't care how it happened. I want your heart to be alive because I know how deeply you can love. It's in the stories you tell about your marriage. It's in the song lyrics you write." He picks up her journal. "I wish I could touch the heart that writes these beautiful words, but you won't let me in. So I keep my distance and settle for seeing you once a month. I'll wait as long as you need me to wait because I know someday your heart will be free. When it is, I'll be the luckiest man in the world."

"Thank you, Theo." Soledad smiles before turning away from

him with the painting propped under her arm and wheeling her suitcase down the hallway. When she reaches the door, she turns to him again.

"Why are you taking our painting?" Theo inquires.

"You said it was me," she replies, hugging it to her chest.

"Promise me you'll come back."

"I'll be back next month, Theo," Soledad reassures him with a kiss.

"Where are you going?"

"I need to get away from Robert."

Theo looks down the hallway. "I'm the only one who is here with you, Sole."

"Not anymore," she whispers. When she opens the door, she adds, "I'm not sorry you knew Bob was dead. I still wish you did." And then she was gone.

Ms. Magoo

When Nita opens the door to her apartment after driving José to preschool, she can hear the water running through the pipes in the walls. She sets a bag of groceries on the counter and accidentally bumps up against the chipped Formica lip. "Damn," she mutters as she looks at the snag in her sweater. She goes into the bedroom and takes off the sweater. "Mom can fix this one too," she mumbles as she tosses it into the shopping bag next to the bed with the rest of the clothing that needs mending. She slides two plastic containers out from under the bed and takes the sweater Eric bought her out of one and an old t-shirt out of the other.

After slipping the sweater over her head, she stands on the bed to check out the lower part of her body in the mirror. She sits on the bed and leans back to repeat the process for the upper part of her body. She sighs, annoyed that she can't see herself in one piece anymore. This room isn't any bigger than the walk-in closet she used to have when she was married to Jim. She picks a piece of lint off her new silk sweater, sharply snaps the wrinkles out of the t-shirt, and slips it over her head. Stepping into the narrow path between the bed and dresser, she primps herself in front of the mirror.

Nita returns to the kitchen to put away the groceries. Whatever groceries she can't get in the small cupboard above the sink, she puts on the shelf in the closet next to the water heater. She picks up two computer paper boxes from the closet floor and sets them on the counter. Beneath the lid are two parfait dishes and crystal stemware glasses that she rinses out and sets on the counter before returning the boxes to the closet.

She dresses the tiny table in the corner of the living room next to the kitchen counter with a linen table cloth and the vase of roses Eric gave her last night. When the water stops flowing through the pipes in the walls and Eric slides the shower door open, she pours grapefruit juice in the crystal stemware on the table and fills the parfait dishes with strawberries and yogurt. Cloth napkins are folded into flowers and placed next to their plates.

Nita steps back to survey the room and frowns. She hates this place. All the wasted energy she has put into trying to make it look nice. The metal blinds on the windows are still bent. There are scuff marks all over the walls she has repeatedly washed. The couch and two recliners overpower the room. At least the table looks nice.

While buttering the sourdough toast, Eric comes up behind her and kisses the back of her neck. "Mmm, I could get used to this," he murmurs. He places his chin on her shoulder and presses his body against her back. "You're right about the water trickling out of the shower. I'll pick up a showerhead and install it tonight." He reaches around her and pushes on the faucet handle, hoping to stop the annoying drip. He kisses her cheek and says, "I'll fix this too, babe."

Holding her hand out toward the table, Nita says, "Breakfast is ready." She slides the t-shirt over her head and sets it on the kitchen counter.

"Keep going, baby!" Eric exclaims as he leans toward her and into the counter.

Nita moves away from him with a warning, "Careful Eric, you'll snag my new sweater."

He stares at the two pieces of toast on the plate she hands to him. "Is this breakfast?"

"Along with the yogurt, fruit, and juice on the table," Nita explains.

"Where are the eggs?"

She defends her eating habits. "This is what I usually eat for breakfast."

"Are you putting me on a diet?"

"No," she replies, playfully squeezing the layer of fat around his waist as they sit down.

After he tastes the yogurt and strawberries, he grumbles, "They're not sweet."

Nita opens the sugar bowl on the table and slides it toward him.

"Do you have any eggs?" Eric asks again.

"Sorry, I don't do eggs, fried potatoes, ham, bacon, or sausage."

"Well, I do," he tells her. He takes out a notepad and writes *eggs*.

Nita grabs the list out of his hand and reads, "Fix shower and drip in faucet, get door lock for bedroom, eggs." She holds it up to Eric and asks, "Does this mean you are staying here tonight?"

"You bet I am," he replies with a wink. "I wouldn't miss an opportunity to be with my baby, even if she doesn't know how to cook."

"The hours I spent slaving over the stove during my marriage are over. Yesterday, August 13, 2004, the day Julia Child died, I declared a moratorium on cooking and baking," she proclaims as she touches his red nose. "You got too much sun this summer."

"If you didn't look so good in a bikini," Eric murmurs as he scans her body, "I would have spent more time under the water instead of watching my Aphrodite tan her body." He slides the parfait dish to the side and says, "I want you instead of this."

"Tell me why you want me," Nita whispers.

He pulls Nita from her chair and onto his lap. "I want you because you're beautiful and a tiger in bed." He pauses to kiss her. "You make me feel so good, babe."

"You're good too."

"Only good?" Eric pouts.

"Yup," Nita teases him.

"How will I ever keep up with my Aphrodite?"

"All she wants is to be rescued from the bottom of the sea."

"I'm the man to do it," he whispers while devouring her body with his eyes.

"Is that all you think about is sex? It won't help your career."

"Au contraire," Eric laughs. "Clinton's approval rating soared to 76% after his rendezvous with Monica."

Nita slides off Eric's lap and clears the dishes from the table.

She slips the t-shirt on the counter over her head before returning to the table to refill their coffee cups.

He pulls on the bottom of the oversized t-shirt. "Was it something I said?"

"The dings in the countertop snag my clothing," she explains as she pours coffee into their mugs. "You wouldn't want the expensive sweater you bought me to get ruined."

"Take it off, baby," he pleads. "I'll buy you another one. I'll buy you a new countertop and anything else you want. Just take that ugly thing off."

"I don't want my things replaced," Nita replies. "I want a better place to live."

"Do you want me to replace him, babe?" Eric asks.

"That depends on what you mean by replace," Nita teases.

"Doesn't my girl think I'm worth it?"

"I don't know yet," she chuckles.

He leans toward her and says, "I love you."

Her smile quickly turns to a frown.

"Don't you love me, babe?"

"It's too soon for those words."

"No it isn't," he protests. "We're practically living together."

"Spending time with me in this cracker box apartment since we got back from Grand Cayman isn't the same as living together."

"Six weeks is enough time to know you, especially after those five fabulous nights on the island," Eric swoons.

"Grand Cayman was a vacation," Nita points out, "not a regular way of living."

"It wasn't all fun and games," Eric claims. "I worked. You were the only person in the audience, listening to my conference paper on computer protocols when all the techies who were supposed to be there were at the beach."

She sets her coffee cup down. "Be practical, Eric. I've only been divorced a year. I've only known you for six weeks. It's not enough time to know—"

"I know you," he insists.

Nita stands up and says, "No, you don't."

"Sure I do. You're the girl who sits in the front row of my class. You're the girl I've been taking out to dinner after class for the last six weeks. You're the girl I took with her son to the children's museum. I don't need to know anything else about the gorgeous doll I woke up with this morning to know that you're it for me, babe."

"Do you really think the person you see in this awful apartment is me? I used to have a nice kitchen with granite countertops that didn't snag my clothing." Nita walks around the counter into the kitchen and opens the squeaky cupboard door. "I used to have cabinets that didn't make funny noises when they were opened. Now I don't have anything except pathetic choices I shouldn't have to make."

"What kind of choices?"

"Forget it, Eric." She turns away from him to put the butter in the refrigerator.

"Tell me, babe," Eric encourages her.

"Forget it," she repeats. "I'm just having a temper tantrum."

Eric comes up behind her and wraps his arms around her. "I bet I know what's wrong with my girl. Now that she has turned the part time job she had when she was married into a full time one, she earns enough money to get by. But it's hard to get a better paying job with benefits when she doesn't have a college degree."

"I'm going to have to drop out of school to pay for José's preschool," Nita explains.

"I thought you told me it's covered by your work with the church."

"It was until…" Nita pauses and moves away from Eric. "It doesn't matter."

Eric grins at her. "Why don't you move in with me?"

She drops the stemware glass on the counter. "Stop joking," Nita warns while examining the glass to make sure it isn't chipped.

"Better yet," Eric says excitedly, "let's get married."

"What's wrong with you?" Nita scolds. "You're usually so sensible."

Eric ignores the scolding and says, "Let's do it, babe. You'll have everything you want; a nice house filled with pretty things, a big closet for all your clothes, and a kitchen with countertops that won't snag all the outfits I'll buy for you."

"What about my three-year-old son?"

"He comes with you."

"I wouldn't have it any other way," Nita exclaims.

"I'll turn my office into a bedroom. It'll be great, babe!" Eric exclaims. "You can quit your job and go to school full-time, and even get a Masters Degree or Ph.D. I won't even have to pay for it after we get married."

"Who said anything about marriage?"

He leans across the counter and looks into her eyes. "What are we doing this for if we're not going to get married?"

"What about José?"

"I'll pay for his preschool so you can take classes during the day."

Nita stops drying the stemware and forces a smile on Eric.

"Come on, babe. It'll be perfect."

"Forget it," Nita replies as she returns to briskly polishing the stemware. "You don't know anything about me, Eric."

"I know as much as I need to know about my girl," he whispers.

"You don't know why I'm divorced," she whispers back.

"I don't care. We wouldn't be together if you didn't have an affair," Eric teases her.

"He was the one fooling around," Nita replies.

He gives her a puzzled look. "No man in his right mind would leave such a desirable sex pot for another woman."

"It wasn't a woman."

It took a few seconds for Nita's statement to register with Eric. "A hot potato like you married to a fag," he snorts.

"That's not funny, Eric," she barks.

"Sure it is, babe."

"I tell you the reason for my divorce—"

"—which is laughable," Eric interrupts.

"What if I had laughed when you told me your wife left you for another man?"

"It's not the same thing."

"You're right. It's much worse."

"Now that's laughable. You're much better off without a fag in your bed."

"Stop it!" Nita shouts.

"What's the big deal? All I'm saying is you are too much of a tiger in bed to be with—"

"Don't use that word again," Nita warns with fire in her eyes.

"Okay, I won't," he concedes. "I need to sit down for this one." He takes her hand and leads her to the couch.

"Imagine the shock when I found out." Nita starts to tell him what happened.

Eric pulls her onto his lap. "Forget about him, babe. If you stick with me, you won't even have to mention his name. You don't have to worry about me. I love women and want you, even if he doesn't. I'll give you," he winks at her, "all the sex you want."

"Will you shave off your beard?" Nita asks.

"I thought you liked my beard."

"My husband grew one when he came out."

"Get the razor, babe." Eric nuzzles his bearded face in her breast. "I want my girl in my bed every night, and I want to wake up with your beautiful body lying next to me every morning."

Digging Up the Corpse

"I'm not who you think I am," Soledad tells the woman standing over her chaise on the Platja de la Barceloneta. She brings her sunglasses over her eyes and fixes her gaze on the white caps caressing the shore with the hope of easing the panic that has overcome her.

The man on the chaise next to Soledad sits up to acknowledge the woman. "I'm Theo."

She extends her hand to Theo. "I'm Susan."

Soledad leans over and whispers to Theo, "I don't know this woman."

"I'm glad I ran into you," Susan continues as she spreads her towel out on the chaise next to Soledad. "Kenny and I are dating."

Soledad leaps up and stuffs her feet into her shoes. Theo gives her a puzzled look and asks, "Where are you going?"

"Go back to sleep," she orders him. "I'll be right back."

"Wait for me," Susan cries. She stuffs her towel back into her bag and runs after Soledad.

Soledad stops to address Susan. "I'll meet you at the bar in five minutes." She notices Theo has his neck cocked toward them. "Not this one, the one on the beach next door."

She breathes a sigh of relief as she watches Susan walk in the opposite direction of Theo. She walks back onto the sand and tells Theo, "I got rid of her."

"Who is she?"

"Someone I have to interview," Soledad tells him. "I had a temporary lapse in memory. I'll be back in an hour."

She walks down the boardwalk in the opposite direction of the cabana bar where she sent Susan and ducks behind the wall of a tapas bar until Theo settles back in the chaise. She uses the sidewalk by the street instead of the boardwalk, slowing her pace as she nears the cabana bar where Susan is waiting.

"Who's winning?" Soledad asks as she slides on the stool next to Susan and signals the bartender for a pitcher of sangria.

"I haven't seen the score yet," Susan replies. "It's the final game of the Euro 2004 between Greece and Portugal. I don't know anything else about it because I don't follow soccer."

"It's a rerun. You better be careful, Susan, the Spaniards love their football. You're taking your life in your hands with words like that," Soledad teases before getting to the point. "How's Kenny?"

"He's fine. His studio in Providence is going gangbusters, and a number of Boston and New York studios have been displaying his work. He's teaching at RISD now," Susan says proudly.

Soledad pours the sangria into their glasses. "Is he here?"

Susan shakes her head. "He won't be here until the weekend because of a few beginning-of-semester things he has to do before his sabbatical. He's doing a comparative study of Surrealism and Impressionism with—you'll like this one—a political science professor."

Soledad laughs. "That's a stretch for Kenny."

"I'm sure he'd like to see you."

"I would too," Soledad concurs, "but I leave for Paris tomorrow."

"I haven't been there. English teachers can't afford to travel through Europe the way you do. We live vicariously through your column in the *Globe*."

Soledad shrugs. "All the bouncing around I do is not as glamorous as it seems."

"Where have you been since you ran..." Susan hesitates. "I haven't seen you since my fortieth birthday party."

"Oh, I forgot about that," Soledad groans. She takes a long swig of sangria. "1998 was a very bad year."

"Where did you go?"

"I've been everywhere since then. The *Globe* gave me a year leave right after your party. I lived in a beachfront condo in the Florida Keys. It was exactly what I needed at the time. I took long walks, ate fish that were still alive that morning, watched the sunset every night, the sunrise every morning, and wrote song lyrics. I even went deep-sea fishing."

"You needed to run away."

"Something like that," Soledad replies. "After that, I negotiated this European gig with the *Globe*. I've been doing it for the last five years. Now I'm talking to the *Chicago Tribune*."

"They're stealing you from the *Globe*."

"It was my idea. I'm burnt out. I need a life that is more settled."

Susan looks at the sun shining on Soledad's face. "You've come a long way since our Providence College days. I remember the scathing articles you used to write about Reagan's deregulation policies and supply side economic programs—"

"I heard he died a few weeks ago," Soledad interjects.

"He did," Susan replies before finishing her thought, "—and how much trouble you gave the professor when he tried to stop you."

"All I did was write what needed to be written. It's hard to do anymore. These days, the news is more about ruining people's lives than reporting the truth."

Susan empties the pitcher into their glasses. "Did we drink all of it already?"

"It's not as bad as it looks. This is the only European country that uses more ice in the summer than America. As they click glasses, Soledad's thoughts drift off into the azure water of the Mediterranean Sea rolling up into a giant whitecap as it thunders toward the shore.

Susan's words, "What makes a guy gay?" throb in her ears like the pounding surf.

Soledad knew it was coming, but she didn't expect Susan to be so blunt. "What makes you think I would know?" she asks.

"You've known Kenny for years. Do you know why he's still not married at forty?"

"I haven't the slightest idea." Soledad shrugs. "Maybe he hasn't met the right woman yet. I mean until now."

"Did Kenny show any signs of being gay when you were married to Bob?"

"Signs?"

"Yeah, you know, real close male friends or unusual sexual interests?"

"I don't think his friends were gay, but then again, I didn't know them very well. As for his sex life, I will defer to Kenny," Soledad replies tersely.

"I really like him, Sole, but I'm afraid." When Soledad gives her a puzzled look, she adds, "He's an artist. You know what they say about artists."

"No, Susan, what do they say?" Soledad asks with a touch of sarcasm in her voice.

"He has a gay brother," Susan replies. "If a handsome, well-built carpenter who was so much in love with you can turn, there's no telling who is gay."

Soledad studies Susan.

"I don't know how you feel about Robert after what he did to you. I don't have a clue what I would have done if I were you. I do know I don't want the same thing to happen to me. I thought you might be able to tell me what happened to Bob so I'd know whether or not to worry about Kenny."

Soledad tries not to snap at Susan when she says, "You should have asked Bob when you saw him."

"Now that would be uncomfortable!" Susan exclaims.

"But you have no problem asking me," Soledad retorts.

"You and Bob were the perfect couple, Sole. If there was any sign of him being gay while you were married, none of us saw it. You are the only one who would know for sure. How will I know if it happens to Kenny?"

Soledad breathes a laugh through her nose. "I, a woman who didn't know my husband would turn out to be gay when I married him, ought to know what signs you should look for before things get serious with Kenny. That's an absurdly tall order, Susan."

Susan busies herself with wiping the sweat off her glass with her napkin. After a minute or two, Soledad breaks the silence. "It's like dangling participles. You're an English teacher. You can usually tell by the way a sentence begins if it will end with a dangling participle. But sometimes you can't. Some sentence beginnings have obvious signs, while others don't. It's the same with Bob."

"There you are," Theo says. "I've been looking all over for you."

Soledad looks at her watch and slides off the stool. "I lost track of the time, Theo. We need to run, Susan. Thank you for the interview." She takes Theo by the arm and walks through the archway of the cabana.

"Wait, Sole. You forgot your tote," Susan calls out. She hands it to Soledad and says, "It was good to see you. I'll tell Bob I saw you."

"You knew Soledad's husband?" Theo asks.

"I sure do. His brother and I had dinner with him in Boston a few days ago."

Theo looks at Soledad. "I thought you said your husband was dead."

It's My Life Too

The voices at the tables in the hotel atrium build to a crescendo as professors gather the study participants together for their morning panel discussions. Judy is drinking coffee at a small table on the other side of the atrium, reading about the Fourth of July groundbreaking ceremony for the Freedom Tower at Ground Zero in New York City. She is sitting among a group of tourists having breakfast before a timeshare presentation because she doesn't want to be disturbed. She opens her computer and reviews her notes for the conference session.

1. Death is a better metaphor than divorce because it keeps your existence as a couple intact and recognizes the passing of a heterosexual life when one spouse comes out of the closet.

2. It's not like a normal death because the gay spouse isn't actually dead. What dies is the gay spouse's heterosexual identity closely tied to the straight spouse's identity.

3. The new homosexual lifestyle is celebrated as a birth of a buried identity, but the death of the heterosexual life is assumed to be an identity that never existed.

4. The coming out is experienced by some straight spouses as—

Judy looks up from the words on the screen and closes her computer as the clicking of the shoes of her children across the atrium stop at her table. "You're late," she tells them. "Why don't you get a cup of coffee and come with me?"

"I can't, Mom," Jerry says with his eyes on the floor.

"I don't have time to argue with you, Jerry," Judy replies curtly. "I have important work to do." She puts her computer under her arm and walks away.

"I'll talk to him, Mom," Kim tells her mother.

"Whatever," Judy mutters as she continues on without her children.

Kim glares at Jerry as he stops at the coffee bar.

"I can't be a hypocrite, Kim. I don't have to support what she is doing just because she is my mother." He turns to the clerk and says, "Café Americano with a double shot of espresso."

"Make that two," Kim tells the clerk. As they stand by the counter waiting for their coffee, Kim asks her brother, "Do you enjoy hurting Mom like this?"

"Of course not," Jerry scowls under his breath.

"Mom has had more than her share of grief," Kim reminds him.

"What about us? She didn't even tell us we have a gay parent," Jerry whispers sharply.

"Neither did Dad," Kim retorts before smiling at the clerk and saying, "Thank you." She turns back to her brother and warns, "Leave her alone, Jerry. She's been through enough. She shouldn't have to put up with your disapproval too."

"I can't help the way I feel about this," Jerry replies. "It's bad enough that we have a gay parent, but Mom doesn't have to broadcast it to the world."

"I'm not exactly thrilled about it either, but it's her life. We should be grateful instead of criticizing her for her research on families like ours," Kim reminds her brother.

"I don't want any part of it."

"There are more benefits in her work than you know. If you went to one of the sessions, you'd meet all kinds of people who share your feelings. I talked to a young man yesterday who reminded me of you. He felt forced by love for his gay father to enter a world he hadn't chosen to live in. His father's life was such a turnoff that he couldn't be in the same room with him."

"I don't blame him," Jerry grunts.

"You're acting the way that man did. He was angry at his mother for not telling him what his father should have told him years ago. It's easier to do than face the truth. You're confused. You're not alone, Jerry. I'm confused, too. The secure world we thought we had is gone, and what is left we don't know anything about."

"I thought you supported the gay lifestyle."

"I do, but I don't," Kim tells him. "I mean I thought I did. I feel like the woman I met last night who said she was a hypocrite, advocating gay causes in college, causes she thought she believed in, and then not supporting her mother when she came out. It's easy to be supportive of any cause when there isn't anything at stake, but when it is one of our parents who is gay…" she stops.

"What's your point, Kim?"

"It's an impersonal political and moral issue to most people, but for people like us, it's a personal experience. I'm not upset about how you feel. I'm not sure how I feel about it. It's like that woman said. She needs time to work through her conflicting feelings about her love for her mother and her dislike of her mother's homosexual lifestyle," Kim explains.

"You may as well add the straight parent to the list, Kim."

"Your behavior is uncalled for, Jerry," Kim scolds her brother. "Mom is giving us an opportunity to listen to and share our experience with people who have gone through the same thing we are going through right now."

"Sharing experiences is one thing, but it should be done behind closed doors. The sexuality of our parents is a private matter that should remain private."

"Mom's not asking anyone to make anything public that they prefer to keep private. She isn't advocating or condemning homosexuality. She's accepting it as a reality of our time that calls for a place where families of gays and lesbians can get together and share their concerns. The forum isn't public, Jerry. Advocating it is."

"Mom is putting our situation out in the open where everyone can see it, and—"

"I know. I know. You don't like it," Kim interrupts with disgust in her voice. "Sometimes you have to go public, put it in the face of the world, if you want to change how people look at something; especially if that something is difficult to talk about, listen to, and understand." She pauses. "Wait a minute. I know what's bothering you. You don't want Mom in the spotlight because of what it might do to your medical practice."

Jerry bows his head. "People don't want a doctor who has a—"

"Things are different now," Kim interrupts. "Homosexuality doesn't have the same stigma it did twenty-five years ago when gays were restricted to dance studios and art galleries. Now they're everywhere; in universities, factories, stores, courtrooms, construction sites, government agencies, even hospitals. I'll bet we could find one here."

"You're making me look ridiculous."

"You make yourself look ridiculous. You don't have to worry about what your patients think of you," Kim reassures her brother. "Most people don't care that we have a gay parent. The problem is finding a way to connect people like us who do so we can share our experiences. This is why Mom's research is so important."

"I know why she's doing it, but I don't have to like it."

"Put your feelings aside and come with me to Mom's presentation," Kim asks.

"No," Jerry scowls.

"What kind of son are you?" Kim scolds her brother.

"How am I supposed to know when Mom parades my life around the world as if it is her life? I'm not the kind of son Mom wants me to be."

"Don't you dare lay the blame on Mom," Kim barks. "You didn't have a problem free-riding off this conference in Grand Cayman to dive and snorkel, but you won't attend even one of her sessions. She hasn't asked you to do anything except to come to her talk today. She invited us so we could discover how much we have in common with people—"

"I am not one of them," Jerry protests.

Macho About-face

"Well, what do you know," Douglas smiles as he leans across the table to Nita. "That makes you one of us."

Nita opens her protocol notebook and says, "You're the first man I've met who has a gay ex-wife."

"You probably have met others and don't even know it. It's not in a man's nature to admit it," Douglas explains, "even though it is the worst thing that has ever happened to me."

"How so?" Nita asks.

"I don't want to talk about my ex-wife," Douglas replies. "I'm sitting on the deck of *Casanova's by the Sea,* having a drink with a very lovely lady. I can't imagine any better way to be interviewed."

"It is idyllic," Nita agrees. She looks at the waves lapping the shore of this island beach before diverting her attention to the two ships sitting side by side in the harbor.

"I'd rather be here with you than at a conference discussing film critiques with a bunch of academics."

"It's a curse of the trade," Nita replies.

Douglas laughs. "I wouldn't call this a curse."

Nita ignores the comment, focusing on the rhythm of her thumb flipping through her notebook. She's afraid to take her eyes off of the pages and is relieved when she finds one filled with research notes. She quickly asks the first question that pops off the page, even though it is out of order.

"Tell me, Douglas, about your male friends' reactions to your divorce?"

"You're all business," Douglas jokes as he holds his hand over his heart. "Okay, Nita, Dr. Clark's research assistant, but only if you'll have lunch with me. It's my treat."

"I don't know," Nita hesitates, afraid of where this encounter will go. *Douglas is much younger than Eric, far more handsome, and, wow, what a smile.*

Douglas's voice interrupts her thoughts. "I told Judy I was taking you here. She doesn't mind."

"She doesn't like my boyfriend," Nita says softly.

"Lucky for me," Douglas exclaims. Not giving her a chance to say no, he signals to the waiter and says, "We'll need a table for two."

The waiter smiles at Nita. "Follow me, ma'am."

Nita could feel Douglas' eyes following the sway of her hips toward a table on the veranda.

"For you, ma'am," the waiter says as he holds out the chair for Nita. "The best table in the house."

"For the best lady in the house," Douglas adds as the waiter hands him the wine menu.

Nita sticks her head behind the lunch menu to block his broad, tanned shoulders from view. *He's a study participant, a film professor from UCLA, a friend of my advisor,* she reminds herself.

"What kind of wine do you like?" Douglas asks.

Nita replies with the first thing that comes to mind. "I like Chilean wines." She blushes as she reminds herself that this is an Italian restaurant.

"We have Chilean wines," the waiter tells Nita. He turns the page of the wine menu and passes it to Douglas. "The 2005 Chateau Los Boldas is a very good wine."

"We'll have a bottle," Douglas tells the waiter. He turns back to Nita and says, "Okay, I'm ready. You want to know about the reaction of my friends to my divorce. Can I start with something I wrote?"

"Sure."

He looks right into her eyes as he recites, "The day I came clean to my friends, they outfitted her preference in fantasy. It had a bunch of women in bed with my wife, with appetites that could not be sated. I wasn't enough of a man, they snorted, to give her the pleasure she wanted. Or perhaps I was such a fantastic lover that no other man would suffice."

"I didn't know you were so—" Nita stops, turning her head to the sea.

"You didn't know straight men could be poetic," Douglas finishes her thought.

Nita blushes. "I'm sensitive to gay stereotypes."

It makes sense. My wife cut her hair when she came out. For a long time, I couldn't look at a shorthaired woman without wondering if she was gay. You have very beautiful hair," Douglas says as he watches Nita twist the ends of her windblown hair into a quickly spun braid.

"I have the same problem with beards. Jim grew one a year before I found out." Nita tries to blink away the image of being with this handsome man sitting across from her. She is grateful when the waiter returns with the bottle of wine they ordered. The Italian words on the menu distract her from the strength in Douglas' forearm as he swirls the wine around the bottom of the glass.

"Would you like to order?" the waiter asks.

Douglas nods. "Can you tell us about the Fus…ill…i…um, Fu…sil…li," he stumbles through the entrée listing on the menu.

"Fusilli con le Braciole," Nita corrects him.

"It sounds so good when she says it," Douglas tells the waiter. "What is it? It says it's Tony's Grandmother's Special Recipe from Ca…"

"Calabria. It's a region in Italy," the waiter explains. "Fusilli con le Braciole is a regional dish. We take pounded pork, roll it in bread, and mix it with risotto."

"It's too heavy for me," Nita says. "I'll have the Linguini del Mare."

"A very good choice, ma'am," the waiter nods. "What would you like to order, sir?"

"I'll have Fus…forget it." Douglas laughs. "Grandma's Special Recipe for me."

"Would you like an appetizer?"

When Douglas suggests Nita order for them, she tells the

waiter, "We'll share the Ortaglia di Stagione and the Carpaccio Condito for starters."

"Where did you learn to speak Italian so well?" Douglas asks Nita when the waiter leaves.

"I speak Spanish. There's enough overlap for me to read an Italian menu."

"Did you grow up in Spain?"

"I was born in the States, but my father came from Mexico City and my mother from Barcelona. My Uncle Theo, a painter, still lives there."

Douglas holds his glass up to her and says, "To a beautiful woman who likes South American wines."

She lifts her glass and takes a sip of wine. She watches him swish the wine around his mouth before swallowing it. *Hmmm, he's a real catch; cute, charming, sophisticated—stop it,* she scolds herself. *He's a man, not a Mayan god.*

"Ortaglia di Stagione and Carpaccio Condito," the waiter says as he sets the appetizers in the center of the table. "Prego."

"It means *back to work,*" Nita teases.

"You're tougher than you look, Nita."

"Looks can be deceiving," she shoots back to him. "Do you mind being recorded?" she adds as she pulls a tape recorder out of her bag.

"You want me to behave myself, don't you?" Douglas pouts.

Nita blushes as she murmurs, "I'll get in trouble if you don't."

"I know. You have a job to do. Please accept my apology for being so forward."

"It's okay," Nita replies. She looks in her notebook at a research question. *Describe the reactions of your male friends when they found out the reason for your divorce.* She doesn't remember if he answered this question or not. This is not the way she planned to start.

To stall, she says, "Go ahead and eat. I need a few minutes to review these questions. She uses her thumb to scan down the page of questions before turning on the tape recorder. "What was your reaction when your wife told you she was a lesbian?" she asks.

He leans back in his chair and chuckles. "The macho about-face."

"You're playing with me."

"No, I'm not. When men are faced with a reality we can't handle, we use anger to deflect the pain. When we can't get angry, we use humor. The reaction to my wife leaving me for a woman is easier to discuss with absurd terms like macho about-face."

"What does macho about-face mean?"

"It means that I turn away from the guys I tell as soon as I tell them and do something macho, like talk about sports, punch a friend's shoulder, or flirt with a woman. It is the only way I know to cope with the rejection."

"Tell me about the rejection."

"It has been overwhelming," Douglas admits. "There's the emotional rejection that comes from getting a divorce. There's also sexual rejection, but it's not the same as when it's another man. When it's another man, I am being rejected because another man is a better man for my wife than me. But when it's a woman, I am being rejected because I'm a man. My masculinity, my very being as a man was tossed aside when my wife left me for that woman."

He takes a gulp of wine before continuing. "Being with male friends who skittishly joke about lesbians was the only way I could cope with the rejection, that is, until I got tired of the jokes," Douglas says softly. He picks up his fork and pushes the appetizer around on his plate. "I severed myself from everyone who knew. It was the only way I could go on."

Their eyes meet when Nita instinctively reaches over to touch his arm resting on the table. She sees longing in his eyes when they reach into hers and notice the depth of her understanding. Her eyes quickly drop to her notebook and grab on to another question. "Would the reaction of your male friends have been different if she had left you for a man?"

"Absolutely," Douglas exclaims. "When a woman leaves a man for another man, most of his male friends feel sorry for him. But when my ex left me for a woman, they made fun of me."

"What did they say?"

"All kinds of things," he answers. "They teased me about being with two women. Some cracked jokes about me being so much of a man that no other man could satisfy my ex. Others made fun of me for not being enough of a man to keep her interested."

"Really?"

"Sure," Douglas replies. "The reaction isn't much different than that *Seinfeld* episode where George turns them into lesbians and Kramer brings them back. The sexual humor varies depending on how attractive the woman is. If she's nice looking, a sexual fantasy is built into the humor. When she isn't so good looking, they joke about how horrible it must have been to be with a woman who hates men."

"What happens when it's a gay man?"

"Most men don't joke about that."

"What makes it different?" Nita asks.

"It's harder for men to joke about gay men than lesbians. If we do, we'd be making fun of our own sexuality. I suppose it's the same for women, but it seems much worse for men. Macho guys don't have a problem with women being together especially when it meets the criteria of a male sexual fantasy, but there isn't anything funny about a man being with a man, even to men like me, who are more open-minded about our sexuality."

"Why?"

"Deep down, most men know they have little control over their sexual desires. The macho ones don't want to believe it. If they did, they'd have to admit it could just as easily happen to them."

"What about open-minded men?"

"Open-minded men are more in touch with their female nature, and therefore have a broader frame with which to look at homosexuality. They don't crack jokes about my sex life. They give me a quick gesture of empathy before moving on to something else."

"Linguini del Mare, ma'am, and Fusilli con le Braciole, sir." The waiter sets the dishes in front of them and refills their wine glasses.

Douglas takes a bite. "This is really good. How's yours?"

"Delicious," Nita replies after swallowing a morsel. "You were talking about broader frames."

Douglas grins at her. "When do we get to eat?"

"I was planning on doing both at the same time. It's the American way."

"I want to enjoy this meal with you, but I can't when I'm talking about her."

"I'm sorry." Nita forces her hands into her lap instead of reaching out to him.

"No need to apologize. You're doing a great job. I need a break, that's all. Before we dig into this tasty meal, I will tell you that I don't think the breadth of frames is gender related, but they do influence our reaction to the news. Narrow frames lead well-intended people to assume there wasn't anything normal going on between my wife and me. People with broad frames of reference understand that it isn't that simple. I have found that out of the mouths of the narrow minded come stupid jokes, but the more difficult questions of open-minded people come out clumsily."

Nita points her fork at Douglas and asks, "Will you tell me if I say something stupid?"

"You haven't so far."

"Has Dr. Clark?"

"Judy? Gay people usually don't react stupidly to this news."

"Do you think she's gay?"

"I don't care. I like what she's doing."

"How do you know Judy?"

"I met her a few days ago when I ran into Paul, a mutual friend of ours," Douglas explains. "I haven't seen him since I was a graduate student at UCLA. He's one of the open-minded people I told you about. When I told him about my wife, he introduced me to Judy."

"I haven't been to California. What's it like?"

"I like it, and I don't. The weather is as good as it gets anywhere in the world, but it's so plastic."

"The people or the area," Nita asks.

"Both. It's tiring to listen to people worry so much about the way they look. The traffic is horrible because they don't have a decent public transportation system. It doesn't fit my down to earth nature. I'd like to make a move, perhaps to Chicago."

"It's a great city. I grew up on the northwest side, near O'Hare."

"Judy likes it too. We're talking about a faculty opening at Northwestern University."

Nita tries to keep her excitement down as she asks, "What is your research field?"

"I study the role of the arts in political and social debate, primarily in films."

"It must be nice to get paid to watch movies," Nita teases.

"It is a hell of a lot of fun." Douglas leans across the table and whispers, "If you tell anyone I said it, I'll have to kill you."

"How is everything?" the waiter asks when he returns to the table and empties the wine bottle into their glasses.

"It's delicious," Nita and Douglas reply in unison.

He turns to Douglas and asks, "Would you like more wine?"

"No, thanks," Nita replies quickly in case Douglas plans to order another bottle.

They continue getting to know each other after the waiter leaves. "Judy told me you have a son. How old is he?" Douglas asks.

"He turned three a few weeks ago, on June 21st. I have a picture with me." She reaches into her purse for her digital camera, turns it on, and flips through the pictures. "Here he is," she proclaims proudly as she hands Douglas the camera.

"He is a handsome young man," Douglas tells her.

"He looks just like his father, but my father doesn't like it when I say so."

"Why?"

"I think he worries that Jose will turn out like Jim because he looks so much like him." Nita laughs uncomfortably. "I know it's absurd, but he can't help it. My father is old-fashioned. When he sees my son cooking or baking with me, he insists on taking my son outside to play baseball or into the living room to watch a soccer game with him. As a matter of fact, he was watching the final Euro 2004 soccer game with my son when I called yesterday."

"The macho about-face at work on the minds of young men," Douglas comments with a chuckle.

"He means well, but he's as bad as Archie Bunker when it comes to these kinds of things." She laughs. "What's really strange is that my dad shares a birthday with Carroll O'Connor, and my son was born on the day he died." She smiles at him. "I don't know what I would have done to get through this crazy year since my divorce without either of them."

"You're lucky. My wife couldn't have children." He flips to the next picture in the camera and asks, "Is this your father?

"No, it isn't," Nita states politely as she snatches the camera out of his hand.

"Who is he?"

Nita quickly pops the morsel of lunch on her fork in her mouth. She fans her hand in front of her mouth to indicate that the food is hotter than it is.

"Is he the man Judy doesn't like," Douglas asks.

Nita puts the camera back into her purse. Douglas watches her take a few more bites of her lunch. She finally caves in to the pressure of his eyes on her, wipes the corners of her mouth with the napkin, and says, "We've only gone out a few times. He's an IT professor."

"That man is your professor!" Douglas exclaims impulsively.

Nita looks out at the Caribbean Sea so he can't see the sting of his comment in her eyes.

"Forgive me, Nita, for being so rude. I have a terrible habit of speaking before I think."

She forces a smile on him and swallows. "It's okay," she lies. "I really like this dish." She turns her head toward her plate and slides a few morsels into her mouth.

They quietly eat their lunch as Douglas searches for a way to break the silence. After an awkward minute or two, he asks Nita, "Do you like movies?"

Nita looks up from her plate to say, "I do."

"What films interest you?"

"That's a tough question because I like so many," Nita replies, relieved that they have returned to a safe topic. "I'm a big fan of Katherine Hepburn."

"Most women who take my film class like her. One term paper described her as—"

"—an independent, determined, and caring woman both on and off screen," Nita declares proudly. "I especially like her comeback role in *Philadelphia Story* where she plays an unforgiving pillar of strength, adored by her fiancé and criticized by her ex-husband, Cary Grant. Jimmy Stewart's character, Mike, is the only one who can see her for who she really is."

Douglas is encouraged by the return of her smile. "It's hard for a man to really see a woman. It's why we mess up so much," he apologizes for his earlier comment and quickly returns to their movie discussion. "I'm a big fan of Hitchcock thrillers. My favorite is *North by Northwest,* with the sensuous Eva Marie Saint," he swoons.

"She is beautiful," Nita agrees. "My favorite Hitchcock flick is *Marnie,* starring the young Sean Connery."

"James Bond," Douglas states. When he sees her frown, he adds, "Most women in my film studies program are not James Bond fans even if they like Sean Connery."

"It's the way women are portrayed. Even their names are demeaning. I like movies in which both the woman and man are taking care of each other because we're complex creatures; strong and weak at the same time. As a matter of fact," she waves her fork in the air, "I fell in love with Christopher Plummer the first time I saw *The Sound of Music* because he was strong, principled, and not afraid to learn from and love a good woman."

"Singing your way through love is a poor substitute for kissing."

She blushes. "It would be difficult to put into practice."

The waiter arrives at the table with the dessert menus. "Everything was delicious," Douglas says as the waiter signals for the busboy to clear their table.

"The Trancia al limoncello sounds wonderful," Nita says as she quickly scans the menu.

"It's one of our special recipes, ma'am, from the Amalfitan coast," the waiter explains.

"I'll take it. No coffee, please. I'll have a glass of water from the tap, no ice."

"I'll have the Casanova double chocolate cake," Douglas tells the waiter.

"Very well, sir." He picks up the dessert menus from the table and disappears into the kitchen.

"You're awfully young to be interested in old movies."

"I'm twenty-six!" Nita exclaims.

"I rest my case," Douglas chuckles.

"I watch TV while studying at home. I don't feel so alone with the drone of voices coming out of the television speakers, especially since my divorce. I started watching the Turner Classic Movie channel because there is very little on during the day. I became hooked when I discovered that the issues they touch on in old movies are similar to those we have today."

Douglas grins at her. "You just passed my *Introduction to Classic Film* class."

"Here's the Casanova double chocolate cake," the waiter says, "and for you, ma'am, our special recipe from the Amalfitan coast."

After they dig into their desserts, Nita slides her plate across the table. "Try some of this. It's really good."

"Thanks," he reaches over with his fork. "Why don't you try some of mine while I answer the rest of your questions?"

Nita smiles uncomfortably after they exchange forkfuls of dessert, knowing she has to ask him an annoying question. "Brace yourself, Douglas," she warns as she turns the tape recorder back on. "I have to ask a question of you that I hate people asking of me."

He hangs onto the edge of the table and smiles at Nita. "Shoot."

"Why do you suppose your wife married you?"

Douglas breaks up the bits of cake on his plate into crumbs with his fork. "You're right, Nita. I don't like this question. I'm as ignorant as most people are about this," he replies. "There are so many things I don't have the capacity to comprehend. I don't know why she married me. I don't know if she's been a lesbian all her life or how she came to realize she is. Worst of all, I don't know why her sexual orientation has had such an effect on me."

"How has it affected you?"

He leans toward Nita and whispers, "I'm uncomfortable talking about this."

"With this on?" Nita asks as she turns the recorder off.

"No, with you," he explains. "You are a very attractive woman, Nita."

"Thanks." She turns the tape recorder back on.

Douglas stops her. "The interview is over. It's my turn to ask questions."

Nita feigns a smile. "I may not be as cooperative as you have been," she warns.

"Just tell me what you did when you found out your ex was gay."

"I got as far away from him as possible."

"Where did you go?"

"I went to see a friend."

"Male or female," he asks.

"I went to see Deb, my next door neighbor. We're good friends," Nita recalls.

"Your best friend was the first person you told."

"She wasn't home so I told her husband."

"What did you say to him?"

"I don't remember. It's all so vague now." Nita fiddles uncomfortably with her dessert before saying, "All of a sudden my life was a movie."

Douglas takes a long drink of water. "There's something I want to say, Nita, but I'm afraid you might take it the wrong way."

"Go ahead," she says with her eyes focused on her dessert.

When she looks up at him, he says, "I'm afraid of you."

"Excuse me?"

"Promise you'll hear me out."

"Okay." Nita sets down her fork.

He leans over the table and whispers to Nita, "I know what the coming out of our spouses has done to us."

"What has it done?" she whispers back.

"It has made us sexually promiscuous."

It's Not All Girl Talk

"Our sex life is linked to their gayness by sheer affiliation," the female therapist facilitating the session explains. "When the sexual identity of the person you've been with changes, it has an effect on your sexual identity."

One of the women sitting around the forum circle sighs with relief. "I'm dating a guy who wants to know why I like..." She pauses before adding, "This is embarrassing."

Several of the women nod, knowing exactly what she wants to say. "If it makes you feel any better," a redheaded woman explains, "we all do what you're doing at the beginning."

"Don't feel bad," the sharply dressed CPA wearing a silk blouse, teal sarong, and matching sandals adds. "My ex used to call me a sex maniac if a guy so much as looked at me. I took him to a party a few years back for some friends who had just passed the CPA exam. He was standing right next to me as I was telling a funny story to a bunch of guys," she says while kicking the foot of her crossed leg in exasperation. "All of a sudden, he pulled me by the arm and escorted me to the car. He yelled at me all the way home about the way I was flirting with the guys."

"He wasn't jealous of the attention you were giving to them," a matronly woman in a floral sundress speculates with a chuckle. "He was jealous because the boys were giving you the attention he wanted from them."

"Don't ever believe something is wrong with being attracted by or attractive to the opposite sex," the therapist insists.

"When you have a gay ex, you can't win." The redhead shakes her head in disgust. "I'm dating someone who thinks the only reason I like sex is because I'm trying to prove something to myself."

"It works both ways," a young woman with piercing brown eyes joins in. "The guy I'm dating overdoes the sex thing to make sure I know he isn't gay."

"Is he the one I saw you with in the lobby bar last night?" the sharply dressed woman asks. When the young woman nods, she adds, "He's too old for you, honey."

"Don't settle for the icebreaker," the matronly woman advises. "There are better men down the road for you."

"Take my advice, honey. Don't get serious with anyone for a while," the redhead chimes in. "Enjoy the attention, but be careful of the ones who use your story to get you in bed."

The conference room door slowly opens as a couple slips into the room, trying to be unobtrusive, and nods to Nita sitting at the back of the room.

"Sign in here," Nita whispers as she motions toward the table next to her.

"Thanks," the woman whispers as the man leans over the table and signs in.

Nita turns her attention back to the voice of the elderly woman in the floral sundress. "I'm afraid to tell my boyfriend." She laughs. "He's not really a boy. I just don't know what to call him. *Man friend* makes him sound like an ape. The term *significant other* has connotations more appropriate to our exes."

The CPA nods her head sympathetically. "The first one I told broke up with me. I think he was afraid to be with a woman who has a gay ex-husband."

"Everyone who has a gay ex should get tested for AIDS," the facilitator points out.

"It was more than that," she continues. "I could see in his eyes the instant I told him that he thought I was a freak."

"You don't need a man like that in your life," the redhead reassures her.

The man who signed in whispers to Nita, "Is this the session on identity?"

"No, it's in room ...," Nita pauses to look at her clipboard. "Follow me," she whispers and leads them out of the room. "We're glad you came, Barb and," she looks at the man's nametag, "Kenny. The session is in the room two doors down the hall."

"Thank you," they reply in unison.

Nita turns around and notices Jerry sitting in the chair outside of Judy's session. She walks over to him. "I thought you were going to your mother's presentation?"

Jerry shakes his head as Nita sits down next to him.

"What's wrong?"

"I'm a terrible son. I can't go in there."

"Why not?"

He looks up at her with fear in his eyes. "Why does my mother's work bother me so much?"

"What is it about her work that bothers you?"

Jerry buries his head in his hands. "I don't want to talk about it, think about it, or hear about it. When my mother brings up the topic, I run from her as fast as I can. I don't know what she expects me to do."

"Maybe all she wants, Jerry, is your support," Nita suggests.

"How can I support her when I'm ashamed of what she does? I know I don't have any reason to be ashamed of her, but I am."

Nita's thoughts immediately go to her parents' refusal to acknowledge her situation. "It must be hard for you. It's also hard for women like me to get the support we need, especially from the people closest to us."

Jerry looks up at Nita. "You too?"

Nita nods.

"I can't go to my mother's session," Jerry insists as he sinks back into the armchair.

"Then come with me to a different one," Nita suggests. "Let me show you what your mother is doing for people like you and me."

Jerry follows her toward a conference room and stops outside the door. "Why does it bother me so much that I have a gay parent?"

Nita shrugs, hoping these fears won't plague her son down the road. "I want to attend this session on identity. You don't have to do anything except sit in the back of the room with me and listen."

She opens the door and smiles at Paul, who is facilitating the session. They sit down in the chairs by the door as a therapist is advising a stately black woman who has shared her story. "If you ask yourself why, you'll just go crazy." The spectacles of the therapist are so narrow that she can only see through them when she looks down at the paper in front of her.

"It sounds as if you and your husband were happy," Barb empathizes. "Hang onto the happiness not onto him."

"It's impossible for a gay man to be happy with a straight woman!" a short, stout woman wearing an oversized cotton t-shirt exclaims.

"My ex and I were happy," the black woman defends her marriage. "We did everything heterosexual couples do together, but no one wants to believe me."

"Because you're fooling yourself," the stout woman insists as she folds her arms and covers the words "Grand Cayman" printed on the front of her t-shirt.

"No she isn't." Kenny stands up to defend the black woman, who is just barely managing to maintain her stately demeanor. "My brother was happily married for years to a wonderful woman and is now in a long-term gay relationship."

"My husband was happy with me, too," the black woman, near tears, repeats to Kenny.

"Your beliefs about your marriage are being questioned because you may not be ready to accept the truth," a handsome therapist with a shaven head explains.

"You don't know anything about my marriage," she snaps at him.

"No one can know for sure, one way or the other, without having been there," Barb insists. "Since this woman is the only one who lived it, we need to take her word for it."

"Anyone who doesn't is dishonoring her marriage," Kenny adds.

The female therapist looks over the top of her spectacles at the black woman who has lost her composure. "You might be hiding behind a façade," she tries again to reach her. "In that case the beliefs about your marriage would need to be dismantled so you can go on with—"

"It seems to me," Kenny interrupts the therapist, "that you may be the one hiding behind theories that support what you've been trained to believe about homosexuality. You're assuming that she is wrong without putting any thought into what she has told us."

"I agree," Barb declares. "If she is right, and we have no reason to believe she isn't, you are dismantling a part of her identity that she values."

The stout woman unfolds her arms and puts her hand on her hip as she addresses Barb. "She's fooling herself if she believes her husband was faithful to her during her marriage."

"You wouldn't like it if she said your marriage wasn't the sham you claim it is, but you have no problem believing this woman is wrong simply because her situation is different from yours," Barb replies with fire in her eyes.

"There isn't a one size fits all answer," Paul interjects. "Sexuality is complicated. Research has shown that there are physiological, psychological, and social reasons for our sexual nature. Research has also shown that we need to categorize life around us in order to make sense of the world. We sometimes put things in the wrong categories because our frames of reference don't include what is beyond our experience."

Paul turns to the black woman and asks, "Can you tell us your husband's name?"

"It doesn't matter," she mutters while shrinking into the chair.

Paul turns to Barb. "What is your brother's name?"

"Bob," Barb replies.

"What is the name of his partner?" Paul asks.

"William."

"Our ex-sister-in-law's name is Soledad," Kenny adds.

"We're caught in a common either/or conundrum," Paul explains to the participants. "If Bob's desire for a same-sex partner is a physiological state, as is the prevailing belief, then it's hard to believe he could have had a heterosexual relationship with Soledad. In that case, Bob's relationship with William would be respected, while his marriage to Soledad would not be. However, if his homosexuality is a psychological state, as was believed to be in the not-so-distant past, the interpretation would change to valuing Bob's marriage with Soledad, but not his relationship with William. These one size fits all categories don't work very well when trying to make sense of complex phenomena like sexuality.

"It's this kind of either-or thinking that has led this woman to hide her happy marriage in the closet her husband left behind," Paul suggests, hoping to bring the woman back into the conversation.

"And make up stories about my marriage that are acceptable to the people closest to me," the woman adds.

Paul smiles at the woman before addressing the therapists in the room. "We can't support this woman's experience with a simple perspective shift because it can lead to the same prejudice it is intended to eliminate. The only thing that changes is the object of prejudice."

"What do you mean?" the stout woman in the oversized t-shirt asks Paul.

"By looking at homosexuality solely through the physiological lens, gay relationships have a tendency to be categorized as an inherent part of nature while the reality surrounding the straight marriage is assumed to be a facade. Many times the marriage is a sham, but many times it isn't. If we put aside our either/or thinking and look at sexuality through a complex lens, we can see that these two seemingly opposing realities may not be mutually exclusive. It also makes it easier to see that this woman's marriage may have been as valuable a part of her husband's life as his gay partnership is today."

As Nita catches Jerry's eye, she wonders how her son will feel about her marriage to Jim.

"We encourage these kinds of discussions because they get to the heart of your confusion," Paul adds.

The black woman regains her composure and smiles at Paul. "You can't do that with family and friends, or even a therapist."

The room resonates with the groans of knowing women.

"The therapist I saw after my ex came out wanted me to tell him what happened in our bedroom," she explains. "I told him I didn't care."

"I remember telling my therapist how upset I was when there was speculation among my friends about whether or not I was gay after I brought an old college girlfriend to a New Year's Day party," the stout woman explains. "I could see by the way the therapist looked at me that he, too, was questioning my sexual orientation. I remember wishing I hadn't told him or my friends that my ex is gay."

The therapist's funny looking glasses hang on a chain from her neck, clearly revealing the affected concern she bent on the women. "Women therapists are better at—"

"Another fallacy," the black woman interjects. "Take my advice, honey, therapy isn't worth a damn to straight spouses. The female therapist I went to reached across the desk, patted the top of my hand, and said, 'Your poor husband.' I was mumbling, 'What about me?' all the way out the door."

"You're well on your way through the lack of support stage," a elderly woman with short graying hair says. "The first thing you hear when you go to a therapist is …"

"It's not your fault," the women shout in unison. The roaring laughter is followed by, "Duh."

"The next thing they say starts with …"

"It's a good thing that—," they chime in unison.

"—it wasn't a woman," one woman adds.

"—you don't have kids."

"—as if it's easier on us than it is on our children."

"People are sympathetic toward children, but if we say negative things about our gay husbands, we're accused of being homophobic," the stout woman adds. "I don't mind so much anymore that he is gay, but I still don't understand why he bothered to marry me."

Paul breaks into the conversation to address the therapists in the room. "These women are suggesting that therapy doesn't focus on the real source of betrayal or the identity issues of straight spouses."

"It's not just our identity. It's our children, too," a loud voice from the back of the room-interrupts Paul. The group turns to the young woman standing across the room from Nita and Jerry. "It has been hard for me," she begins as she walks toward the front of the room, "but I worry more about my five-year-old son. Someday he'll..." She pauses. "What will I say to him when he finds out his father is gay?"

Nita looks over at Jerry and wonders, *How will I tell my son?*

Breaking the Silence

"Mom is making a spectacle of our life."

"It's a conference for people like us, Jerry. Not one about our life," Kim explains.

"It's still embarrassing."

"She's a social scientist. It's her job to address controversial realities of our time," Kim defends Judy. "It's not any different than what you do when you address important medical issues."

Jerry glares across the table at his sister. "I do not put our personal life on public display for everyone to see."

"What do you expect her to do?"

"She should have told us in private," Jerry begins.

Kim leans over the table and reminds her brother. "She did, Jerry, a few weeks ago."

"It's 2004!" he exclaims. "She tells us twenty years after their divorce, and I'm not supposed to be upset."

"Stop it," Kim scolds her brother. "Mom paid for us to come to this conference in Grand Cayman because she wants us to hear what people like us have to say about…" She pauses to take a sip of water. "She hopes that listening to the experiences of families of gay people will help us get used to the idea."

"The famous Judy Clark," Jerry mocks, "is ruining it for all the people who want to keep their private matters private."

"You better not upset Mom tonight," Kim warns her brother.

Roland comes to the table to uncork the bottle of wine Kim brought to the restaurant. "Welcome to my restaurant. Be prepared for a romantic evening," he begins.

"She's my sister," Jerry explains in a matter of fact tone.

"I'm sorry, sir," Roland says.

Jerry laughs. "Sometimes I'm sorry she's my sister too."

"Sir?" Roland inquires.

"He has a strange sense of humor," Kim interjects. "We're waiting for our mother."

Roland smiles at them. "Would you like me to pour the wine?"

"There she is," Kim says as she stands up and waves at Judy walking up the path.

"We'll let it breath a little," Jerry tells the waiter as Judy sits down with her children.

"Where did you find this place?" Kim asks her mother.

"Nita told me about it. She came here last night with Eric," Judy rolls her eyes. "The way it works is Roland cooks what he feels like cooking, and we pay what we feel it is worth."

"What a strange idea," Jerry says.

"It's an awesome place," Kim disagrees. "I can't think of a better way to spend an evening with you, Mom, than eating a gourmet dinner on a linen table cloth in someone's backyard on a tropical island."

"How about eating it in a backyard that is not a mosquito-ridden rainforest and doesn't have a dog under the table," Jerry retorts.

"Think of it as a courtyard restaurant in Germany," Kim scolds her brother politely.

"I didn't know tropical plants were so common on this desert island," Judy comments.

"They've been brought in," Jerry states the obvious.

"When did you become so sarcastic?" Judy asks.

"He gets it from dad," Kim replies.

Roland returns to the table and asks, "Are you ready for the wine?"

"Yes, please," Judy replies as she swats a mosquito on her arm.

"Do you have any bug spray for my mother?" Jerry asks Roland.

"Yes, I do. I keep it behind those plants for all my guests to use," he replies. "Just follow the path around the corner."

When Judy is out of sight, Jerry sets his glass down and whispers, "Do you have any idea what it will be like for us now that all these people know? The jokes we'll have to put up with when people at home find out that Dad and Jeffrey are together. Let's not forget about our kids."

"Shhh," Kim whispers harshly.

"I don't want anyone to know," Jerry repeats.

"What's wrong," Judy asks as she returns to the table.

"It's nothing." Kim forces a smile on her mother.

Judy turns to Jerry and asks, "What don't you want anyone to know?"

"I don't want to talk about it," Jerry replies.

Kim changes the subject. "I was telling Jerry I've been asked to be one of the attorneys that represent the law firm at the Democratic National Convention later this month."

Jerry smiles gratefully at his sister. "And I was saying I didn't want anyone to know because I'm jealous. I told her she was only invited because she lives down the street from John Kerry."

Kim laughs. "There's a big difference between Beacon Hill and Beacon Street in the Back Bay. I bet you'd be the one with an invitation if the convention was going to be held in Chicago."

"Why would they want me?" Jerry asks. "I don't know anyone in politics."

"Sure you do," Judy addresses her son. "You live on the same street as Barack Obama, who will be delivering the keynote address."

"It's not the same thing, Mom. I live on the same block as a freshman senator from Illinois, but Kim lives within two miles of our next president."

"Presidential hopeful," Kim corrects.

"Hush, Kim," Judy replies. "I couldn't take another four years of Bush."

Roland comes back to the table with a tray of appetizers. He explains how he prepared each of the five different items on the tray and refills their wine glasses.

Judy takes one item off the tray and slides it between Kim and Jerry. "The rest are yours," she tells them.

Jerry slides the tray back toward her. "There's one of each for all of us, Mom."

"I know, honey, but I had a big lunch at the conference today."

She examines Kim's expression and asks, "Are you nervous about the convention?"

"She's nervous because she wants to ask you something," Jerry blurts out.

"No, I don't," Kim grumbles as she stretches her foot out underneath the table and kicks her brother.

"If you won't ask, I will," Jerry warns.

"Okay," Kim concedes, knowing that the question will be better received if it comes from her. "Ready, Mom?"

Judy nods.

"Why did you wait so long to tell us Dad is gay?"

The wicker chair makes a line through the stone as Judy moves closer to the table. "Your father told me a few years before the divorce. I knew something was wrong from the beginning, but I didn't know what it was."

"So he knew and married you anyway!" Jerry exclaims.

"Your father told me he was always gay. He just didn't know it when we got married."

"It doesn't make sense, Mom," Jerry replies. "If he was always gay, he must have known when he married you."

Judy pops an appetizer in her mouth, hoping to settle the churn in her stomach. "Try this one," she suggests to Jerry.

"It's really good," Kim agrees, happy for the diversion.

After setting her fork down, Judy holds her hand on her heart and smiles at Kim. "My daughter is going to be at the Democratic National Convention in a few weeks."

Kim smiles back at Judy. "It will be exciting, Mom," she agrees, turning back to their conversation about her father before Jerry does. "Is this why Dad stayed in the bedroom most afternoons before we had dinner?"

"You remember that?" Judy asks with surprise. "You were only five at the time."

"Four," Kim corrects her mother.

"Why did you stay with him after you found out?" Jerry asks.

"Things were different back then, Jerry. Homosexuality wasn't as accepted as it is now. We had—"

"I don't understand, Mom," Jerry interrupts. "How could he be with you in a heterosexual way and then be with someone else in a homosexual way?"

"Only your father can tell you why he is gay, Jerry. All I can tell you is he started out with the best intentions."

"Why are you protecting him?" Jerry starts another interrogation.

"I'm merely pointing out that your father is in a better position to answer some of the questions you are asking me," Judy explains.

"I don't get it. How it is possible that Dad didn't know he was gay when he married you?" Jerry reiterates.

Judy takes a deep breath. "I wish I had the answer, honey. Why don't you ask your father?"

"We can't ask Dad these kinds of questions," Jerry protests.

"I see." Judy pauses. "Well then, I'll do the best I can. Why didn't he know?" she repeats her son's question. "He probably didn't want to admit that he was gay. It's very common for people to deny what they can't accept about themselves. It was also standard practice in the 1960s and 1970s to try to cure people of homosexuality which probably made it worse for your father."

"We know the clinical answer, Mom," Jerry reminds Judy. "We want to know how he could be with you in that way if he didn't like women."

"Your father didn't dislike women. He didn't like to be with them in that way," Judy corrects her son. "By the time I knew for sure that he didn't have much interest in our..." she hesitates, "in women, we had years of living together behind us, a shared history that included you. It was... he was ..."

"Did you have sexual relations with him after you found out?" Jerry asks.

"I'm not going to answer that question," Judy replies. "I will tell you that things were never quite right in the bedroom."

Roland sets the main course menu on the table. Judy examines the faces of her children as he explains how it will be prepared. He refills their wine glasses and disappears down the path.

"We have another question, Mom." Kim waits for Jerry to nod before she begins. "We were wondering if Dad's coming out was triggered by an event."

"An event," Judy repeats.

"Something that caused him to change," Jerry replies.

"Your father didn't change," Judy corrects.

"Maybe he did," Jerry counters.

"We were thinking that sexuality lies on a spectrum," Kim interjects. "There might be degrees to which people are homosexual and heterosexual, just as there are degrees to which people are happy and sad." She waves her hand toward Jerry so he can add his thoughts.

"I know from my experience in treating patients that no one reacts to the same event in the same way," Jerry explains. "Some people are happy all the time, others are depressed all the time, but most people, being in the middle, need an event to trigger happiness or sadness. Maybe our sexuality, like our mood, depends on the interaction between nature and nurture."

"It's possible," Kim agrees with her brother before Judy has a chance to comment. "People who are on the homosexual end of the spectrum don't need an identity-altering event to be gay. Similarly, an identity-altering event can't turn those of us on the heterosexual end into homosexuals. It's the people in the middle who are most vulnerable to these events. They aren't necessarily bisexual. They could also be straights turned gay or gays turned straight because some identity-altering event interacts with their sexual nature."

"It's an interesting theory," Judy tells her children. "But even if it is true, it doesn't change the fact that your father has always been gay."

"Maybe the identity-altering event occurred before he married you," Jerry suggests. "If important events over the span of our life like puberty, midlife, and old age cause us to reshape our sexual behavior, perhaps an event during puberty or the war may have caused him to shift his interest from women to—"

"I'm pretty sure it didn't happen that way for your dad," Judy interjects.

"Maybe someone messed him up," Jerry suggests.

"Your father has always been—" Judy says with irritation in her voice.

"What Jerry means, Mom—" Kim interrupts.

"I can speak for myself," Jerry barks at his sister.

Kim ignores her brother as he picks up the appetizer tray and passes it to Judy. "If homosexuality and heterosexuality aren't mutually exclusive," she continues, "there may be just as many gay people who don't hide in the closet during their marriage as those who do."

Judy sighs. "It makes sense, but your—"

"Which one is worse?" Jerry leaps in.

"They're both difficult in different ways," Kim speculates, hoping to stave off another one of Jerry's interrogations. "When it's in the closet, the gay spouse ends up betraying the straight spouse by marrying them. If it's an identity-altering event, the betrayal happens at the end of the marriage to both spouses. The gay spouse may even go as far as to blame the straight spouse for the shift in sexual orientation."

"The theory also explains bisexuality," Jerry adds. "A spectrum suggests differences in the strength of the pull toward one orientation or the other."

"It doesn't matter where anyone falls on the spectrum," Judy replies. "It is a very confusing experience for the straight spouse."

"How was it confusing for you?" Kim asks.

"I had to come to terms with the conflict between the married life everyone believed we had and the reality of your father's interest in…" Judy stops and looks at her son. "You're right, Jerry. I am being insensitive to how you feel about this. It must be just as hard to reconcile the difference between the straight father you thought you had and the gay one he actually is."

"I've suspected for a long time that Dad is gay, but I didn't want to believe it. It is easier to believe Mom had a—" Kim stops mid sentence.

"It's okay, honey," Judy encourages her daughter. "You can say it."

"It's not okay," Jerry disagrees. "You lied to us about having an affair."

"Did I?" Judy asks.

"I don't know what else to call it," Jerry whispers sharply. "You knew we'd reach a false conclusion that would hurt our relationship with you."

"And help the one you have with your father," Judy adds.

"You didn't do it for us," Jerry scoffs. "You did it to protect Dad's reputation. Do you have any idea what it's like to be kept in the dark about something like this?"

"I certainly do. Your father was also my husband," Judy reminds her son.

"Then you must have known we'd get hurt by keeping it from us." Jerry folds his napkin next to his plate and motions Roland to come to the table.

"Is everything okay?" Roland asks.

"The appetizers are delicious," Jerry replies. "I have an emergency and won't be able to dine with my mother and sister."

"He's a doctor," Kim explains.

"I'll take care of them, sir," Roland replies.

"Please excuse me, Mom. This is more than I can handle," Jerry explains.

Judy reaches for Jerry's arm as he stands up. "Give me one minute of your time before you walk out on us," she insists.

When he settles into the chair, she leans across the table and speaks in a soft, clear tone. "Your father was very confused about his sexuality, but I stayed with him because he was my husband and a good father to you. Maybe we should have told you about it at the time of the divorce. I didn't because it was, in my opinion, your father's place to tell you. Since you seem to think it was my place, let me ask you something. When is the best time to tell your children that their father is gay? Should I have told you in preschool when I suspected something seriously wrong with our relationship? What about when you were thirteen and your father told me the truth? Should I have told you in high school that your father was discreetly seeing someone? I didn't think about getting a divorce until … ," Judy pauses. "What would you have said if I had told you when we divorced?"

Jerry turns his eyes to the table.

"It would have been just as hard then as it is now," Kim replies.

Judy pats Jerry's hand. "What you're feeling right now, honey, you would have felt no matter when or who told you," Judy explains. "All we did was delay the inevitable. You're right. It wasn't fair to deprive you of the chance to deal with this during our divorce by fooling myself into believing you wouldn't have strong feelings about it. Right or wrong, I did what I thought was best for you."

"You always have, Mom," Kim reminds her brother.

"I know," Jerry replies with quick glance at his mother.

"Good," Judy says as she picks up her wine glass. "Now, let's enjoy our dinner."

"I can't, Mom. I need to be alone for a while." He stands up and says to Kim, "I'll take a cab back to the hotel. I love you, Mom," he tells Judy as he leans over and kisses her cheek.

"Here you are, ma'am," Roland says as he sets two plates of seafood in front of them.

"Thank you," Kim replies.

Judy feigns a smile and murmurs, "I've lost my appetite," as she watches her son walk down the path to the road.

"I'm sorry, Mom," Kim catches Judy's attention with the squeeze of a hand. "We shouldn't have brought this up tonight."

"Yes you should," Judy insists. She wipes the corner of her mouth with her napkin and smiles at Kim. "It's normal for you and Jerry to ask difficult questions when you're confused about who your father is. It's good that Jerry is so open about his feelings."

"He's always been like that," Kim comments.

"And you're too worried about everyone else to say what is on your mind," Judy reminds her daughter.

"I don't know what to say."

"How about starting with when you were four years old?"

Kim sets her napkin back on her lap. "I didn't know what to make of any of it at the time. I still don't. How can I blame Dad for being who he is? And yet I do because of what he took from you."

"Took from me?" Judy echoes.

"I know you gave up a lot for us because of Dad." Kim holds up her hand as Judy starts to protest. "I knew something was wrong when we came home after school to Dad hiding in the bedroom. It wasn't until I was old enough to stay overnight at my friend's house that I figured out why he did it."

"You knew!" Judy exclaims.

"I suspected, but I didn't want to believe it. It was hard not to know after I saw my friends' parents together. They talked to each other over dinner. They would wink at each other across the room while they were watching TV. Dad didn't look at you that way. I knew it wasn't you because he didn't look at any woman that way. He didn't complement you on the way you looked or give you a peck on the cheek the way my friends' parents did. You didn't even go to bed at the same time. You and dad sat in separate chairs across from each other, pouring over your work without even so much as acknowledging each other. The only time you were mentally in the same place was when Jerry and I needed help with homework."

"You noticed all that?" Judy says softly.

"I did, Mom. I can't be upset with you about any of this when I know how much of yourself you gave up to protect us from Dad's secret."

Chasing the Sun

As Soledad looks into the warm, Alaskan sun, she reminisces about the sunset and sunrise she witnessed early this morning. The sun had sunk below the horizon and halted momentarily before lifting its head into the same symphonic spectrum of color that hung in the sky only an hour earlier. It was a reminder of how tenuous her darkness is and how easily her life with Bob is revived and murdered every time she hears the words, "What happened?"

She doesn't want to explain what happened. The spectrum of colors in the sky is enough. The truth of their life together and its inevitable death lies in the contrast that appears when you hold two seemingly opposing states of nature side by side. As one side of Bob's nature took hold, the other side disappeared from sight.

"What's a woman like you doing alone in the wilderness?"

Soledad looks up at a rugged looking man of about thirty. "I'm not exactly alone," she replies.

"You got me there." He laughs. "I'm sorry to say you don't look like you belong here."

"What leads you to that conclusion?" she asks.

"People around here don't paint their toenails."

Soledad quickly whips the sock out of her hiking boot and slips it on her bare foot. "Are you making fun of me?"

"It's my feeble attempt at conversation." He sits on the bench next to her. "Let's start over. I'm your guide, Adam, from Portland."

"Maine or Oregon?" she asks. She leans over and pulls the lace tightly around her hiking boot.

"Maine."

"Well, what do you know," she utters, "another New Englander alone in the wilderness."

"Now you're making fun of me," he contends. "That's okay,

Soledad. I'm looking forward to bantering with you during our three day stay in the Brooks Range." He looks at the clipboard. "You are Soledad, aren't you?"

She nods while stomping her foot a few times into her hiking boot.

"Where are you from?"

"Providence," she answers stiffly. She stands up, places her foot on the edge of the bench, and laces up the other boot. "I don't live there anymore. I'm on my way back to Paris."

"Alaska is a roundabout way to get from Providence to Paris."

Soledad sits back down and sticks her head in her journal.

"You don't seem like a tourist," he continues. "You look like someone who lost the other half of the couple."

"You sound like someone who works for the FBI," she shoots back at him without looking up from her journal.

"I don't mean to pry," he apologizes. "I am interested in the people who take these trips. Knowing about you helps me guide you through the wilderness," he explains while swatting away the mosquitoes that are hovering over his DEET-covered skin.

She snaps her journal shut. "Okay Adam, I'm a journalist and song writer. I live in Europe," she recites. "I came to Alaska on holiday after a few meetings in Chicago and Boston."

"When I saw you on the bench all by yourself I thought..." he pauses. "I know what it's like to go through a divorce." There is an awkward silence between them before Adam asks, "Would you like to me to show you around the camp?"

She shrugs. "I don't have anything better to do." She places the journal and pen in her backpack and allows his extended hand to lift her off the bench.

"The population of Bettels hovers around fifty in the summer when the outfitters are here. The long harsh winters push most of them away by Labor Day. Only the local Indians stay year round. Bears are the only other life around here. We do everything we can to keep them away. These bells let them know where we are, and the tightly sealed barrels over there to keep them from our food. That's the ten cent tour. If you want the rest, you'll have to wait for the book."

"Do the Indians in this area speak Ath … tha … pask?" Soledad stumbles on the word.

"Athapaskan," Adam says. He smiles at Soledad. "I'm impressed."

"It's the curse of a journalist." Soledad laughs uncomfortably before returning to Alaskan facts. "I read that their social framework is matrilineal, and marriage inside of the clan is strictly forbidden.

"That's right," Adam replies. "Developing mutual obligations through marriage outside of the clan is necessary for survival in this resource poor and demanding environment."

"I also read that regional bands consolidate their resources and jointly make decisions. Male leaders emerge only if they exhibit superior hunting abilities or physical strength."

Adam smiles at Soledad. "I think you should lead the tour," he teases while hoisting her bag into the storage compartment. As he leans with her against the float plane, he opens a baggie and squeezes the center of the sandwich to separate it into two halves. "Here, take one," he offers.

"Thank you, but no," she says.

"You're going to need your strength," he coaxes her.

"I have some food in my backpack."

"You'll either have to eat it on the plane or give it to me when we get to camp. We can't have hungry bears licking their chops at you while we're sleeping."

After she settles in to the small, uncomfortable seat on the float plane, Soledad looks out the window at the natives gathering next to the airstrip. This scene takes her back to Prudence Island, where the townspeople's entertainment depends on the ferry schedule. She shakes the thought from her mind, shifting her attention to the guide's briefing on the dangers of the Brooks Range and giving her a last out with a full refund.

The plane rises over the wide tundra that surrounds the outpost.

The guide's husky voice vibrates to the tune of the float plane's propeller. "Alaska is a sparsely populated state, with about two people per square mile. It doubles when you take out Anchorage and Fairbanks. Arctic Alaska is," he draws a triangle on the map with his finger, "from the Kotzebue Sound to Point Barrow to the Demarcation Point. We will be staying right here, in the Gates of the Arctic National Preserve, between the Noatak and Alatna rivers.

Planes, well suited to travel over sparsely populated and uninhabited regions, are the only way to get around. This man right here," he says, patting the grungy looking pilot on the shoulder, "is your only way in and out of here." He points to an oval lake in the distance. "There she is, home sweet home for the next few days."

After they step off the pontoon, the guide walks them through the tasks of dragging the plane toward the shore, unloading the gear, and pushing the plane back toward the center of the lake. They stand on the tundra shore in silence, capturing the image of the plane as it glides across the water and slowly fades to a tiny dot, trekking back toward civilization. They remain focused on the spot where the plane has abandoned their sight until the engine roar echoing through the wilderness ceases to be heard.

As they pitch their tents, Soledad takes note of the lack of distinction between women and men when it comes to what is necessary for survival, whether that wilderness is physical or psychic. The physical wilderness she was dropped in an hour ago is more comforting than the psychic wilderness she was dropped in when Bob left seven years ago.

Confusion about their life together is as far reaching as the Alaskan tundra surrounding her today. It's not the vastness that's disturbing. It's the permanency of it. The float plane will return in three days to take her out of the physical wilderness, but there isn't a plane that can lift her up out of her confusion about Bob. She asks the same questions over and over and spins around argument after argument that leads to nowhere. She doesn't know how to break this cycle. She knows there are many others like her who are wandering around in this same wilderness, but she hasn't found anyone who really knows the experience. The vastness of their confusion keeps them apart.

When they have completed all the tasks Adam has directed them to do, they sit together on the ground. "Aah," Nick moans as he stretches his body out over the permafrost tundra. "It's nice of Adam to bring us to a place with air conditioning coming out of the ground." Within seconds, he leaps up, swatting the air around him. "I've never seen so many mosquitoes in my life."

"The Arctic Circle is a breeding ground for mosquitoes in the summer because the permafrost leaves the ground below the soil unreceptive to water as it thaws," Soledad recites what she has read.

"Why aren't they attacking you?" Nick asks her. "The skin of women is usually sweeter than mine."

"You need to apply DEET mosquito repellant directly to your skin or wear one of these." Adam hands Nick a mosquito net.

"Or stay in your tent like they are," Abby adds.

"They still swarm around you, but they won't land if you use DEET." Soledad laughs. "I wonder if it works on men."

"Being here with us is a sure way to keep them from landing?" Nick teases.

"What he means to say is you're too sophisticated to be here all by yourself," Abby explains.

"She just went through a divorce," Adam announces.

Soledad swats a mosquito from her shoe. "He left."

"You'll get over it in time," Nick encourages her.

"I don't know about that," Soledad mumbles.

"What happened?" Abby asks.

Soledad cringes at these two words and swats another mosquito from her leg. "He's a wonderful person," she defends Bob. "We were good together until he went down a path that didn't include me."

"The path of another woman," Nick replies, "is a familiar story."

"No, no, that's not it at all," Soledad denies. She searches for a reason that will appease Nick and comes up with, "I'm the one who wanted out."

"How long were you together?" Abby asks.

"Fourteen years. I wouldn't give up all those years for anything, no matter how it turned out."

"The NRA should lobby for a gun that can kill these little buggers!" Nick exclaims as he swats the mosquito from his arm.

Soledad is grateful that the swarm of mosquitoes hovering over them has distracted Nick. "Are you a member of the NRA?" she asks.

"He is," Abby answers for her husband, "a full-fledged card carrying member who lobbies against gun control."

"The world has gone crazy. With the Iraqi war in full swing for over a year, gun control will be a secondary issue in the presidential campaign despite the recent rise in violent crime in schools. It's one of those issues that will be bantered around during the election by Kerry and Bush."

"I don't know," Nick starts.

"Soledad is right," Abby interrupts her husband. "The world has gone crazy."

"Do you think the sale of handguns and assault weapons should be permissible under the law?" Soledad asks Nick.

He laughs. "That's a strange question to ask in the middle of a wilderness of hungry bears."

"I'm a pacifist, so I don't own a gun. However as an advocate of constitutional rights, I won't impose my own beliefs about guns on others."

"Gun control makes it harder for people who have a healthy respect for guns to protect themselves from criminals who act like a bunch of mean, hungry bears," Nick explains. "Those liberal lobbyists who don't have a clue how to use a gun believe that gun control will keep guns away from criminals. But it doesn't. Criminals will always have access to guns, no matter what the laws are. And bears will always have sharp claws, no matter how often they use them. So, Soledad, if you're asking me if I would shoot Abby if she had an affair, the answer is no. But I shouldn't have to give up my constitutional right to protect myself from criminals just because someone else would."

Mark comes out of his tent. "Most people misunderstand the NRA. I'm a procurement officer," he explains with a chuckle. "Before you ask, no, I don't buy guns. I buy promo material for NRA-sponsored education programs that teach groups of gun owners like women and hunters how to use them responsibly."

"You didn't know you are hiking with a bunch of NRA proponents," Abby states.

"It's a first." Soledad laughs. "Being in the Arctic Circle with a bunch of NRA members who are exercising their right to bear arms sounds pretty good to me right now."

"Actually, I don't work for the NRA," Nick adds. "I supply them with decals for their education programs."

"I don't own a gun because I'm divorced and hate my ex-wife," Mark teases Soledad.

Soledad blurts out a false confession. "And I never married my ex-boyfriend so I have no reason to own a gun," she banters back.

"You're not divorced?" Adam inquires.

"I never said I was. We lived together for seven years."

"I thought you said you were with him for fourteen years," Nick reminds her.

"We were living together for seven of the fourteen years we knew each other," Soledad adjusts her story.

"Why didn't you marry the guy?" Nick asks.

"Neither one of us wanted to get married," Soledad adds to the yarn. "We met in college. We both felt that marriage would put pressure on us to live up to the gender expectations of our parents and get in the way of our careers. He's an attorney in Boston, and I'm a journalist. Over time, our careers took us so far in opposite directions that I couldn't find a trace of the person he used to be."

"What changed?" Abby asks.

"When we started living together, we saw no reason to get married because neither one of us wanted kids. He changed his mind, and I didn't. I'm much too independent to be married. So we split." Soledad stretches her neck to the sky, grateful that no one she knows is around to refute the yarn. "It's so beautiful here. There's no one around for miles."

"Are you ready?" Adam asks.

As they trek through the Brooks Range with the heat of the sun circling the sky, Soledad sees many parallels between their physical surroundings and her psychic world. She is as unreceptive to the unsolicited advice she gets about her life with Bob as the ground below her feet is to water. The warmth of her years with Bob followed by its abrupt, frigid ending leaves her heart as permeable as the soil that thaws and freezes above the permafrost. Her life has been in as much of a constant state of flux for the last seven years as the immature, acidic soil of the Arctic tundra. She is as vulnerable to shallow relationships as the thaw lakes are to the shallow-rooted growth that surrounds them. There is, however, one consolation. She maintains respect for their relationship by hiding behind people's misperceptions of its demise.

They follow Adam up the side of the mountain on a dried up river bed looking for water. Adam stops at a patch of ground moisture. They kick the rocks aside and trace the moisture to its source. Before long, Nick's shout, "I found it!" echoes through the wilderness so clearly that any creature in the Alaska tundra would know they were there. The water is not gushing out of the ground as Soledad expected. It is leaking from a tiny hole in the ground like an old-fashioned bubbler that barely works. The excitement of finding it, however, has made filling the water bottles seem like minutes instead of an hour.

As she sits with these new strangers on the top of a mountain in the Brooks Range drinking the best water on earth, she can feel her restlessness dissipating. That is until Nick leans toward her and whispers, "You should have married him and had his children."

Soledad expels her ire in a deep sweeping breath and turns back to the vast emptiness in front of her, happy that she can't remember his name.

You Want Me Please

What have I done? Nita wonders as she watches the stranger standing at the foot of her bed slide his swimsuit up over his hips.

"You are one hot young lady," he says, ogling her as she gets out of bed. She can feel his eyes caressing her breasts as she steps around his t-shirt next to the bed. She sweeps her damp beach cover from the floor and quickly wraps herself in it. The smell of sea salt comforts her.

As she looks down at the rumpled linens on the bed, an unfamiliar hand glides across her back and lands on her waist. The warm moisture of his breath touches her neck. She is trapped between the stranger and the bed. In one sweeping move, she slides her feet toward the foot of the bed and pivots her body away from him. She lunges through the patio door and notices his friend sitting on the chaise lounge below her room.

Through the screen door of the room next to her, she hears the television broadcast the news that Marlon Brando died. The announcer claimed that *his rugged sex appeal and rebellious nature established him as one of Hollywood's best method actors.*

As she leans her back against the patio railing, her eyes focus on the strange man sitting on the edge of the bed putting on his sandals. She closes her eyes and reopens them several times. But the stranger who looked so much like Marlon Brando only an hour earlier is nothing more than a mussed up, slightly overweight, middle-aged guy from Baltimore who just cheated on his wife.

She waits to reenter the room until she sees him rummaging through his pocket to make sure he leaves with everything he brought in. As she walks through the patio door, the breeze pushes her swim cover closer to her skin. He gives her that same crooked smile he gave her on the snorkeling trip when he sat down next to her and introduced himself. She forces a smile on her face as she walks around the foot of the bed to the door.

When they reach the door, the stranger says, "You sure know how to..."

Her lips press against his, silencing the words she doesn't want to hear. She keeps her lips tightly sealed as he responds with a sloppy kiss. She reaches her arms around his waist and unlatches the door. "Bye," is the only word she says as the weight of her body forces his feet to slide backward out the door.

Nita sits on the bed, looking out at the sea rising up from the place where the deep azure sea changes to aqua green after slamming into the reef. The calming sound of the surf is abruptly disturbed by the voices of the strangers echoing through the air outside her room. She doesn't get the patio door closed soon enough to block the words—"You got her,"—that they exchange as they walk down the beach.

She closes the curtains and falls face first on the bed, but is quickly drawn back on her feet by the repulsive odor of the sheets. She picks up the phone. "Could you please send someone to change the bed linens?" She listens to the response. "When is the shift change over?" She looks at the clock by the bed. Forty-five minutes will give her enough time to shower. "Thank you," she says as she hangs up the phone.

Nita turns on the faucet of the whirlpool bath and tests the water temperature with her foot. Since she can still feel the stranger's sweat on her skin, she jumps in the shower while the water in the tub rises and scrubs her body as hard as she can with a loofah sponge to remove of all evidence of the stranger from her body. She steps right from the shower into the whirlpool tub, pausing only to flip the jets on and turn the faucet off. She sinks down in the steaming hot water and rests her head on the porcelain back.

Nita doesn't like what is happening to her. She was a virgin when she married Jim and was faithful all through their marriage. It all changed six weeks after her divorce, on the night he spoke those three little words to that strange man on the other end of the phone. Since she found out the real reason for her divorce, the number of sexual trysts, let's see, she uses up the fingers on both of her hands. She sinks beneath the water when she realizes that she doesn't have enough fingers to count the latest encounter.

Nita resurfaces. She found this one on a snorkeling trip, admiring her youthful figure, her silk skin, and her face innocent of makeup, shining as bright as the sun. She gathered the straw around her lips, took a sip of the iced punch, and lifted her dark eyes up from the straw.

He took his sandwich out of the bag and offered half of it to Nita. Nita looked at the roast beef hanging out of all sides of the bread and shook her head no. She watched him wrap his lips around the sandwich and devour half of it in just one bite. Beneath his unshaven face, she noticed his broad jaw greedily tear away at the sandwich clump bulging from his cheek. Her eyes were fixated on the vacillation of his Adam's apple protruding from his long thick neck as he washed the sandwich down with an entire bottle of water. She could still see the imprint of his teeth in the hard white bread as he shoved the rest of the sandwich in his mouth. She found herself strangely attracted to the ruggedness of a man with the social graces of a horse.

She steps out of the Jacuzzi tub and wraps herself in a clean, thick towel. She twists another one around her wet hair and positions it like a weight on top of her head so it won't slide off. She walks back and forth from the patio door to the bed, waiting for the maid.

She doesn't plan on sleeping with any of them. Whenever she hears the voice of a strange man, speaking the three little words she heard Jim say to the pleading voice on the other end of the phone, she finds herself magnetically drawn to him. Through a passionate encounter with these three words, she is able to validate for a moment what it means to be a woman.

The disentanglement is always temporary, lasting only as long as his sweat lingers on her skin. When she's showered and dressed, the words settled back into the same place, tangled up in Jim's whisper to the strange man who called that day, the one with the plead-ing in his voice. It was the same *I want you,* in the same tone, with the same yearning in his voice that he used when he was with her. Her hungry search for normalcy in these three little words is pri-mal. She lusts for their return to an intimate phrase between a man and a woman.

Nita hears a light tap on the door, followed by the turning of a key by the maid. "Good evening, ma'am. I'm here to change the bed linens. I can come back," she says when she sees Nita wrapped in a towel.

"No, please change the sheets," Nita insists as she grabs some clothes out of the drawer. "I'll only be a minute." She closes the bathroom door, briskly rubs her hair with the towel, and throws on a tee and a pair of shorts. Within a minute, she is out on the patio as the maid rids her bed of the scent of the hunt. She opens her eyes to the darkness that has settled into the heavens. She promises herself that she will not continue this hunt. This time, she promises herself she won't break her promise.

She jumps as the man sitting on the patio next to her asks, "Don't I know you?"

"Dr. Higgins!" Nita exclaims. She blushes, hoping he didn't see the strange man leave her room or hear what they were doing.

"Please call me Eric. I didn't mean to startle you, Nita," he apol-ogizes, tripping over the table leg as he gets up. He sets his sun-glasses on top of his head and leans on the railing facing her patio. "Shouldn't you be in Evanston writing a paper for my class?"

"That would be too logical." Nita laughs. "Actually, I'm here on official business for the university."

"Hosting events?" Eric asks.

"I'm facilitating breakout sessions at Dr. Clark's conference next week."

"Really," Eric says with surprise.

"My mother took off the week before the Fourth of July week-end, so I left my son with her and came down a week early."

"Well, what do you know? I came early for a paper presentation at a computer science conference next week," he explains. "Hey, why don't we have dinner, that is, if you're not doing anything tonight?"

She looks at her clothes. "I'm not dressed for it."

"I'll wait."

"Thank you, Dr. Higgins, but no."

"Eric," he corrects her. "How about having dinner with me tomorrow night?"

"No, Dr. Higgins."

"A drink," he pleads. "If you want, we can talk about algorithms. We can talk about the switch from network control protocol to transmission control protocol that made the internet possible."

"You are very persistent."

"Do you need anything else, ma'am?" the maid standing on the other side of the patio door asks.

"No, thank you," Nita tells the maid. She whispers to Eric, "I have to tip the maid."

"I'll see you tomorrow," Eric shouts, leaning over the rail as she goes inside and closes the door.

After the maid leaves, Nita draws the drapes and cracks the patio door open so she can hear the ocean roar through the night. She looks at the crisp white sheets inviting her to lie down. She drops her night tee to the floor and crawls into bed. The freshness gliding along her skin as she stretches out between the sheets soothes her. When she rests her head on the pillow, her eyes fall on one star shining through the skylight, the brightest among the billions of stars in the sky tonight. Tears roll out of the corner of her eyes, building from a few quick drops to a steady flow. She rolls over on her side, knowing that whatever relief she gets tonight from this star will disappear as quickly as the darkness when the east brings to her another dawn.

He Creeps Back In

"I was on my way out the door," Judy replies flatly with the phone propped up on her shoulder against her ear.

Carol's voice shakily rattles off the words, "Jeffrey left me."

"What do you want me to do about it? I haven't seen you in twenty years," Judy utters impatiently.

She hears a long sigh from Carol before the words, "Jeffrey moved in with Pete," fall into her ear.

"When?" Judy exhales and falls back into the chair as if she has been hit in the stomach.

"I don't know," Carol answers. "The kids told me last night that they are going to get married next month."

Judy focuses her attention on the academic robe hanging on the back of her closed office door. She releases her anger with a raspy, sarcastic comment. "Is this a surprise?"

"You knew?"

"No," Judy snaps back as she reaches over to turn the desk lamp off. "What did you expect me to say?"

Carol clears her throat nervously. "I was hoping we could meet to talk about it."

"I have to go," Judy replies tersely.

"Please," Carol begs. "You're the only person who knows what it's like for me."

"I can't." She pushes the receiver button down before Carol can say anything else.

"Jeffrey," Judy whispers, cringing at the shiver his name evokes in her spine. She sneers at the memory of Carol's invitations, knowing they were only extended to keep her in line so Jeffrey could see Pete. The gnawing heart burn she had every time they went out as a foursome bubbles up all over again. She leans back in her chair and closes her eyes for a few minutes.

She knew that someday she would get this phone call from Carol, but she isn't prepared for what will inevitably follow. She can't protect her children from it anymore. Pete's closeted lifestyle has kept Jeffrey from being a larger part of her children's lives. Now that the closet door is open, Jeffrey has a chance to be a constant presence in their lives.

Judy tells herself that a dose of reality might be good for all of them. The problem is how to infuse the truth into Kim and Jerry's misperceptions of their father without hurting them. She knows Pete's refusal to tell their children the truth will cast a shadow of mistrust over her relationship with them that has not been there before.

Judy places her elbows on her desk and buries her head in her hands. *What was I thinking? What made me think that Pete would continue to be discreet after the divorce? What made me think my children wouldn't be interested in knowing the real reason for our divorce? Do they have a right to know how messed up our sex life was while we were married? Where does truth telling end and privacy begin?*

Secrecy about Pete's life has forced their children into creating a story about her marriage that has no other choice but to deceive them in the end. The half-truths they have been fed are worse than lies because they are entangled in a believable alter reality. She knows this because they are the very same half-truths she was told while she was married to their father.

Judy angst builds with her memories. She is afraid that her children will end up as messed up as she was after her divorce. It's clear that her psychic struggles were the result of living with a man who has been confused about his sexual identity for most of the twenty years they were married. She knows this news will affect her children beliefs, value systems, and identities. Her fears are grounded in her experience, in her psychic struggle after her affair with Paul, and in the way some people still question her sexual orientation because of her work with families of gays and lesbians.

Judy is livid about finding out from Carol instead of Pete. She calls his office and gets right to the point. "Carol called."

"You know." There is a mixture of guilt and relief in Pete's voice.

"Do the kids know?" Judy asks.

"No. I was about to call you. "There have been some..." he pauses, "developments."

"Developments," Judy inquires impatiently.

"Yes," Pete replies. "We need to discuss how much we want the twins to know."

"What else is there to know?"

"Can we meet this afternoon?"

"I'm busy," Judy lies.

"Please, Judy, it's important," Pete insists. "We can grab a quick supper before I make my rounds at the hospital."

"I need a few days to talk to our children." She checks her calendar. "The only time I am available next week is for lunch on Wednesday. Meet me at my condo." She hangs up before he has a chance to object.

• • • • •

"My children are ashamed of me," Pete pouts to Judy.

"They need time to get used to this, that's all," Judy tries to reassure him. "Jerry is taking the news harder than Kim. He always has."

Pete sets his tea cup down and recaps their earlier conversation. "My son thinks I don't respect our marriage because of Jeffrey. Doesn't he know we'd still be married if I wasn't gay?"

Judy runs her finger around the rim of the mug.

"Are you upset by this?" Pete asks with surprise.

"What did you expect?"

"I thought you, of all people, would be happy for me."

"I wouldn't describe what I'm feeling right now as happiness for you."

"My love for you hasn't changed just because I don't want to sleep with you."

Judy feels a sharp sting in her gut. "Let's focus on our children."

"What I mean is sex isn't all there is to love. The twins should know that."

"They're confused."

"What do they have to be confused about?" Pete asks.

"They don't know what kind of father or man you are anymore," Judy explains. "I know exactly how they feel. I don't think they should have to be hurt by this."

"And you think I do?"

"You seem much more worried about how Kim and Jerry feel about you than how they feel about themselves. I'm worried about them. Jerry, in particular, is very confused right now."

"And you think this gives him a right to stop loving me?"

"I didn't say that, Pete. It is hard for our children to know who to love when the person they thought you were isn't really the person you are."

"I'm still their father."

"I know that and so do they. It doesn't change the fact that you betrayed our thirty-seven-year-old children by hiding your gay lifestyle behind the façade of a straight father."

"We betrayed our children," Pete says.

"We," Judy repeats.

"You knew I was gay and didn't tell them."

"Do you really think it was my place?"

"I should have told them," Pete admits, "but when I didn't, you should have—"

"Don't you dare lay it on me," Judy warns.

"We both behaved as husband and wife when we went to all their soccer games, dance recitals, and school plays," he reminds her.

"We behaved the way parents behave," Judy corrects him.

"How about all the Saturday nights we hung out with mutual friends or went to family events and holiday parties? We even slept in the same bed."

"What is your excuse for the twenty year delay after we divorced? I seem to recall that you were going to tell them after you settled into your new place. You chose, instead, to tell them I was having an affair."

"You did have an affair, Judy, with that visiting professor from UCLA."

"And how would you describe what you were doing?"

"I told our kids we both were having affairs," Pete insists.

"Did you tell them that my year-long affair happened at the end of our marriage while you were having one the entire time we were married?"

Pete turns his eyes toward the table.

"You told them only as much as you wanted them to know," Judy snaps. "A truth that supports a lie about who you really are is worse than a lie."

"If you wanted them to know more, you should have told them more."

"Don't give me that crap, Pete. If you really are as honest as you are claiming to be, Kim and Jerry would not have found out that you are gay a few days ago from me."

"You didn't seem to mind that they didn't know," Pete reminds Judy.

"You're being ridiculous!" Judy barks. She takes a deep breath before continuing. "Blaming each other won't help our kids. What's important to understand is that the confusion Kim and Jerry have about who you are as a man and their ability to lay the foundation for a new way of looking at you has been delayed."

"I can't help—"

Judy holds up her hand to stop his rebuttal. "We'd have a different set of problems if we had told them when you first came out. But we didn't. Now you're lashing out at me because you're mad at our son for the way he's reacting to your news. It's preventing you from seeing that his refusal to be a part of this vow-exchanging thing is the result of his mistrust of you rather than his lack of love for you."

"It's called a marriage ceremony in Boston."

Judy ignores Pete's comment. "You're completely forgetting about our daughter. Kim is much more polite than Jerry, but I can tell you she doesn't want to be part of the ceremony either."

"Are you telling me that neither one of my children will be there?" Pete asks.

Judy nods. "Their reaction is legitimate, no matter how much it may hurt you."

"If they don't approve of my lifestyle, they can't be very proud of me as a father."

"It's not your lifestyle that is objectionable. It's how they found out about it that bothers them. They're not very proud of you, or me, or themselves right now."

"Why?"

"They're confused, Pete. Think about it. We're hypocrites, teaching them to be true to themselves and using our marriage to hide who you are from them. I would venture to guess that they're angrier about the straight father pretense than because you're gay."

"You pretended too."

"You're right, Pete!" Judy exclaims. "I gave up a lot of myself by staying with you. It's about time we stop circling around the problem and face reality. You're a liar, and I'm a fool. No wonder our kids are ashamed of us. How can they ever believe anything we tell them? It makes me sick to know how many times they will be upset as they go back, over and over again, and rewrite their memories of our family life and their relationships with you and me. Every time they run into an old friend, they will wonder if they knew our secret and think less of them because of it."

"But I'm the one who's gay," Pete protests.

"Explain that to the rest of the world."

"This doesn't have anything to do with them," Pete mutters.

"Oh yes, it does," Judy snaps. "Our children don't have any control over how others will react to them, and they are not comfortable enough with your lifestyle to brush it off."

"They shouldn't blame me for the way other people react to me."

"React to them," Judy corrects. "Aren't you being overly hard on them for the way they feel about this new development?"

"It's not a new development."

"It is to them," Judy exhales her frustration. "Let's take a break, Pete."

Pete follows her into the kitchen. They don't talk as Judy takes the spinach out of the refrigerator and hands it to Pete. As he tosses it in the pan with the warm bacon, vinegar, and sugar, Judy asks him if he heard Ronald Reagan died. She knows he is upset when he keeps his eyes focused on coating the spinach with the warm bacon dressing and nods.

She tries again. "Tell me about your trip to Washington to protest the war in Iraq."

"What difference will it make? Iraq formed a new government last week, but it won't help. The Pentagon proposed a troop withdrawal, but it won't happen. Same-sex marriages were made legal in Massachusetts last month while state referendums banning gay marriages are being drafted all over this country. I am happy for the first time in my life, and my kids are ashamed of me."

As he fills the plates and dresses the salad with tomatoes and croutons, Judy goes out to the balcony and sets the table. When she returns to the kitchen, she slices the French bread and fills their glasses with red wine. Pete pumps the air out of the bottle and hands it to her. She puts it back in the cupboard.

Judy follows him out through the screen door. When they sit down at the table, Pete leans back in the chair on her seventh floor patio and looks out at Lake Michigan. "I liked living here. With you," he adds as an afterthought. He sighs as if to prepare himself for another difficult conversation. "I'm sorry, Judy, for making it so hard for you."

He knows it isn't the right time when Judy stabs the spinach with her fork and shovels it in her mouth. She doesn't look at him or say anything until she finishes the salad.

"Did you like it?"

Judy nods. "Thank you, Pete."

"What should I do, Judy?"

"Nothing, Pete. Let's not worry yet. Our kids will be fine once this has time to settle in."

"Medical doctors don't let things settle in or spend years studying problems the way you do, Judy. We fix them right away."

Judy sighs, knowing that she must find a way to alleviate another looming altercation. "Some medical problems don't go away overnight. A broken leg, for example, takes at least six weeks to heal. You put it in a cast and wait as the fractured bone slowly grows back together. It's the same with this, Pete. Their straight father image of you has been fractured. They'll be fine if you give them time to heal."

"How do you know?"

"Because they are our children," Judy barks. "Because they're smart enough to know that you will never be the straight man they thought you were. And because I went through the same thing!" She sighs. "Forget about the ceremony and start from where the twins are right now."

"Where are they?"

"They're struggling with why you married me even though you are gay. Jerry is upset about believing you were a straight father and I was the cause of the divorce. Kim is out of touch with her feelings because she's too busy worrying about me. I'm taking them to the conference in Grand Cayman to help them get through this."

"Are you suggesting that as long as our kids think I can't love you the way a straight man would, they can't love me as a father without betraying you?"

"Oh, they love you," Judy defends her children. "Jerry, in particular, is not ready to accept your life with Jeffrey without feeling that he is betraying me."

Pete leans forward in the chair. "Then he might come to the ceremony if you tell him it won't bother you."

Judy shakes her head in disgust.

"Come on, Judy. Talk to them," Pete pleads.

"I will not force our children to do something they are not ready to do," Judy insists.

"What am I supposed to do?"

"Get over it and leave our children out of it!" Judy barks.

"Then you are the one who doesn't want our children at the ceremony," Pete accuses.

"They are the ones who don't want to go," Judy corrects him. "I'm the one who won't force them to go if they don't want to go."

Pete folds his hands in his lap and bows his head.

Judy massages her temples as she says, "You have to remember that it's only been a few days since they found out you are gay."

"How much time do they need?"

"As much time as they need," Judy states the obvious.

"But—"

"Give it a rest, for your own good," Judy warns. "I know all about the psychic wilderness they are in right now and the time it takes to find their way out of it. Remember how long it took you to come to terms with your homosexuality?"

Pete puts his elbows on the table and rests his chin in the palms of his hands. "Years," he mutters. "I can't afford to wait that long."

· · · · ·

It's after five when Judy returns to her office. She paces the floor, upset with Pete for telling her more than she wants to know. She doesn't have time to digest one development before he springs another one on her.

She looks at the stacks of research papers on her credenza. "I must be nuts," she mutters while hurling the stack labeled *Homosexuality* across the room. "She plops into the chair and mutters underneath her breath, "I'm a fool. What has all my research about his sexual orientation done to help women like me? I need help more than he does," she sputters while tossing the stack of research papers labeled *Coming Out* in the garbage. As she gathers the papers strewn across the room, she grumbles, "I'm sick of picking up his messes," and tosses them in the garbage.

A light tap on her office door brings her attention to a good friend and colleague with an office next door. "Are you okay, Judy?" he asks.

"I'm having a bad day," Judy explains.

"Do you want to talk about it?" he asks.

"No," she replies, resting her elbows on her desk.

"Hey, Judy, did you hear gay marriages are now legal in Massachusetts?"

Judy studies her gay colleague. "Can you tell me what makes a guy gay?"

"I think you need a drink," he suggests.

"Give me five minutes," Judy replies. "I have to make a phone call."

She picks up the phone and waits for an answer. "Nita, this is Dr. Clark. I want to add another session to the Cayman conference." She listens to Nita's response. "Do we have time to send out notices six weeks before the conference?" She smiles at the voice on the other end of the line. "Good. Meet me in my office tomorrow morning." She pauses. "Pack your bags, Nita. You're coming with me to Grand Cayman."

Judy puts her head on her desk and closes her eyes for a minute. Carol's words, "I need to talk to someone who knows," are pulsating through her ears. "Damn," Judy mutters. "Why did I have to take that phone call?"

She walks out to Ana's workstation and rummages through her trash can to find the telephone slip with Carol's number. When Carol answers the phone, Judy asks, "Do you still want to meet?"

You Can't Take It Back

Soledad and Bill stroll along the riverside walkway amid a large crowd of people at the Water Fires, watching the wood-filled boats slowly move along the river as the torch runners stoke the bonfire braziers on the water. Wafts of burning oak, cedar, and pine float toward them as vocals derived from Tibetan chants resonate from the speakers under the bridge at the intersection of the three rivers in downtown Providence.

"My European friends don't understand the appeal of Bush to Americans," Soledad says.

"He isn't that bad."

"Oh yes he is!" she exclaims. She pauses before switching gears to avoid a disagreement about the Iraqi war. "Did you read my article on outsourcing?"

"No," Bill replies.

"The Republican Party's election platform on jobs is based on tax incentives and deregulation. They claim that Kerry's proposal to end tax subsidies won't stop companies from falling prey to the cheap labor lure in Asia. But this isn't the point."

"What is your point?"

"They don't want anyone to know the truth, Bill. The value of the U.S. dollar—"

Bill yawns. "What are you going to do about the job at the *Tribune?*"

"—is closely tied to outsourcing," she finished her thought before responding to his question. "I don't know."

"Why don't you come back here for me?" he suggests.

"It won't work."

"Why not?"

She sighs. "I was going to tell you at dinner that I'm seeing someone in Barcelona."

Bill stops walking. "You are!" he exclaims.

When Soledad notices the stinging tears hidden in his eyes, she puts her arm around his shoulder. "I'm sorry it didn't work for us, Bill."

"It's okay." Bill composes himself and smiles at her. "Good for you."

"This could be the real thing if the logistics don't get in the way. It'll be hard because I live in Paris and Theo lives in Barcelona. Living in Chicago and working for the *Tribune* would make it even harder," she explains. "I talked to the *Globe* yesterday about continuing my work from Barcelona instead of Paris. They're amenable to it, but I don't know if it's the right thing to do."

"You're still afraid to get involved," Bill declares.

"It's not fear. I don't have any roots in Europe, and the roots I used to have here in the States don't exist anymore."

"I could be your roots."

"So can Theo," Soledad states clearly. "We tried six years ago, Bill, and it didn't work."

"I still have strong feelings for you," Bill insists.

"Strength isn't enough for me. I need someone who can bend and allow me to bend, the way tree branches do, without worrying, the way you do, about the relationship breaking in two. Theo knows how to bend. So did Bob."

"I wouldn't want to bend over as far as Bob did," Bill teases.

Soledad blinks away her ire and says, "You know too many of my ghost stories."

"Seven years is enough time to get over him," Bill comments.

"Maybe true love only comes along once in a lifetime. Maybe twice," she whispers as the music echoes from the speakers under the bridge.

Passion quarrels with will,
Capturing his flame,
Holding her spirit at bay.

The sacred loses shape,
Its manifest beauty, an ash
Lingering,
Shrouded in possibility
And nourished by imagination.
The purity of promise,
Lurking in the shadows
Hiding from life's blemishes
Only to tarnish itself.

"Water douses fire and fire evaporates water," Soledad murmurs. "I read that Barnaby Evans designed these fire sculptures by applying the mutually destructive and regenerative forces of fire and water to highlight the ephemeral nature of life." She points to the braziers on the river. "The scent of these logs and their flames crackling through the night air with this music as a backdrop to the simplicity of these brazier sculptures would make any Spanish surrealist proud."

"You're still very intense," Bill comments. "One minute you're spewing out a bunch of facts and the next you're as mesmerizing as the bonfires in the river."

"I can't be one without the other."

They walk up the stairs below the bridge near Brown University to get a cup of hot cocoa. They watch the street performers scattered along the path on the east side of the river while Bill fills Soledad in on the mayor of Providence going to jail last year. "He wanted the water fires to be a symbol of the city's rejuvenation. In 1998, the year you went on leave, the water fires became a regular summer event."

Soledad looks at her watch. "The last train to Boston is at midnight."

"Why don't we take the gondola back up the river, unless you'd rather stay here overnight with me?"

"I'm going back to Boston tonight," Soledad insists. "Let's walk back along the river."

"A gondola ride would be better," he coaxes her.

"Thank you, Bill, but no."

"Pleeeease, Sole, do it for me."

"Gondolas are a part of a past I'd like to forget," Soledad explains.

"What's the big deal?" he whines. "You'll be close enough to feel the heat of the fire."

"If you must know," Soledad replies sharply, "the first thing Bob and I did after we were married was take a gondola ride around the Venetian canals. The last thing we did together before things fell apart was take a gondola ride at a water fire."

"Nothing's changed," Bill mutters. "You still idealize your marriage to a gay man. I suppose you still won't admit that he was having sex with men while you were married to him."

"What do you know about it?" Soledad snaps, remembering how much he used to annoy her with his nonsensical talk about her marriage.

They walk all the way back up the river in silence. It isn't until they reach the train station that he breaks the silence. "Why do you get so upset when we talk about your ex?"

"My train leaves in ten minutes," she replies tersely and proceeds swiftly to the commuter train platform with Bill following close behind.

When they reach the platform, Bill asks Soledad, "What did I do wrong?"

Soledad turns to Bill. "I'd like to tell you, but it'll only take us back to where we used to be. If I tell you that I'm upset about your attitude toward my marriage, you'll find a way to turn it into a conversation about my ex-husband. If I tell you I don't want to talk about it, you'll tell me I'm in denial. One thing I learned while we were dating six years ago was to leave my marriage to Bob out of our conversations."

"I wouldn't be a very good friend if I didn't tell you the truth."

"A friend wouldn't cheapen my marriage in the name of friendship," Soledad scowls. "Just because I can't tell you what made Bob turn to men at the end of our marriage doesn't change the reality of what we had during our marriage."

"You're fooling yourself about your marriage to a gay man," Bill insists.

"How do you know? I didn't see you in our bedroom at night, at our kitchen table in the morning, or fighting alongside of us over the silly things that annoy most couples."

"I don't have to be there to know that you're still wrapped up in a dream."

"You're a psychologist!" Soledad exclaims. "You're supposed to validate my reality, not create one of your own. I can't tell you why Bob is gay, or if he was when he married me, or what he was thinking when he was with me." Her voice escalates as she adds, "I don't know when his interest in gay men began, and I certainly didn't see any signs of it before we married or I wouldn't have married him."

"I'm only trying to help," Bill insists.

"Uh uh," she disagrees. "You're using my marriage to satisfy your own perverted curiosity about men who come out of the closet."

"That's uncalled for."

"Is it? Questions about what he might have been thinking or what he did when we had sex are sick. Whenever I tell you the way it really was, you don't believe me. You insist that I'm imagining the life I lived with Bob when, in reality, it's your imagination, working overtime to accommodate your beliefs about homosexuality. You'd rather get off on talking about my ex-husband than enjoying your time with me."

"You're still upset about your ex-husband?"

"It's your attitude that bothers me. You set it up so I can't win."

"You don't get ..."

"You're the one who doesn't get it," Soledad snaps back. "You don't have room for the truth, and I don't have any interest in defending my life with Bob to you."

The Discovery

Judy and Pete
1965-1985

Soledad and Bob
1983-1997

Nita and Jim
1998-2003

It's No Picnic

Soledad is tired of all the lies that have invaded her life. Journalistic integrity has always been important to her, and yet it is difficult to find any honesty in the sound bytes of information she has to report as news. The truth is buried in the details of the story, intertwined with the meddlesome intrigue paraded around by the media as news. It is difficult to tell the truth anymore when it is subject to embellishment or ripped to shreds by her editor.

She scrolls through the list of events she wanted to cover last month. On August 6, 1998, over two hundred people died and forty-five hundred were injured when U.S. embassies in Kenya, Dar es Salaam, Tanzania, and Nairobi were bombed by a terrorist group linked to Osama bin Laden. The U.S. retaliated two weeks later against suspected al Qaida camps in Afghanistan and al Shifa chemical plant in Sudan. Her request to cover these stories is denied. So is a request to do an in-depth series on the devaluation of the ruble after the Russian government defaults on their bonds. Instead, she is assigned to the team covering Bill Clinton's embarrassing affair with Monica.

Everything Soledad has learned about journalism tells her she shouldn't use speculation or opinion in her news stories. News reporting is supposed to be an objective portrayal of the facts. Opinions are reserved for the editorial page. Everything else is rumor. This morning, the features editor insists that her news stories and commentaries are factually dry and suggests incorporating argument and speculation into her work to make it more appealing to the reader.

Most days, Soledad finds herself staring at a blank computer screen, contemplating the truth about her fourteen year marriage to Bob and the very idea of their existence as a couple. Was their life together real or imagined? Was their sexual intimacy the only part of their marriage in question? Is there any truth in any part of their coupled being?

Personal integrity is also important to her, but what kind of integrity is there in having had a heterosexual relationship with a man who turned out to be gay? She despises the fact her intimate life with Bob is nothing more than a speculative drama, a politically intriguing debate, a news story of the commercial endeavor, all because he fell in love with and married her. She doesn't know if he knew who he was when they got married. All she knows is the truth lies somewhere in his coming out, a process she is ill-equipped to understand much less explain.

Soledad is tired of the burden of ownership of Bob's coming out. She doesn't want to be left with the deed to their assets or the burden of selling them off. She doesn't want the deed to their friendships after he walks away from everyone who was part of their married life. The last thing she wants is the deed to his truth, an asset she values and can't maintain because he is the only one with access to all the facts. How can there be any truth in his omission of relevant facts? How can there be any truth in her story without these facts?

Soledad tries to hold on to the friendships she and Bob had during their marriage, but it has become harder and harder to do without transferring the deed to the truth back to Bob. The hope of being relieved of this burden when Bob finally opens the closet door a year after the divorce is short lived. All opening the door has done is stimulate an appetite for what happened during their marriage and an apprehensiveness to enter it through Bob. All the open door has done is leave Soledad saddled with the burden of explaining its contents.

She knows the closet door has been opened when she hears the words, "My son was a fool for leaving you," being pushed through the sea air by her ex-father-in-law at a surprise birthday party for Susan, a college friend and neighbor of Bob's family. Soledad doesn't know when she accepts the invitation that Bob will be there along with her ex-father-in-law's hope of bringing her back into the story in order to change the facts about his son.

• • • • •

The wind pushes her long hair off her shoulders as the ferry begins its journey from Bristol to Prudence Island. Soledad looks out over Narragansett Bay and revives the image of their sailboat anchored near the shore of the island. She recalls the times they participated in weekend regattas, baked quahogs at the cottage, and watched the moon rise while skinny dipping in the bay. She can still see the millions of stars that hung over their boat the night they sailed up the Block Island Sound. And then there was the day the new owner dropped her off at the Bristol ferry dock where she wept her way back to the home she used to share with Bob on the East Side of Providence.

The townspeople still hang around the dock outpost on the island to greet family and friends returning home from school and jobs. She waves to Susan's father standing on the porch of the post as the ferry nears the island. They drive about a mile down the road, following the shoreline to the driveway next to the cottage of her ex-father-in law. Her nose is drawn to the smoke rising from several charcoal grills in the yard. She is surprised to see her ex-father-in-law standing next to one of the grills, brushing his famous home-made barbeque sauce on the chicken.

"I didn't realize you'd be here," Soledad says as he approaches her with his hands wiped clean by the apron he is wearing.

"When I heard you were coming, I decided not to go to Vermont for Labor Day. I wanted to see you." He holds her arms length away and scans her body. "You look great, Soledad. When was the last time I saw you?"

"It's been a while," Soledad replies, not wanting to remind him of her ex-mother-in-law's funeral shortly before the divorce last year.

"I have to run home for more sauce. Why don't you come with me?"

Soledad follows him down the hill toward the house. They walk through the breezeway and into the kitchen where her eyes are drawn to the large window in the adjoining living room overlooking the bay. She notices a picture of her and Bob in their sailboat still sitting on the piano next to a picture of her deceased mother-in-law. She turns around to the creak of the back stairs and finds Bob standing in the kitchen doorway.

"Look at who I found!" her ex-father-in-law exclaims to Bob. "She gets better looking every day, doesn't she?"

"Hi, Sole," Bob greets her politely.

"Bob," she replies.

They are uncomfortable standing next to each other in the kitchen. Soledad nervously shifts her weight from one foot to the other. Bob crosses and uncrosses his arms around his chest. Both of them are waiting for a reason to leave. When Bob's dad takes three large jars of sauce out of the refrigerator and sets them on the counter, they lunge for the containers. Bob's dad reaches them first.

"Keep this beautiful daughter-in-law of mine company, Bob," he says before rushing out the back door.

"I wouldn't have come if I had known you were here," Soledad tells Bob.

"It's not your fault." They walk into the front room and stand side by side at the front window, looking out at the bay. "I heard you sold the sailboat," Bob says.

"Yeah, last year," she informs him. "How do you like living in Boston?"

"I like it. We just bought a condo in the Back Bay."

"How's business?"

"I'm doing commercial real estate now. You can't believe how much money there is in the development going on all the way up to Concord."

"I thought you were still restoring old homes."

"I lost interest in it."

Soledad looks over at the man standing next to her with his eyes fixed on the place where their sailboat used to be moored and wonders who he is. He still has the same muscular physique, but on the inside, everything has changed. He used to despise the crowds of Boston. He was opposed to development of the area north of Boston. He hated commercial real estate even more than new construction. He promised himself he wouldn't sell his work short for money.

But look at him now. Not only does the man who used to sleep with her now have a male lover, he is also doing all the things he promised himself he wouldn't do. There isn't any trace of the man who married her in any of his words. It took only a year for the man she loves to die.

"I need some air," she whispers. Her feet quickly gallop out the door and down the steps to the water. She drops herself onto the sand. Wrapping her arms around her legs, she brings her thighs to her chest and rocks back and forth. Even the sand is cold today.

Soledad looks out at the empty sailboat moored offshore. She blinks several times until she sees a couple come up from the galley. They float toward the middle of the bay as they put up the main sail. They raise the same spinnaker she and Bob use to sail when the wind was light.

"We've been looking all over for you," her ex-father-in-law's voice floats toward her.

Soledad stands up and forces a smile on her face. She loosens the rocks with the tip of her shoe as she walks toward him. "I used to come down here all the time."

"I remember," her father-in-law winks. "I used to keep an eye on you and Bob before you were married."

"That was a long time ago," Soledad reminds him.

He looks at Soledad with tears in his eyes. His voice echoes in the wind, "My son was a fool for leaving you."

"Excuse me." Soledad turns away from him. She takes long

strides up the hill away from her ex-father-in-law standing on the narrow patch of sand along the shoreline in front of his cottage. She makes it halfway up the hill when the word "surprise" falls down the hill from the house where Susan's family and friends are gathered.

She spots Susan at the top of the hill talking with one of their mutual friends. She stops to catch her breath before walking through the crowd to greet her old roommate. "Happy birthday Susan," Soledad shouts.

"Soledad!" Susan cries.

"Congratulations, you're officially a member of the over forty club."

"Please, don't remind me," Susan groans. "I haven't seen you since … you look good. Where have you been?"

"I still live on the East Side."

"I'm glad you are here. Come with me." When they are out of earshot of the crowd, Susan stops and looks around. "We didn't know," she whispers, "until Bob brought that man to the island last weekend."

Soledad looks around the backyard, searching for a place to hide. She notices a group of islanders staring at her, whispering amongst themselves, probably about Bob's visitor.

"Do you know?" Susan asks.

"Do I know what?"

"If the man Bob brought to the island is his lover," Susan whispers.

"Of course I know," she lies. "Excuse me, Susan. I promised to help with the barbeque." She plans to duck behind the garage and head to the pier, but Bob's father intervenes. He leads her toward Bob who is talking with the neighbors. "You remember Soledad, Bob's wife," he introduces her.

"Ex-wife," Soledad and Bob correct him simultaneously.

"My son is lucky to have married this terrific lady," Bob's father says proudly.

"She's the lady with the sailboat," Susan's dad reminds them.

Before Soledad can get away, Bob's father says, "Come with me, Bob. You too, Sole. I need some help with the rest of the stuff in the refrigerator."

As they follow him back to the house, Bob whispers to Soledad, "I'll talk to him."

"We need these bomber buns cut, Bob," his father instructs as Soledad and Bob stare at each other across the kitchen island. "Sole, you can toss the salad in this bowl with my homemade Italian dressing in the refrigerator. I'll take the potato salad and coleslaw over."

Soledad smiles at her ex-father in law and sweeps the two containers from the counter. "I've got it, Dad," she says. Little does she know that these will be the last words she will ever say to him.

"It isn't going to work, Dad," she hears Bob warn his father through the kitchen window.

"What do you mean?" he asks.

"Don't act so innocent. You know exactly what you're doing."

Soledad lengthens her stride, hoping to move out of earshot of Bob's scolding. She is trapped, entangled in the intrigue of whatever transpired when Bob brought his lover to Prudence Island.

When she reaches the side of the garage, her feet skid on the grass, stopping just short of the cement apron where the owners of the gossip are standing. "They were married for a long time," the voice she recognizes as Susan's explains.

"Fourteen years," a man's voice replies.

"How could she not know he was gay?" a voice she didn't recognize asks.

"No one knew," Susan tells them.

"I don't get it. What made him turn?"

"He must have always been that way," another voice declares. "I wonder if she knew."

"She must have known."

"It wasn't obvious to me," Susan defends Soledad.

"It may not be to us, but she was his wife. She must have known something."

Soledad rushes back to Bob's father's house. Halfway back, she changes her mind. She stands on the lawn, unable to move, like a statue holding two Tupperware containers of food in her arms. She doesn't want the pity of their friends. She doesn't want to go back to the hope that Bob's dad has of changing their story. She walks toward Susan's party, this time entering the barbeque area more directly so she can be seen. She keeps her head low as she sets the containers on the serving table in the garage.

"There you are, Soledad," Susan calls out. "I want you to meet someone."

"In a minute," Soledad replies. "I have to get the rest of the food." She keeps her eyes on the movement of her feet out of the garage.

"Isn't she the one who ..." their voices fade as her legs carry her farther down the lawn. As she nears the walkway on the side of Bob's father's cottage, she can hear voices traveling through the open kitchen window.

"I don't want to be with her."

"It's only a weekend."

"Stop it, Dad. I don't have any intention of getting back together with Sole."

"You better be nice to her."

"You be nice to her, Dad. I didn't invite her."

Soledad doesn't recall exactly when her legs began to trot down the road toward the dock, but she is happy to arrive just as the five-fifty p.m. ferry is preparing for departure. She waves to the crew as she runs up the ramp.

The wind moistens her eyes as the ferry begins its trek toward Bristol. Coming to the island hasn't helped her put her life with Bob into perspective the way she hoped it would. It has left her with a wish to purge herself of the deed to his closet and the truth of their existence as a couple. She yearns for a place where no one knows her, where she doesn't have the burden of telling their story without all the relevant facts and feeling stares boring through her back as whispers are exchanged about her life with Bob.

The sun casts a shadow of their sailboat across the sparkling water of the Narragansett Bay. She leans on the railing and hums the song she sung the last time she sailed the bay, the night before handing the helm over to the new owner.

> Chasing the sun over the horizon,
> She calls forth a gentle breeze
> To hold his fading to a glow
> And draw her into knowing.
>
> The dampness clinging to her face
> Polishes their skin to a golden jewel,
> The brilliant alchemy hanging around
> Hypnotizes the earth to stillness.
>
> The nugget of gold below the horizon,
> Dances a wish across her face,
> As streaks of fire crackling through the air
> Fall away and fade to gray.

The sun brings the shadow of their sailboat closer to her as it moves toward the west. The sound of the plank slamming against the concrete dock traverses the water with the wind. She disembarks. The sailboat must remain in its place, anchored to their life on the bay along with the weekend bag she left in the spare bedroom of Susan's parents' home.

The Couch Is on Fire

Fifteen years after they married, Pete tells Judy he is gay. She is relieved. He has finally put into words what they both have known for a long time. She stays with him for five more years, living a socially acceptable existence, closing her eyes to his lifestyle for the sake of her children.

Their daily routine doesn't change. They continue to converse over breakfast about the news events in the *New York Times* and discuss the joys and concerns of their children over family dinners every Wednesday and Sunday. They spend time together with other couples on Saturday nights, sleep in the same bed every night, and make love once a year, on Christmas Eve, far more out of comfort than for ecstasy.

At the core of their marriage is distance. Pete goes out every Friday night and doesn't return until Saturday morning. He doesn't tell Judy what he does, and she doesn't ask. Deep down, Judy knows, and Pete knows Judy knows, but they never speak of it. They both intimately know what lurks in the shadows of any room they are in together and choose to leave it there.

With Kim and Jerry in high school, Judy throws herself into her next book about the history of women's rights. An equal rights amendment ending the legal right to discriminate against women was first presented in Congress in 1923 and numerous times since then. The latest effort, adopted by the House in 1971 and the Senate in 1972, is a few states short of the three-fourths required for ratification. With the deadline extended to June 30, 1982 and state ratification unlikely, Judy's book will present the arguments that have been used to stop its passage throughout history.

Judy is a highly respected researcher of women's rights and gender equality in the workplace. Graduate students flock around her because she is a rigorous researcher who challenges and takes care of them. Research is her life. She dismisses her friends and colleagues accusations that she is a workaholic. She doesn't have friends outside of colleagues who are beginning to avoid her at social events because she is too intense about her work. She is too busy with her book this year to go to the annual weekend in Door County with her old college friends. She doesn't have anyone to confide in, but she doesn't mind because she has her work.

One Friday night as Judy is pouring over her research, a recently hired visiting professor stops by her office. He leans against the door frame and says, "I thought I was the only lunatic who works late on Friday night."

"I'm not working. I'm taking a stroll through my thoughts," Judy says.

"Where are they taking you?" he asks.

"Nowhere," Judy replies. "They're waiting for the red light to turn green." She stands up, hungry for company. "Come on in. Aren't you Paul James, visiting from UCLA?"

"I am." He steps into her office to shake her hand. "And you must be Judy Clark, world renowned for your work on equal rights." He continues to recite her accomplishments and ends with, "Congratulations on your full professorship. I saw the promotion memo yesterday."

"Thank you."

"Does this mean you won't be around anymore on Friday night?"

"Didn't you hear? I'm a workaholic." Judy laughs. "What's your excuse?"

"I don't know anyone here. It's my third week in Evanston," Paul says. "I hang out here until seven or eight, have dinner and go home. Sometimes I take in a movie."

"I use to do dinner and a movie with my kids until they started high school. Now they prefer the company of their friends to me." She motions toward the chair in front of her desk. "Have a seat, please, but give me a minute to clean up this mess."

"Thanks." Paul laughs nervously as he sits down. He flips

through the *Tribune* on her desk as she neatens the tall piles of papers that separate them. "It looks as if Jimmy Carter is going to lose the election to Ronald Reagan because of the Iran hostage crisis."

"It's been nine months since the American embassy in Tehran was taken over by students," Judy replies. "I hope it's over soon."

"It won't be because Jimmy Carter is a pacifist in a world that resorts to violence to solve problems," Paul suggests. He turns the page when Judy doesn't respond. "It looks like we'll have to wait a month to find out who shot JR?"

"Who's JR," Judy asks as she flips through a pile of papers.

"From the TV series *Dallas*," Paul explains.

"Oh, yeah," she mumbles. She looks up at Paul with a video in her hand. "Sorry, I was looking for this documentary. Okay, who shot JR? I don't watch television very often."

"What do you do?"

"Oh, all kinds of things."

"Can you be more specific?"

"I work and take care of my kids." She smiles at him uncomfortably, not used to the attention. "I'm pretty boring."

"Let me be the judge of that. Will you tell me what you did today?"

"Today?" Judy asks.

"Yeah, today," Paul repeats.

"I don't want to bore you," Judy objects.

"You don't bore me. Come on, try me."

Is he flirting with me? Judy wonders as she smiles at Paul. "I met with my graduate students, worked on my women's studies book, and read about the release of RU-486, an abortion pill in France."

"What are you doing tomorrow?"

"I take tennis lessons on Saturday. I'm going to the art museum with my mother. And I have to find time to develop a lesson plan for this Apartheid documentary before class on Monday." Judy hands him the video.

"I heard you give yourself more homework than you give your students."

Don't look at him, Judy warns herself. *He'll level me with those warm blue eyes.* Judy laughs nervously. "I told you I'm boring."

"What are you doing tonight?"

"Tonight?" Judy asks with surprise.

He looks at his watch. "It's too late for dinner, but how about a movie, unless you have someone waiting for you at home."

Oh, he's good. "I don't know," Judy hesitates as he hands the video back to her. "I should watch this," she objects until she sees his deep blue eyes twinkling at her across her desk. "Okay, why not? My husband is playing basketball with the guys tonight," she adds to let Paul know she is married.

"Would you like to see *Ordinary People?*" Paul eyes drop to the video in her hand. "Or would you like me to take you over to the media center to watch this video?"

"What a choice," Judy banters back. "It's between a movie about a messed up family or a documentary about a messed up country."

"We could go for a drink," Paul suggests.

Her office becomes a regular Friday afternoon haunt. They hang out there until everyone else has gone home, looking through the weekend section of Friday's *Sun Times* for something to do that night. She suggests movies, plays, and music groups but avoids Jazz clubs for fear that they'll run into Pete.

Judy likes that Paul is cerebral like Pete, but exactly the opposite in two important ways. He makes her laugh. The way he roars at funny scenes in movies gives Judy no other choice but to laugh along with him. He also enjoys being with her. He will do things with her that she enjoys, like tennis, even though he's a terrible player, and exposes her to things she needs, like meditation, by inviting her to go with him to yoga class.

Their friendship is platonic until he goes back to Los Angeles over winter break and they realized the depth of their feelings for each other. On their first night out after his return, he confronts her about her marriage over a drink after a *Second City* improvisation show.

"I don't mean to pry into your personal life," he says, "but there's something I need to know."

"Shoot," Judy replies calmly as she tries to control the angst shooting through her veins.

"Doesn't your husband mind that we go out?"

Judy's smile disappears as she shrugs away her fear of losing him. "Why should he mind?" she asks innocently. "We're just friends."

"I would."

She turns her head to the table to avoid Paul's blue eyes piercing through her. "Pete doesn't know."

"I'm not comfortable with that," he declares.

"What I mean to say is he doesn't want to know. We have," she pauses, "an arrangement."

"He's seeing someone," Paul suggests.

Judy nods. "We don't talk about it."

"Do you know who she is?"

"I only know it isn't a she." Judy clears her throat and keeps her eyes on the table. "It's been going on for as long as I can remember. He mustered up the courage to tell me last summer."

"What are you going to do?"

"My children don't know. I don't know how to tell them. I'm not even sure I want them to know."

"It must be hard on you," Paul empathizes, covering the top of her hand with his. She doesn't know if it is the gentleness of his voice or his sympathetic touch that shoots like fire through her entire body. The same flame rushes through her when he gives her a hug as they stand between their cars in the university parking lot. The warmth of the fire stays with her as she drives home, unlocks the door, and crawls into bed alone.

Their good-bye hugs get longer as time passes. Soon they are ordering in Chinese food at his place and fondling each other like teenagers. When Judy can no longer contain the fire in her heart, they do it.

Judy drives home that night with a mixture of guilt and ecstasy. She thought she had made up her mind about sex. It is a burden of marriage, something to get through when your husband wants it. She has never been more wrong about anything in her life. Her body is alive in a way she has not known before.

Thoughts of her evening with Paul are still smoldering when Pete opens the door on Saturday morning. Guilt douses the fire so fast that she gasps for air. She watches Pete disappear into the bedroom, as usual, without much more than a courteous greeting. She has let him off the hook for what he does on Friday night, but she hasn't considered exercising the same freedom for herself until now. Is this thing with Paul within the bounds of her arrangement with Pete or a violation of the bonds of their marriage? The Friday night no-talk norm prevents her from finding out. She eases her anxiety by convincing herself that Pete doesn't want to know what she does anymore than she wants to know what he does on Friday night.

Judy has all she can do to contain her feelings for Paul when she walks past his office or sees him in the cafeteria. She wants to jump into his arms, the way young lovers do, and never let him go. Afraid of what others may suspect, she makes it through Monday without caving in to her desires.

He stands up when he sees her at the door of his office on Tuesday afternoon. "Are you okay?" he asks.

Judy smiles at him. "Take me home with you?"

Paul grins. "Are you serious?"

She nods. "Pete is out of town. My kids are with my parents overnight. We can take tomorrow morning off."

They end up in his bed within minutes of entering his apartment. Afterward, she lies in Paul's arms, telling him about her life with Pete and the twins. Paul listens to her vacillate between the happiness of being a mother and the sadness of being a wife. "I'm trapped. I can't leave because I love my kids."

Paul tries to comfort her. "Let me take you away from the heavy burden you're carrying."

Judy's seriousness disappears as they eat breakfast in bed the next morning. She giggles the entire time they are reading the same page of the *New York Times* at the same time.

"I like it when you smile," Paul tells her.

"Pete and I don't share a *New York Times* at the breakfast table much less in bed."

Paul picks up the manuscript on the nightstand next to the bed. "I don't want to talk about Pete. I want to read your book."

Judy takes a shower while Paul reads the chapter about problems the Illinois Legislature has with ratifying the Equal Rights Amendment. He is sitting in the chair with the chapter in his lap when she returns. She sits on the ottoman in front of him and asks, "What do you think?"

"I really like it. It's an interesting and thorough representation of the issues, many of which I haven't considered."

"What don't you like about it?"

Paul eyes her for a minute before saying, "It's obvious you put a lot of work into it, but your personality isn't coming through in your words. Writing objectively the way we have been trained to write as academics distances you from a topic you obviously care about a lot. You describe the need for the amendment and the impact it can have on women's issues like abortion and the military draft, but it leaves me wondering why people in Illinois would be against it because the emotional aspect is missing."

"Emotional aspect?" Judy repeats.

Paul leans forward in the chair. "You're in their heads, Jude, but not in their hearts. To know what is at stake for the opposition you have to get into their hearts. I know you can do it because I've seen your passion." He reaches over and kisses her.

When their lips part Judy says, "I used to have passion, but I lost it the first time I had sex with Pete."

"What about now?"

"What do you think?" she teases.

He gets up and takes her hand. "I need more evidence."

They begin seeing each other twice a week. Judy makes arrangements for the twins to spend Friday night with her parents on a regular basis so she can stay overnight with Paul. She changes her Saturday morning tennis lesson to a private one on Tuesday afternoon so Paul can join her. Since Tuesday is Pete's night with the twins, she goes to Paul's apartment after their tennis lesson. They lie in bed as they banter ideas back and forth and eat Chinese food out of paper containers. She goes home around nine to see Kim and Jerry before they go to bed. Pete stays in the den watching the news. He doesn't ask where she has been, and she doesn't offer. She says goodnight to him, heads down the hallway toward the bedroom, and falls asleep with her thoughts on Paul.

The dual life goes on for the rest of the semester. She starts the day sitting across the breakfast table from Pete with the *New York Times*. They browse through their separate papers, discussing issues like the economic sanctions against Apartheid. She ends the day discussing the news in more depth with Paul. She reveals her concerns over the use of money or withdrawal of resources to solve civil rights issues in South Africa and her fears about how the 1960s activism has turned into limousine liberalism.

Paul's impending departure at the end of the academic year forces her to face reality. Judy has to make a choice. She can leave Pete and her job behind, disrupt the life of her kids, and follow Paul back to California; or she can stay behind and wait for Paul to get an appointment at one of the university hospitals in the Chicago metropolitan area.

Paul is willing to resign from his position at UCLA and hang out at Northwestern until he finds a tenure-track position, but Judy won't let him. She doesn't want him to give up the dream he has been working toward for years. She couldn't live with herself if he gave up his chance to work at the prestigious University of Chicago Medical Center. She convinces him that a few years apart will give him time at UCLA to build his research reputation and her time to get her personal life in order.

Judy is full of hope when Paul departs the week before the fall term begins. Her hope diminishes with each passing day as she imagines him in her office, wanders past the restaurants they used to frequent, and parks her car in front of his apartment building on her way home. She anxiously awaits his daily phone call, where he feeds her hope with future plans. It gets her through the day. It keeps her warm at the night. Anticipation for another phone call gets her out of bed in the morning.

Judy's excitement builds as she counts down the days until Paul's visit over winter break. As they drive down to the loop, he feeds her hope for their future when he tells her about his meetings with faculty at the University of Chicago and a possible appointment at the hospital a few years down the road. The love that is so obvious during his two-week stay is consumed by fear as soon as she drops him off at the airport. Lurking in the back of her mind is her biggest worry: How long she can hope for what isn't possible?

Paul's departure brings Judy to the heart of her emptiness. After a month of futzing with her work and ignoring her children, she tells Paul it's over. She ignores his calls, brushes herself off, and returns to her marital routine. The emptiness grows into a bigger hole in her heart as his calls dwindle from daily to weekly to occasional until, a year later, her voice mail no longer contains a message from Paul.

Paul has changed everything for her. She can't get away from the reality of being cheated out of love by being married to a gay man. She's torn in two. She can't pretend her marriage is an acceptable arrangement, but she can't leave Pete without disrupting the lives of her children. The marital routine that used to be an acceptable form of freedom is now a prison.

Judy can't stand being around Pete anymore. She gets up at dawn and leaves for work with an excuse for him and the *New York Times* under her arm. She eats breakfast at the University coffee shop with her fresh newspaper untouched. She goes home early when Pete works late and works late on the days he gets home early. She forces herself to be cheerful when he cooks dinner for her and the kids on Wednesday and Sunday. She sheds ten pounds in a month and another five the next month. The twins are too busy being teenagers to notice she is miserable.

When summer arrives, Judy asks Pete for a divorce. He talks her into staying until the twins are in college. She accepts his proposition even though she wants out by convincing herself she has more freedom than she ever had and finds relief in knowing her captivity will end. Three more years is a minor sacrifice compared to the seventeen she has already invested in this sham. She throws herself into writing her most famous book about sexuality and dedicates it to PJ, the initials Paul used to sign on his notes to her.

Things don't change much on the surface, but deep down, Judy is stuck between two doors. The door that shrouds her marriage and the one leading to Paul have been closed. She has kept Paul's love and Pete's secret safely tucked away for so long that she doesn't know who she is anymore. Is she the wife who hates the thought of sex or the woman who set fire to Paul's couch? Maybe she's both. Maybe she's neither. And if she isn't either of these women, then who is she?

She finally gets up the nerve to send a signed copy of her book, on the *New York Times* best-seller list, to Paul's office the semester after her divorce. The package is returned to her unopened with a note that he has left UCLA to accept an appointment as Chair of the Psychiatric Department at the University of Chicago Medical Center.

Judy is so thrilled that his dream came true that she cancels everything she planned for the day and rushes off on the train to Hyde Park to personally deliver her book and the news of her divorce. The anticipation of seeing him quickly turns to regret when his secretary informs her that Paul is on his honeymoon.

Judy is crushed. Her heart is as empty as the return train out of the Hyde Park station. The rattling of the car past one empty station after another soothes the ache in her heart. She takes a piece of paper out of her pocket and unfolds the feelings she was going to share with Paul. *My marriage is a lie and you are my dream, awakened to be seen, promising to the future all that was lost or never had.* She crumbles it in a ball and tosses it out the window.

Paul was her chance to be. She was an authentic person for the first time in her life. The passion he awakened in the bedroom permeated her life. It roared through her laughter and brought depth to her work. It also made her ache when he boarded the plane to Los Angeles. Now, her heart hurts too much to feel anything.

No one knows her heart the way Paul does. She let him in. She tossed him out. He has passed through her heart faster than the scenery shooting across the window. Her love for him is a hungry inferno, dampened by circumstance and left to dry up and blow away with the wind. Her future is gone. Even her tears are gone. All that is left of her heart she wraps around her work.

Touch Me Not

Since their divorce five weeks ago, Jim hasn't spent any time with their three-year-old son, even though he has liberal visitation rights. José gets so excited about his Daddy's visits that he cries himself to sleep when Jim cancels at the last minute. So when Jim agrees to take José to his grandmother's birthday party today, Nita decides not to tell José until they arrive at his place. She lets José ring the bell as she says, "I wonder if Daddy is home today."

"Daddy!" José rushes toward Jim. Jim lifts him into his arms and gives him a great big hug.

As he carries José down the hall to his room, he says to Nita, "I'm expecting the realtor to call. Can you get the phone if it rings?"

Nita steps out of the small foyer toward the sound of the radio in the living room. She sits in her favorite chair and scans the room, remembering the weeks it took to fix up this room. Her sweat is in the paint on the walls and the furnishings in the room, but all she sees now is a cloud of betrayal suspended over her hard work.

Nita jumps when the phone rings. The voice of a man at the other end of the line hesitates before asking for Jim. "Just a minute," she tells the man. She covers the receiver and shouts down the hall, "It's for you, Jim."

"Thanks, Nita," she hears Jim's voice on the line in the bedroom.

She is about to hang up when the voice whispers to Jim, "I miss you." She brings the phone back to her ear.

"Can I see you tonight?" the man asks Jim.

"I have my son for the weekend," Jim replies. "We're going to a birthday party for my mother."

"I'll come over tonight and make Pollo Enchiladas en Mole for both of you."

"Can you make something else?"

"I forgot. She ruined it for you," the voice complains.

"I can't talk right now. I'll see you tonight."

"I can't wait to see you, Jimmy. Do you know how much I want you?" the man murmurs.

"I want you too, babe," Jim flirts back.

Jim and the mysterious man hang up, leaving Nita with a humming drone in her ear. She quietly places the phone in the charger, plops down in the chair, and closes her eyes. Her heart is pushing her stomach to her throat the way it does when an elevator races down to the first floor. It all makes sense: the heavy drinking, the coming home at three in the morning, his insistence about not having an affair with a woman, his impotence the last time he tried to make love to her, and the words he repeated over and over to her, "It's too late. I can't live with you anymore."

The radio announcer, who is describing the second anniversary memorial services for the victims of the September 11th attack on the World Trade Center, pauses momentarily before turning to the news in Hollywood. *John Ritter died yesterday. He was taken to St. Joseph Medical Center in Burbank after experiencing severe nausea and vomiting while ...*

Her stomach jumps back to her throat as Jim's newly bearded face invades her sight. How can he be the same man who slept with her night after night when they were married? She leaps out of the chair and into the bathroom where she empties the contents of her stomach into the toilet. She takes a sip of water out of her hands and splashes some on her face before returning to the living room. She searches for her ex in the person standing before her, but all she sees is a man making love to a man.

"Are you okay?" Jim asks.

Nita nods. "Can I pick José up tonight? I forgot that he has been invited to his cousin's birthday party," she lies.

"No problem," Jim replies calmly. "I didn't have anything planned anyway. I'll drop him off tonight on the way home from my mother's."

"Please," she says as she walks down the hallway to the door.

• • • • •

Nita finds herself at the front door of her former neighbor. "Debbie is at her mother's with the baby," Zach informs her. "I have to get something from the office. Why don't you come with me? We'll talk in the car."

After Nita reveals what she overheard, Zach says, "Deb and I have wondered about that for a long time."

"You have?" Nita murmurs.

"I'll only be a few minutes," Zach explains. "Will you be okay while I run in?"

She nods.

As Zach opens the door, Nita suppresses the urge to jump out of the car and run away. Too many questions are swimming in her head. *If my friends suspected, why didn't I know? They were in our wedding. If they thought Jim was gay, why didn't they tell me before I married him? What kind of friends are they anyway?*

When Zach returns to the car, he says, "I hope you don't mind. I called Deb and told her what you told me. She'll be home in about an hour. We can talk over lunch."

Nita nods.

"Are you okay?"

Nita nods.

"You must know the divorce isn't your fault."

Nita nods.

"Say something, Nita, so I know you are okay."

"If he's gay, what does that make me, a gay lover?"

"It makes you a wife who has a chance to start over. Look at the bright side, Nita. At least it's not another woman."

"If it were a woman, I could fight it. But with a man, I ..." Nita's voice fades away as she stares out the window. "I feel violated. I can't imagine how this is better than another woman."

"You don't have anything to feel guilty about," Zach tells her.

"My body has been touched for the last five years by the man who…" Nita shivers. "I've been sleeping with a man who sleeps with men. What does that say about me as a woman?"

"It doesn't say anything about you as a woman," Zach tries to reassure her as he pulls the car into the garage. After he takes the key out of the ignition, he turns to Nita. "Why don't you give me your keys? I'll put your car in the garage so Jim doesn't see it."

She turns to Zach and asks, "Do you find me attractive?"

"You're very pretty."

"Do you find me sexually desirable?"

"It's obvious to everyone."

"Am I desirable to you?"

"Don't ask questions like that, Nita. I'm married to your best friend."

"If you weren't married to Debbie, would you find me sexually attractive?"

He fidgets in his seat. "Debbie will be home shortly."

"Do you find me sexy?"

Zach opens the car door. "Let's go inside."

"Do you want to have sex with me?" Nita asks, brushing her finger down his arm.

"Don't, Nita," he places her hand back on her lap. "It isn't fair of you to ask me these questions, and it wouldn't fair of me to answer them."

Nita leans over the consol, pressing her body firmly against Zach's chest.

"What are you doing?" Zach pushes her away angrily.

Nita falls back into her seat. As Zack brushes himself off, she asks, "Don't you find me desirable?"

"Stop it."

"Do you find me desirable?" Nita repeats.

"Yes, I do!" Zach shouts. "Any man in his right mind would need every ounce of strength to push you away, but I wouldn't be helping you if I slept with you. I don't take advantage of my friends, especially when they are vulnerable."

Nita puts her face in her hands and cries, "I wouldn't be able to face you or Debbie ever again."

Zach relaxes. "I'm glad to see you've come to your senses."

Nita sinks down in the passenger's seat. "I'm sorry, Zach. I didn't mean it."

"It's okay. You've had a big blow today, bigger than I can imagine."

"Jim is a disgusting liar. He touched me after..." She shivers. "What kind of a woman am I? I hit on my friend's husband."

"It's to be expected, I suppose, when you find out your husband is gay. Better me than someone—"

"—with fewer scruples," Nita interjects. "This is so embarrassing."

"Forget it, Nita. Go in the house. Deb will be home in," he looks at his watch, "about five minutes. She wants you to stay for lunch."

"What about you?"

"I'm going to the store."

"Do you want me to stay?"

"Of course I do, Nita," he reassures her.

"Are you sure?"

"Look at me," Zach draws an imaginary line down the middle of the console, "but stay on your side of the car."

Nita laughs.

"That's better. No harm has been done as far as I'm concerned."

"Are you going to tell Deb?"

Zach shakes his head and says, "Not unless it happens again. You and Deb have been friends for too long and these things have a way of ruining friendships." He hands Nita the keys to the house and holds out his hand. "Where are your car keys?"

She rummages through her purse as she continues to apologize.

Zach clasps Nita's car keys inside his fist. "Go inside and wait for Deb," he instructs Nita. "I'll be back in a few."

She notices a car pulling into Jim's driveway when she gets out of Zach's car. As the garage door is closing, she sees a bearded man get of the car.

The Pall Bearer

Soledad takes off the rubber gloves and answers the door.

The man standing on the door stoop says, "We came for the pickup for the *Sisters of St. Joseph Orphanage.*"

"Come on in." She leads them into the great room. "All of this goes; this couch, these chairs, coffee table, end tables and the dining room set," she tells them somberly as she touches each of the items. She leads them down the hallway to the bedroom. She steps aside so the two men can enter the room while she stands at the door and says, "Make sure you don't forget these boxes of linens or this bedroom set."

"Are you sure?" one of the movers asks. "It's made of solid oak."

"I'm sure someone can use it," Soledad replies nonchalantly. "Everything goes except the desk and chair in my office."

"We don't have enough room in the truck for such a large pickup. We'll have to do this in two trips." He signals to his partner to take the couch.

"If you can't take it all now, start with the bedroom set," Soledad insists.

"Yes, ma'am."

"I'll be out back if you have any questions."

As the men are removing the furniture she and Bob have accumulated during their fourteen year marriage, Soledad sits at the table on the back patio with her newspaper. She looks at the front page headline, *England Grieves for their Princess,* and shakes her head, knowing that many people have given up their fifteen minutes of fame so Princess Diana can have front page coverage a week after she died. She passes over the pictures of her coffin arriving at the airport, the mourners leaving flowers outside the gate of Kensington Palace, and the sidebar rumoring that she was pregnant. She flips the page to the world news. Her eyes scan the headlines ... *Eighty*

Seven Killed in Beni-Messous Massacre, Athens Chosen for 2004 Summer Olympics...and come to rest on the headline at the bottom of the page, *Mother Theresa Dies.*

She snaps the paper shut and looks down toward the Seekonk River. "Excuse me, ma'am." The man's voice draws her eyes through the screen to one of the movers and another man wearing a Roman collar. "This is Brother Patrick," the mover explains.

"I'm Soledad." She stands up and motions for Brother Patrick to join her on the patio.

He steps outside and states his purpose. "I thought I'd come by and personally thank you for your generous gift."

"My pleasure," she replies.

"We don't usually get such generous gifts. Do you mind if I ask why you chose our organization?"

"I chose a Catholic orphanage because I lost my both of my parents when I was eight."

"I'm sorry."

"It was a long time ago." The moving man with a clipboard in his hand opens the screen door for Soledad.

"Make sure she gets a detailed receipt," Brother Patrick tells him.

"It's all itemized," the mover replies as he hands the receipt to Soledad.

Brother Patrick lays his hand on Soledad's head and says, "God bless you," before leaving with the movers through the open garage door.

With the bedroom emptied of furniture, Soledad wipes down the walls and steams the carpet. Once the room wafts of Pine Sol, the heavy rubber gloves are removed and tossed in the garbage. She flops on the couch and quickly jumps back to her feet. *Did they lie here too?*

Soledad goes into her office and breathes in the fresh scent of Pine Sol. She wraps her hand around the handle of the closet door and turns it quickly. She leaps away from the open door as if she were expecting to find a mouse inside. She slams the door shut.

She opens the door and slams it shut again. She repeats the process several times before stepping back into the center of the room. She glares at the closed door and takes another deep breath. When she reopens the closet door, she falls back into the chair and rolls into her desk. Her eyes sweep across the shelves of photo albums lined up in neat rows. How can she divide what lies inside?

When Soledad hears a car pull into the driveway, she peeks out the window and sees Barb lifting her swollen body out of the car. She rushes to the door and watches Barb waddle up the driveway. "How's the little one," she says as Barb enters through the side door. She feels the kick as she hugs Barb.

"Feisty," Barb replies as she rubs her hand on her stomach, "but not quite ready to be on her own."

"Come on in. I'll make some tea. You'll have to excuse the mess," Soledad apologizes as they step around the boxes stacked on floor next to the living room wall.

Barb's eyes fall on stack of boxes in the corner of the kitchen. "Are you sure you want to do this, Sole?"

"Yes." Soledad states firmly.

"I know how upset you were when I interfered at the wedding," Barb begins. "You may get mad again when you find out I came here to talk some sense into you."

"Why should you be any different than anyone else?" Soledad says with sarcasm.

"You and Bob are making a terrible mistake. Both of you are losing far more than you're gaining."

Soledad stares out the window and lets her mind drift away. Barb gently touches her shoulders and says, "Talk to me, Sole. I'm on your side."

"I know," Soledad acknowledges, turning from the window to fill the tea kettle with water. "Your parents were here yesterday with the same message. I'll tell you the same thing I told them. There isn't anything anyone can do about it. I'm not even sure it matters anymore."

"It does matter, Sole. You and Bob are so sure, but in your haste, perhaps you, both of you that is, haven't put enough thought into what you are doing." Barb removes the only two mugs left in the cupboard and places them on the table. "Take time to think about this before doing anything. You and Bob are happy. Do you want to throw it away?"

"We were happy," Soledad remembers, "but things change."

"Are you having an affair?"

"No, I am not," Soledad looks directly at Barb before returning to the kettle whistling on the stove. "Your parents asked me the same thing."

"Is Bob?"

"Is Bob what?" Soledad replies curtly.

" … having an affair?"

She hands Barb a mug of hot water. "I think he should be the one to answer that question."

"We have asked him, Sole, but he won't tell us anything. He claims that none of this is your fault. He is certain that he loves you. He knows he was lucky to have you as a wife. He is sure he can't turn the clock back and change what has happened. He says a lot but doesn't tell us anything."

"He's right."

"Why are both of you talking in circles?" Barb inquires. "You're throwing it all away without attempting to fix it. I don't know what happened at your brother's wedding, and it was wrong of me to interfere. I know one thing. You and Bob belong together. Can you deny that you have a good marriage?"

"We *had* a good marriage," Soledad replies, "but it's not that simple. Sometimes life throws us curve balls that change everything, especially the good things. You should know this better than anyone else."

"It's not a fair comparison. My ex-husband is an alcoholic," Barb reminds Soledad.

"And Bob is who he is. I don't have any control over that either."

Barb ignores the comment. "It's different with you and Bob. You got married for the right reasons. You love each other. Now you have a problem, one problem, one night two months ago at your cousin's wedding, the only night in fourteen years of marriage. Let it go. Hang on to what is good."

Soledad's finger travels around the rim of the mug as she wanders into thought.

Barb breaks the silence. "Perhaps it has been too easy for you and Bob, so much so that this problem looks bigger than it is." She holds her hand up to stop Soledad from responding. "I wouldn't be here if I didn't care about both of you. You and Bob need to be reminded how lucky you are. Most people would give their right arm to have the kind of relationship you have. Don't throw it away," Barb pleads.

"It went away on its own."

"Every marriage is difficult from time to time," Barb continues. "You told me so yourself. Remember the night I was worried about a big blowout I had with Rich shortly after we were married? I was afraid I had made a mistake, you know, getting married a second time. You told me something that night I haven't forgotten. Do you remember?" Their eyes lock momentarily. "You told me that marriage is like skiing, that it isn't the steepness of the hill that makes the problems insurmountable, but rather the inability of the couple to make good turns. You know what? You were right. If I had given up as easily as you are now, we wouldn't have our beautiful little girl and," she smiles, patting her stomach, "another one on the way."

"You are so sensible about these things," Barb reminds Soledad, "so please take your own advice and don't give up."

"I don't have a choice." Soledad stands up, uncharacteristically scratching the chair legs across the hardwood floor. She rushes over to the sink and slams the mug on the counter. "Everyone wants me to fix this, but I can't," she rants. "This is what Bob wants. He must have it. I can't and shouldn't talk him out of doing something like this."

She turns her back on Barb, hoping to regain her composure. "You should know me well enough to know I'd walk through fire to save something worth saving. I can't save our marriage because I can't change who he is."

Soledad gathers up the shards of the mug scattered across the counter and tosses them into the garbage. "I know you mean well, Barb, but you have to understand that our marriage is over, and there isn't anything you, I, or anyone else can do to save it. So please, for my sake, for Bob's sake, for your own sake, let it go." Her eyes gravitate to the window. "The movers will be here shortly," she mumbles, "and I still need to pack some boxes."

Barb studies Soledad long lean figure standing by the window. Placing the palms of her hands at the edge of the table, she lifts her swollen body from the chair. "Okay," she says. "Let me help you with the packing. I have a few hours to kill before I pick up Janie from my in-laws."

Soledad turns around and smiles. "Thank you, Barb."

Barb follows Soledad to the closet in the den possessing the only remnant of her life with Bob of which she will not part. Soledad brushes her fingers along the spine of the photo albums neatly stacked on the closet shelves Bob built. "This is all that is left," she murmurs.

Soledad opens the cover of each album before handing them off to Barb, one by one, to pack in the empty boxes on the floor. When the shelves lays bare, they sit on the floor in front of the open closet door and mark each box with the year the pictures were taken. They roll the boxes from side to bottom to side to top, in unison, to seal Soledad and Bob's married years inside the boxes.

Soledad carries her sacred treasure, one box at a time, to the trunk of her car with Barb at her side. The impromptu ritual is as automatic to them as breathing, the calm shock that occurs in the aftermath of a trauma, ensuring that everything valued isn't lost in the numbness of the day.

With all the boxes secure in the car, Barb pulls a wrapped package from her purse and gives it to Soledad. "Kenny made this for you. He wanted to give it to you personally, but he didn't have the nerve to come here today. He feels awful about what happened at the wedding." Barb instinctively pulls Soledad toward her swollen belly. "We love you, Sole," she murmurs.

After Soledad watches Barb's car disappear around the corner at the end of the street, she returns to the den. Her eyes touch upon the empty closet as she stands in the middle of her office and opens the gift box. It contains a hand-blown glass gondola of a man and woman embracing as a gondolier escorts them around Venice. She watches the light reach through it and fall on her desk as she reads Kenny's simple message, "Love remains when all else changes."

After carefully returning the gondola to the box, she buttons her coat up around her neck and reaches for the doorknob, pausing only to touch upon the dusty floor of his empty closet. She exhales, "I love you too," and closes the door.

Gay Whisperers

"Nita has always come to us, no matter what, but this time, she hasn't told us anything except that her marriage is over." Ana looks up at Judy, nervously folding and unfolding the clean tissue in her hand into a neat little square. "A few weeks after the divorce, Carlos scolded her, insisting that she explain to us what had happened. Nita contorted her face with disgust, claiming that she had no desire to talk about that vile, repulsive liar who called himself her husband. She stormed out of the house, making it clear that she wouldn't be around until we stopped nagging her."

Ana blows her nose. "I had lunch with her a few times since school started, but she hasn't seen her father since the end of July. Last week she called, strangely upset that Elia Kazan died, on September 28, 2003, Jim's thirtieth birthday. Old movies are her latest obsession. The background noise helps her concentrate when she is studying at home. It's her only option, she claims, because no one at school likes her anymore."

When Ana instinctively reaches over to pick up the ringing phone, Judy holds her hand up and says, "Let it go to voicemail."

"Thanks." Ana smiles at Judy and continues. "She called to find out if we were going to get together for our Friday night family dinner and movie because there was a movie she wanted us to see."

"Her father thought she was going to bring *On the Waterfront, Gentlemen's Agreement,* or some other movie directed by Elia Kazan, but she stretched out on the floor with her sister, Nikki, intently watching *Day Trippers.* It's about a woman who suspects her husband is having an affair. She goes with her family to New York in search of her husband and discovers he is having an affair, but it's not with a woman."

"Oh," Judy utters as a familiar sinking feeling disquiets her stomach.

Ana washes down the lump in her throat with a swig of water. "I didn't know what to say, so I didn't say anything." She sniffles. "After Nita went home with Nikki, I mentioned to Carlos that I suspected Nita had rented the movie because she wanted to tell us something. 'The whole idea is absurd,' he said. 'Why would Jim prefer anyone to our daughter when she has everything a man would ever want?'"

"This morning, Nikki tells me Nita stayed the weekend with her. Last night when Nikki returned to the living room after putting the kids to bed, she found Nita sitting on the couch with Jose sleeping in her arms, staring at the static on the TV. Nikki asked Nita if what happened in the movie is the reason for her divorce. Nita nodded. She didn't cry. She didn't say anything expect that she wants us to know so we'll leave her alone."

Ana sighs and looks up at Judy. "What have we done to our daughter?" Judy hands Ana the box of Kleenex. "I don't know where to begin. This kind of thing must happen all the time with all the men who are coming out, but I wouldn't have imagined that it would happen to my daughter. I don't know how or even if I can help her."

"And my husband," Ana continues, "is an old-fashioned man who believes a man ought to be a man in every sense of the word. How do I tell Carlos? He'll be furious." Ana's eyes widen as she leans forward with emotion churning through her words. "All I want to do right now is rip Jim's eyes out. Why didn't Nita tell us the truth instead of renting that silly movie?"

"Because she can't," Judy replies. "She doesn't know what is true anymore. She doesn't have the words to make sense of it, so she feeds you clues, like the movie, hoping you will help her make sense of what has happened to her. She's too torn by her conflicting feelings to make sense of it," Judy explains, surprised by the insight that is forming on her lips. "On top of this is the politically correct absurdity of instant acceptance. It doesn't work that way." Judy stops to contain her own anger. "If you're questioning your beliefs, Ana, imagine what Nita must be doing right now."

"Oh," Ana utters through the hand covering her mouth. "How can I help her when I don't know how I feel about this?"

"Use the movie as a way to help her make some sense of this."

"I don't know where to begin," Ana states reluctantly.

"No one does," Judy reminds herself. "We have so few tools to deal with this. Tell her you know. She brought the movie to you, so use it to help her find the words she needs to make sense of this. Let her know you'll be there when she's ready to talk."

"Thanks for the advice, Judy." Ana looks at her watch. "It's time to get back to work. I've taken up enough of your time."

Ana." Judy catches her eye as she hesitates at the door. "Why don't you take the afternoon off to be with her?"

"Thank you, I will. Is there anything you need from me before I leave?"

"Did you send that new hire notice over to administration?"

"I will on my way out."

"Before you do, change the job description to the one we use for an undergraduate research assistant." Judy holds up an envelope. "This is the publishing contract for my next book about families affected by gays and lesbians coming out of the closet. Do you think Nita might be interested in working with me?"

"It would keep her away from the television."

"Why don't you get the paperwork ready and I'll talk to Nita?"

"I appreciate anything you can do." Ana says as she shakes her head. "I wish I knew what to do."

The Elephant Is in the Room

Judy leans back in her chair as the door closes behind Nita's mother. Her heart is heavy because she knows that Nita faces the same circuitous path out of this mess as she did after her divorce. Judy's parents were so good at turning their heads away from what they didn't want to see; knowing what, for their generation, was a totally unacceptable lifestyle. What surprises her is that things aren't much different for Nita. Her father refuses to acknowledge it. Her mother is terribly worried and uncomfortable with what happened. Nita is just as confused about how to tell her parents as Judy was. Her parents have turned away from her signals the same way Judy's parents did.

Nita has been sucked into the very same eddy of confusion Judy was in twenty years ago. The very foundation of her femininity, everything she believes to be true, has been shattered. Nita needs her parents' sensibility, but she probably won't get anything more than their silence. Ana is too sensitive about it to be of much help to Nita. And how much support will she get from her old-fashioned father? Judy wonders how much progress has been made in the last twenty years if all Nita can do is the same thing Judy did—let the riptide heave her into the deep and release her for a long swim to the other side of the storm.

Judy remembers the night in the fall of 1985, when she tried to tell her parents about Pete in much the same way as Nita has, and failed in much the same way as Nita has. When her father came through the door that night, Judy was leaning back in a leather chair with her feet resting on top of her desk.

• • • • •

George smiles, remembering how, when Judy was younger, she sat the very same way in his office chair, waiting for him to come home when she needed to talk to him.

"Hi, honey," he hails, leaning over her and brushing her bangs aside so he can kiss her forehead.

"Hi, Dad," Judy says flatly without opening her eyes.

"Your mother went to the store to pick up groceries for dinner," he reports. "She didn't think you'd want to go out after having such a tough day, and I wouldn't go with her because I didn't think you wanted to be alone." He grabs one of the chairs from the table, wraps his legs around the back of it, and sets his chin on its back. "How is my girl?"

"I'll tell you about it when Mom gets here."

"Only if I don't have any other choice," George grumbles. He studies her as she flips through the freshly printed manuscript.

"Oh, Judy!" he shouts excitedly, "I read the manuscript for your new book. This one will put you on the map."

"Yeah right, Dad," she chuckles. "You say that about every book I write, and none of them has put me on the map."

"They are on my map." He petitions her forgiveness. "Can I help it if I am proud of my daughter?"

The foyer buzzer sounds. Her father turns his pants pockets inside out and shows her a key. "I forgot to give your mother the key."

Judy presses the buzzer next to her desk to let her mother into the lobby downstairs. "So Dad, what don't you like about the book?"

"Nothing. Not a thing at all," George maintains.

"Then tell me, what do you like about it?"

"Everything in it and my little girl," he responds lightheartedly.

"Some help you are." Judy pouts playfully as she hands him the book. "Here it is, hot off the press. Can you make us a drink, Dad, while I let Mom in?"

"Sure." George takes three glasses from the shelf above the bar as Judy walks down the hallway to the foyer. "One quarter vodka and three quarters orange juice for Edna, and," he proudly hums, "a Glen Levitt with a splash of water, just a splash, and a twist of lime for Judy."

George hears the door open followed by Edna's voice echoing through the foyer, "You look tired, Judy." He visualizes the hug Judy is getting from her mother. "What a terrible ordeal the trial must have been. Honey, tell your mother what…," George follows their fading voices toward the kitchen with the drinks.

"I thought we'd have your favorite meal tonight." Edna holds each item up as she takes it out of the bag. "I bought fillet minion for your father to grill. I'll make garlic mashed potatoes. You can toss a salad with these fresh greens. And," she continues to rustle through the bag, "I brought your favorite treat, Cherry Garcia ice cream and Kahlúa."

"Yum," Judy exclaims when her mother gives her a hug.

"They don't call it comfort food for nothing," Edna proclaims.

George notices the worried look on Edna's face when she glances at him over Judy's shoulder. He rubs his hands together and says, "Let's get to work."

Edna busily scrapes the skin off the potatoes while Judy washes the greens. "Save some garlic for the potatoes," Edna instructs George as he blends the olive oil, garlic, pine nuts, basil, and Romano cheese.

"Save some of that Romano for the salad," Judy adds.

George flips the blender off. "I already did," he replies, holding up several cloves of peeled garlic and a small dish of grated cheese. He pours half of the pesto from the blender over the tuna fillets and sets the oven at one hundred degrees. "This will speed up the marinade. I'll start the grill." He opens the screen door and steps out to the patio.

"I already put the coals on the grill, Dad. The lighter fluid is in the storage cabinet," Judy instructs through the door.

George can hear the humming of his wife and daughter in the kitchen as he lights the coals. Not wanting to disturb them, he leans against the rail while puffing away on his pipe and caressing his daughter's name on the front cover of her new book. After admiring the sun shining off the buildings in the distant Chicago skyline, he sinks into the chaise lounge and flips quickly through Judy's book before returning to the den. He mixes himself another drink at the wet bar beneath the large picture window overlooking Lake Michigan. He taps his pipe bowl against the side of the ashtray on the table next to the window framing Northwestern University. His eyes brush over the three stacks of papers labeled with post-it notes and rest on the manuscript Judy was reviewing when he arrived. He flips it open and reads the first thing he sees.

> An unwanted drama is unfolding. His identity is hidden by their union, and the union is dying. What becomes of her? She wishes she could yell at him, but he'll only say, 'I can't help but be who I am.'

The manuscript slides out of his hand onto the floor. George sets his pipe on the table and carefully resorts the pages. The thumb and forefinger of each hand form a V cup around the manuscript, first top right to bottom left and then top left to bottom right, before he places it under the book where he found it.

He falls into one of the swivel chairs facing the patio door, but the wild thumping of his heart pushes him out of it. He paces the length of a long row of mahogany bookcases that house an eclectic collection of writings before returning to the table. His fingertips brushing across the document are quickly withdrawn as if he is touching a hot burner. His eyes return to the stacks of journal articles. Two large stacks are labeled "homosexuality" and "coming out." The book that was on top of the manuscript he looked through is labeled "impact on spouses."

His eyes race faster than he can walk to the patio where the auburn clouds hanging in the east reflect the end of the day in the west. George hangs onto the railing and slams down his drink, waiting impatiently for the brandy to warm him. As he spreads the red hot coals over the grill, he reminds himself that it would not be uncommon for a sociology professor to write about this kind of thing.

George watches his daughter through the patio door slicing a tomato while chatting with her mother about her book. "The part I really enjoyed," Edna says proudly, "is your comparison of people's perceptions of the same sexual behavior when it is exhibited by women and men. There's also something in this book that I haven't seen before."

"What is it, Mom?"

"This book has heart," Edna tells her daughter. "You peel away at the layers of sexual behavior, social norms, feeling, and desire as if you were peeling this onion."

Judy's thoughts immediately wander through her heart to Paul.

"When will the book be published?" Edna asks.

George opens the screen door and steps into the kitchen with the book in his hand. "It's already published." He hands Judy a pen and asks, "Will you autograph it for me?"

Judy pretends to scribble her signature over the note she already wrote inside the front cover and passes the book back to her father. "Are you ready to sear the tuna?"

· · · · ·

When they finished eating, George rushes into the kitchen and returns with his hands behind his back. "I have something very special for my daughter." He covers Judy's eyes as he waves a dish of Cherry Garcia ice cream topped with Kahlúa in front of her nose. "Can you guess what it is?"

Judy tastes a spoonful. "Hmm," she feigns ignorance, "cherries and chocolate and cream all together in an icy clump." She smacks her lips. "The sauce is especially tasty." When he uncovers her eyes, they widen with surprise as she squeals, "Thanks, Dad."

George sets a dish of ice cream in front of Edna. "I eat when I worry about you," he explains after his wife and daughter exchange an amusing look as George begins to devour an oversized bowl of ice cream.

"Tell us about the trial, honey," Edna suggests.

"There's not much to tell because everything is worked out in advance. Pete and I sat in the judge's chamber while he reviewed the documents. He asked us a number of questions and, with the slap of a gavel," Judy mimics by touching her fist to the table, "twenty years of my life are over. I'll be okay. Pete and I haven't been close for a long time. You see, he's been, um, how do you say, seeing…"

"Is Kim enjoying her semester in Florence?" George interrupts.

Judy stares at her father as Edna's warning, "Geooorge," resonates through the room.

"What about the settlement?" George asks.

"It's equitable," Judy declares.

"Equitable!" George exclaims. "He's having an affair, and you say the agreement is equitable."

"I'm not going there, Dad," Judy warns. "I know Pete isn't a good husband, but he is a good father. He will take care of the twins. The settlement requires that he set aside an annuity with enough money for both Kim and Jerry to get advanced degrees. What he brings in from his medical practice is enough to take care of anything else they need. Everything else, including the equity in his medical practice and both of our retirement plans, has been divided equally. So both of us, sadly, own half of what we did yesterday." She holds up her hand to stop her father from interrupting. "It's more than enough. I don't want alimony. I am a tenured full professor with a decent income from Northwestern. I don't have any debt, not even a mortgage. What more can I ask for?"

"A husband who doesn't have a woman in his hip pocket," George replies.

"That's not exactly it, Dad," Judy jumps in. "We're more like old friends than husband and wife. I don't remember exactly how or when it happened. He did try, many times, but his efforts failed. We went, um, how would you say," Judy stammers, "our separate ways. It's not his fault that he is—"

"Eat your ice cream before it melts, Judy," George insists.

Edna turns her head sharply toward George. "Stop it, George. And why are you drinking so much?" She takes the glass out of his hand and sets it firmly on the table. "I don't want to hear another word from you until—"

"It's alright, Mom," Judy breaks in. Her mother settles back into her chair. Her father turns his head toward the table. "Are you okay, Dad?"

George nods, eyeing the melting ice cream in front of her. "Go ahead, Jude."

"Our divorce is the recognition of the reality that we have grown in completely different directions. I know that your generation believes marriage is forever, that spouses are supposed to stay together through thick and thin, hang in there no matter what. I used to believe this too, so I turned my back on, um, his problem. I did it to save our marriage for the sake of the twins, but there are new reasons for divorces today, reasons that don't lend themselves to marriage-saving techniques." Judy pauses. "That is, when he is, you know, um, how would you say …"

"How are the twins handling this?" her mother asks.

"They seem to be okay. It's probably a good thing they're not home. Pete and I plan to visit each of them at school next semester after they return from their studies abroad to, um …" Judy's voice fades off, "tell them the real reason for the divorce."

"Don't think we haven't noticed, honey," George tells his daughter.

"We've been worried about you for a while." Edna gathers up the dishes. "Take care of your father while I take care of the dishes," she adds and disappears into the kitchen.

"Hey Dad, I rented a movie directed by Arthur Miller, and to top it off, Kate Jackson," Judy nudges her dad, "your favorite Angel, is in it."

"Kate Jackson!" George exclaims as Judy hands him the video jacket. "In *Making Love*. Hmm, what's this?" He silently reads the jacket. *An ideal marriage between Claire, a television producer, and*

Zack, a doctor, disintegrates when he confronts his latent homosexuality. He looks at his watch. "It's getting late. We'll watch it another time."

"It's nine thirty on a Friday night. None of us goes to bed this early."

"Well, you should. You've had a tough day." He kisses her cheek. "I'll help your mother with the dishes."

"But the movie," Judy protests as she follows her father into the kitchen.

"Another time, honey."

"Go to bed," Edna insists as she turns Judy's shoulders and pushes her out of the kitchen. "We'll let ourselves out after we clean up."

"You're treating me like a two-year-old," Judy objects.

"Every once in a while, all of us need to be treated as if we are two years old."

"If you insist," Judy concedes. "Night, Mom. Night, Dad."

As she walks through the den to her bedroom, Judy notices a piece of paper sticking out from under the couch. She picks it up and examines it. It is the third page of the paper she was editing when her father arrived. When she puts the page back in its place, she notices her father's pipe is lying on the table next to the manuscript.

Judy listens to the murmur of her parents' voices from the kitchen while putting on her pajamas. Her stomach is churning, waxing and waning the way a series of light slaps awakens the skin, relieving her of the numbing onus of the day while hurting her at the same time.

She had planned to tell her parents the truth, but she didn't. She thought they would guess, but they didn't. Or had they? Her mother ignored her stammering, and her father didn't ask about the manuscript that he obviously had scanned. He even refused to watch a movie starring one of his favorite actresses.

Wrapping her arms around the video, she lays her head on the pillow as her parents' voices in the kitchen are like a lullaby cooing her to sleep. It isn't too late to tell them. She musters up enough energy to lift her head from the pillow, but a new awkwardness pushes back at her. All she can do is crawl beneath the covers as an eddy of incredulity takes her to a place where she, like a deaf mute, silently pleads to be heard.

The Fault Line

The judge looks up from the document at Jim. "Is it true that you have filed for the dissolution of your marriage to Anita Maria Burroughs in the Circuit Court of Cook County, Illinois, Department Domestic Relations?"

"Yes."

"Is it also true that the extreme and repeated mental cruelty of your wife caused irreparable damage to the marriage, rendering the continuing of the marriage impossible."

"Yes," Jim replies.

The phrase, *extreme and repeated mental cruelty,* penetrates Nita's brain like poison. She glances over at Jim and focuses on his newly bearded face, taking a gulp of air to settle her stomach. She watches his head bob up and down to the statements of the judge. As she examines the judge reviewing the documents, she is hypnotized by the rhythmic motion of his lips and the rotation of his eyes back and forth from the document to Jim.

The drone of his voice echoing through the chamber is the music she needs to drown out the words she doesn't want to hear. She looks down at the date displayed on her phone—July 28, 2003. The song she heard on the radio after the announcement that Bob Hope died is still ringing through her ears. *And then I see the laugh is on me, but thanks for the memory.*[1] She has no memory of what she did to cause Jim to do this to her. She can't change what is about to happen because he won't admit he is having an affair. She can't do much to save her marriage when she doesn't know who the other woman is.

"Excuse me, Ms. Burroughs." The Judge's edgy voice brings her thoughts back into the room. He glares at her over the top of his glasses before returning to the document. "Other than the agreed-

[1]   Thanks for the Memory, Writers: Leo Robin/Ralph Rainger Artist: Frank Sinatra and Bob Hope

upon support for your son, do you permanently waive for yourself any claim of allowance, support, maintenance, or alimony, past, present, or future, and agree to be barred from asserting such claim either now or in the future in any court whatsoever?"

"Yes."

The judge continues mumbling a rote string of words. "A Judgment for Dissolution of Marriage is hereby granted to James Michael and Anita Maria Burroughs. Said marriage is hereby terminated, and the parties are both freed from the bonds and obligations thereof. This court reserves jurisdiction of the subject matter of this case and of the parties heretofore the purpose of enforcing the terms of this Judgment for the Dissolution of Marriage and the terms and provisions of the Marital Settlement Agreement." He slaps the gavel on the desk and smiles at Nita. "Now, dear, you can go next door and get married."

I'd rather have a lobotomy, she rebounds silently as she stands up, pushing her long black hair to one side of her face so that her dark eyes have a chance to pierce through the judge. She wants to run out of the room, away from the judge and Jim, but her feet are stuck to the floor. Even if she could move, she doesn't know where she would go. So she does what she has always done and follows Jim through the door of the chamber, down the elevator, through the large atrium, and to the steps in front of the courthouse building.

When they reach the bottom of the stairs, Jim turns around and extends his hand to Nita.

She pulls her hand away and asks, "How could you do this to me, Jim?"

He gives her a puzzled look. "I wish you the best, Nita," he says before turning away from her and walking down the street.

Keep Me from Me

"I can't cancel my trip now," Soledad explains to Bob as she glances out the bay window in the living room. "My cab will be here in fifteen minutes."

"Do you have to go to Moscow?"

"The Russian-Chechen Peace Treaty was signed this weekend. There's no one else who can cover the story."

"I thought you're responsible for covering economic issues not political ones."

"They go hand in hand," Soledad explains, "especially when economies are transitioning from government control to free markets."

"Don't go," Bob murmurs.

"I have to go." She leans into the bay window and looks both ways down the street. "Where is that cab driver?"

"Please stay with me, Sole," Bob insists.

"You know I can't." She softens her voice because she doesn't want to leave him on a bad note. "I'll be home before you know it."

"What am I supposed to do for three nights without you," Bob moans as he plops on the couch.

"Stop whining," Soledad snaps. When she looks over at him and sees how upset he is, she adds, "We'll talk when I get back on Thursday."

"Your cousin's in-laws will be staying with us for the wedding," Bob protests.

"We'll have several hours to talk before they arrive."

"Since when do I have to make an appointment to talk to my wife?"

"That's not what I mean." Her edginess grows as she looks through the window at the empty driveway. "Why didn't you tell me last night when we had time to talk about how you feel about my traveling?"

"Because you're rarely home anymore," Bob complains. "Not even on our wedding anniversary."

"We're back to that again," Soledad says sharply. "What do you expect me to do about something that happened a year ago?"

"Please don't leave, Sole," Bob begs.

Something in his voice makes Soledad turn around. "What's wrong, honey?"

"I don't like what is happening to us. Everything has changed. I wish I understood."

She sets her purse on top of her suitcase and sits on the couch next to Bob. "What's changed?"

"When was the last time you met me after work on a Friday night at one of the mansions I'm renovating? You used to walk through it with me and give me all kinds of ideas before we went to that Thai food restaurant on the river. Now I come home to my sleeping jet-lagged wife."

"I get up as soon as you come through the door," Soledad defends her behavior. "There is rarely a lull in our conversation while I make dinner for you, and afterward, we lie in bed and talk for hours into the night."

"It's not the same when you leave Monday morning and return Friday night."

"Afternoon," Soledad corrects.

"Either way, you can't be with me when you work on another continent. Sure, we talk on the phone every night, but it's not the same as it is in person. I need to be with my wife every night of the week."

"Bob," Soledad exclaims, "I didn't know you miss me that much!"

"I miss you so much that I even wish you were here to sleep through a movie, wake up to the credits, and expect me to recap it for you on the way to bed."

Soledad smiles at Bob. "I love you too, honey."

"There is more to it, Sole. I'm afraid something might happen."

"What can happen?"

"It's what can't happen. You can't have my child."

"Yes, I can," Soledad insists.

"You've already had two miscarriages."

"We've only been trying this time for a month."

"How can it happen when you're not here?"

"I'm tired of being away from home as much as you are." The sound of a horn in their driveway brings both of them to their feet. Soledad signals to the driver from the window before addressing Bob. "I told you last night that I'll talk to my boss about working out of the Boston office. I'm far enough along on the project where it shouldn't be a problem."

"Will you?" Bob asks with a tone of desperation in his voice.

"Something is wrong, Bob. I can feel it." When the cab driver honks the horn again, Soledad asks, "Will you be alright?"

Bob nods as Soledad kisses him good-bye. As he watches the cab pull out of the driveway, he whispers, "Don't leave me, Sole."

Wedding Night Jitters

"You're going out on our honeymoon!" Judy exclaims.

"I always take a walk before I go to bed." When she stands up, Pete adds, "I always go alone."

"Alone," Judy repeats as she sits back down on the bed in her negligee and watches Pete put his shoes on.

He gives her an inquisitive look. "Why are you dressed like that?" he comments sharply.

Judy looks at herself. "This is what women wear on their wedding night."

"It makes you look cheap."

"Our friends gave it to me. They told me that you'd like it."

Pete covers his face with his hands. "Sex ruins everything," he mutters.

"What?"

Pete leaps up and paces the floor a few times before saying, "It spoils everything."

"It makes everything better," Judy claims.

"How do you know when you haven't had sex before?"

"It's supposed to make our relationship stronger."

"You've been reading too many books, Judy. It's supposed to, but in reality, it gets in the way." Pete sits on the bed next to Judy. "When I imagine our future, I see me making dinner for you and our children. I see your soft face in the morning as you sit across the breakfast table from me and read the *New York Times,* but nowhere in this picture do I see a sexual act."

"Don't you want to have sex with me?" Judy asks.

"Sex isn't everything."

"It's like the sunset; alluring, colorful, vibrant," Judy whispers.

"And short lived," Pete adds. "Darkness always follows. I need some air."

Judy is flabbergasted as she sits on the edge of the bed in her negligee, staring at the door closing behind him. This isn't what she imagined her wedding night to be. She is supposed to feel Pete's touch through the silk fabric of her negligee. His arms are supposed to reach around her as he kisses her neck. She is supposed to feel the crispness of the sheets as they slide under the covers together and make love for the first time.

She doesn't remember exactly when she fell asleep, but she is awakened by a kiss on the forehead and Pete's voice whispering, "Wake up, sleepy head."

Judy sits up against the headboard and opens her eyes to Pete sitting on the edge of the bed fully dressed. Through the bedroom door she sees someone from the kitchen staff setting up the breakfast cart in the sitting area. She tugs at the sheet partially covering her until she loosens the tautness on Pete's side of the bed. "When did you get back?" she asks.

"You were sound asleep by then," he replies. "Since I was up early, I booked the eight a.m. dive trip for us."

After Pete tips the waiter and lets him out, he leads her from the bed to the table. He holds out the chair for her and serves her breakfast. Judy notices a *New York Times* folded neatly like a napkin next to each of their plates.

"I'm going to take a shower. Enjoy, my love," he says as he unfolds the paper, places it in her lap, and disappears into the bathroom.

Judy is reading the paper when Pete returns to the table. "I'm back, my dear," he announces as he smiles at her, before snapping open the newspaper and burying his head behind it. She peeks over the top of her paper to the front page headline on his, *Gemini III Manned Crew Orbits the Earth.*

"What are you reading?" Judy asks.

Pete drops the paper below his eyes. "The University of Michigan had a Vietnam war teach-in yesterday."

"What's a teach-in?"

"It's a public forum with lectures, debates, and musical events protesting the war," he explains. "And what are you reading?"

"The civil rights marchers made it to Montgomery."

"Page number?"

"Bottom of the page two," Judy replies.

Pete turns to page two and lifts the newspaper back over his eyes. After he finishes reading the article, he sets the paper on the table and addresses Judy. "Remind me, my love, how Dr. King convinced authorities that eight thousand Negroes could march in protest."

"It was after James Reeb died last week. You remember him. He and two other white ministers from the north were beaten in front of a southern white segregationist hang out. The Selma hospital refused to treat him."

Pete shakes his head. "Some people say it wouldn't have happened if the publicity from the beatings at the first march hadn't brought twenty-five hundred people from all over the country to the second march. Others say it would have been worse if they had marched."

Judy closes her paper. "They didn't march the second time because they tried to get a court order to stop the police from interfering and it backfired. A restraining order violating First Amendment rights was issued. Sadly, it took a senseless murder of a northerner not the Civil Rights Act to give them the right to march in protest."

"I thought the Civil Rights Act was supposed to stop this nonsense."

"It doesn't," Judy explains, "because the act outlaws racial segregation without placing checks on the power of states to discriminate at the voting poles or in the political arena. The voting rights bill that Johnson sent to Congress last week will help, but I can't see it stopping these horrible murders of Negros and White Northerners who support their rights."

Pete frowns at Judy. "You are much too passionate."

"You think so?" Judy asks.

"I do."

Judy gets out of her chair and sits on Pete's lap. "I'm passionate about you, too. We can do what we missed out on last night."

Pete grabs her waist and moves her off his lap. "We don't have enough time," he insists. "Take a shower while I check on our dive trip." The door to the honeymoon suite, once again, closed behind him.

• • • • •

"We're off," the dive captain says as he signals the skipper to leave the dock. "We'll be diving at the tip of the 900 foot sheer vertical drop of the Cayman Trench. The Cayman Trench is 24,795 feet deep. Does anyone know the name of the deepest trench in the world?"

"It's the Mariana Trench in the Pacific," Judy says.

"That's right, ma'am. It's 35,895 feet deep." The captain holds up a sample card. "You'll see all kinds of fish on the dive. This one right here, the parrot fish, is a sequential hermaphrodite."

The man sitting next to Judy spits out a laugh. "Some of the females are gay?"

"Sequential hermaphrodites are transsexual organisms," Pete explains. "The environment rather than DNA determines their gender."

"Are you a scientist or a fisherman?" the man asks Pete as the captain adds, "With seventeen female born for every male, the process is necessary to perpetuate the species."

"Neither," Pete replies. "I've trolled the lakes in Northern Wisconsin with my church group when I was a kid, but I learned of hermaphrodites when I was in college."

"I am a deep-sea guy myself," the man says. "I'm Jeffrey. This is my wife, Carol."

"I'm Pete," he introduces himself without mentioning Judy.

"We're on our honeymoon," Judy adds.

"Congratulations," Carol replies. "When did you get married?"

"Yesterday," Judy replies proudly as she reaches over and squeezes Pete's hand.

"I design gardens," Jeffrey says.

"I thought I recognized you!" Judy exclaims. "Pete, he's the garden designer written up several times in *Lawn and Garden Magazine*."

"I could do your garden," Jeffrey says to Pete.

"We have an apartment," Judy explains.

"But we have a terrace that…" Pete pauses. "What did you say your name is?"

"Jeffrey," he replies as he gives Pete a business card. "We're going on a day-long fishing excursion tomorrow. Why don't you come along?"

The skipper turns off the boat engine. "Don't touch the reef while we're down there. It's anywhere from eighty to one hundred million years old, but the mucous membrane takes about ten years to grow one quarter of an inch. Hey you, keep your hands off her," the captain teases a middle-aged man fawning over a young woman, "We'll be able to tell if you touch her while we're diving by the red rash that will show up on her skin an hour after we surface. The good news, young lady, is that the human skin repairs itself much more quickly than the coral does."

"Why do middle-aged men make fools of themselves like that?" Pete whispers to Judy. "He doesn't respect her. She thinks love and sex are the same thing."

"Women don't confuse love and sex. Men do," Judy corrects Pete. "It's the only real difference between men and women."

"Women think about sex and men don't," Pete tells Judy.

"I don't think so," Jeffrey chimes in. "Men think about sex all the time, and women don't think about it at all."

"Maybe men are hardwired to think of sex, and women are hardwired to think about sex," Judy posits with a tone of irritation in her voice.

"It's the way it has to be," Carol agrees. "When women think about sex, they are thinking about being with a man who has good genes to pass onto their children. It's a good thing women control the selection process, because men don't have any qualms about having sex with anyone. They'll even have sex with a man."

"Not to change the subject," Pete interjects. "The deep-sea excursion you mentioned earlier sounds interesting."

"You can get tickets on the dock," Jeffrey explains.

"Let's do something on our own," Judy suggests.

"Don't you want to go?"

"I'd rather be alone with you," Judy protests. "It's our honeymoon."

There's a Man in My Bed

When Soledad leaves her cousin's wedding reception, she knows her marriage is over. She is hoping to have enough time to digest what she saw when she came home from Moscow, but the altercation with her brother-in-law has forced her to take it all in at once.

Little does she know when she arrives home Thursday afternoon the significance this altercation will have in the demise of their life together. It is the catalyst that thrusts them into a new phase of their lives, one in which fate fashions the inseparable into two separate identities. From that night on, they are pushed apart the same way identical magnetic forces reject each other, just as easily as they were drawn together when the opposing forces of the same magnet brought them together fourteen years earlier.

Yet that night holds such a small piece of the truth. It isn't until a year after their divorce, when his family has already imprisoned Kenny's altercation with Soledad into a neat little yarn, that Bob brings his friend home, providing evidence to rip their prosecution of Soledad to shreds.

Bob's family has accused Soledad of a murder she didn't commit. His silence gives them an opportunity to draw a picture of the crime from the limited pieces of the truth they have and shrouds them from the events that transpired during the forty-eight hours preceding the wedding.

· · · · ·

Soledad takes an earlier than expected flight home so she can tell Bob that she will not have to go back to Moscow. Her news series, arguing that the Russian-Chechen Peace Treaty is likely to be short-lived because of the nature of the Chechen people and their relationship with the Russian government, has been accepted by her editor. She gets out of the cab, excited to tell Bob that her editor also agrees to let her write the series from the Boston office. She opens the bedroom door to a strange man in their bed with her husband.

It isn't like the movies. She doesn't shoot them. Bob doesn't chase her out of the house without any clothes on while his lover patiently waits for him. "I'll be back in an hour. He better be gone," is all she says before closing the bedroom door and leaving the house.

Soledad stops the car in front of a long row of tombstones in the cemetery on the East side of Providence and walks a few rows in. She sits on her calves with her head on her knees and sobs in front of a tall stone cross engraved with the lettering, *Frieda and Gerald Spetzmann, beloved parents of Soledad.* Fifteen minutes later, she is back on her feet, wiping her eyes on her sleeve. "Don't worry Mommy and Daddy," she whispers before returning to the car.

Bob is sitting in the chair by the window when Soledad returns. She sits next to him with her chin pointed upward away from Bob. "This isn't the best time to talk about what I saw in there," she says calmly. "My cousin's future in-laws will be arriving at the house in a few hours. I think it is best to set our problems aside for the next forty-eight hours so we can live up to our obligations as a couple for my cousin's wedding. Do you agree?"

Bob nods.

"Okay. I'll get the guest room ready. You can change the … the sheets in our … in the …" She bolts out of the chair. "Wash the sheets," she insists before walking into the guest room.

When the soon to be in-laws of her cousin are getting ready for the rehearsal dinner on Friday night, Bob pulls Soledad aside and says, "I can't go, Sole."

"You promised," Soledad whispers.

"I know," Bob whispers back. "I can't."

"You're in the wedding."

"I'm sorry. I can't be with you right now."

"When I left a few days ago, you said you couldn't live without me," Soledad whispers sarcastically. She catches herself and says, "Forget it."

Bob tries to apologize. "I can't help it, Sole. I'm upset you saw us like that."

"I'm upset too, but I'm not going to ruin my cousin's big day," Soledad whispers angrily. "His in-laws are in the next room. You're one of the groomsmen. Please, Bob, get dressed."

"Please don't make me go," Bob replies.

"It's not fair to let him down like this."

"I promise I will be there tomorrow. I think it's better if I don't go tonight."

"What'll I tell my aunt?"

"Tell her whatever you want," Bob says.

Not wanting to make a scene, Soledad leaves him at home and armed herself with an excuse for Bob of a sudden and violent stomach ailment.

· · · · ·

When Soledad returns to their bedroom that night, Bob asks, "Did you have to tell her?"

"What did you expect," she replies in a harsh whisper. "You should have known my aunt wouldn't let it go. I got tired of her prodding during the rehearsal dinner, so I took her aside and told her that you didn't come because our marriage is in serious trouble."

"Did you tell her to call me?"

"I told her to leave it alone, but she wouldn't. She insisted on calling you to remind you that you are part of the family and belong at the wedding."

"Did you tell her everything?"

"I didn't tell her what I saw in here," Soledad whispers. "Did you change the sheets?"

"Yes, Sole. They're crisp and clean the way you like them."

Soledad jumps off the bed as soon as she lays on it. "I'll sleep on the floor."

"Why don't you take the bed?" Bob suggests. "I'll sleep on the floor."

"I can't sleep in a bed that was used for..." her voice trails off as she leaves room. She returns with the extra pillow and blankets from the linen closet.

The next day, Bob lives up to his promise of walking down the aisle with Soledad, but he disappears immediately following the ceremony before pictures he is supposed to be in are taken. He is missing in action until Soledad finds him at the club bar right before the reception.

"I've been here all afternoon," Bob volunteers.

"You're drunk," Soledad accuses.

"I'm calming my nerves," he corrects her.

"I don't care what you do after this reception, but I'm begging you one more time to cooperate. Please come to the head table," Soledad pleads.

"I'm going to sit with my family," Bob insists.

"I've tried very hard all day long to forget what I saw so it won't spoil things for my cousin. Do you really want to ruin his big day?" Soledad asks. "Come on, Bob. This is the last thing we have to do together."

She breathes a sigh of relief as he gets up from the barstool. She forces a smile on the crowd when their name is announced. Her persona shines with self assurance as they parade across the room to the head table. All the events of the previous forty-eight hours are coiled up in her persona; so tightly wrapped around her that she is unable to inject any grief on anyone, including Bob, for the sake of her cousin and his new wife.

Dinner's on You

The aroma of Mexican food fills the kitchen air as Nita stands at the stove with a wooden spoon in her hand. She took the afternoon off to prepare Jim's favorite dish, Pollo Enchiladas en Mole, from scratch. She scoops the sautéed chicken and onions out of the pan, and with the back of the wooden spoon, spreads it out over the tortillas. She arranges the rolled tortillas in a glass baking dish, pours her freshly made mole sauce over them, and places them in the oven. She checks the refried beans and adjusts the flame on the rice.

Nita snaps the white linen cloth out across the table top and smoothes out the wrinkles. The table is set with her best china, crystal stemware, silverware, and linen napkins. She plucks two roses from the vase by the window, separating the pedals from the stems and sprinkling them around the fresh flower arrangement in the center of the table.

She steps back to survey the table before fussing with the napkins and spraying the air with the perfume in her purse. *Music,* she reminds herself as she turns on the radio and pushes the scan button.

> —*was a role model for generations of woman. Katherine Hepburn's death yesterday at her home in Old Saybrook, Connecticut, is the end of the golden era in Hollywood*—

> —*It's 5:55 on a beautiful Monday afternoon*—

> —*porch that collapsed in Lincoln Park Sunday, July 29, claimed it's thirteenth victim*—

> —*and Democratic presidential hopeful, Howard Dean, astounded*—

Nita pulls the clip out of her long black hair and shakes it out across her shoulders. When she recognizes the music of Pedro Iturralde, a Spanish saxophonist, she hits the remote button to stop the scanning. With a little over an hour before Jim is expected to arrive home, she hops into the shower.

Their five-year marriage has had its ups and downs. They do most things together and quietly converse in bed after they make love. When the intensity can no longer be sustained, they spend more time apart and fall asleep in front of the TV before dragging themselves to bed. The cycle has repeated itself many times since they were married.

But this time is different. In the last year, Jim has rarely been home. His new job requires that he work second shift. Most nights he tacks on a third shift. He usually sleeps most of the day before leaving for work by mid-afternoon and arrives home at eight in the morning. He insists that the overtime and shift differential have been saved, but none of the extra money has shown up in their bank account.

Nita is certain he is having an affair. Whenever she confronts him with her suspicions, he assures her that he is not seeing another woman. He follows this up with a tirade about not understanding what he is doing for her. He is working hard, he claims, so she will have all the things that she wants. She's the one looking for a bigger house. She wants him to pay for her college education. These things cost money. The fight always ends with Nita leaving the room in tears.

Nita knows her marriage is in serious trouble, but she keeps the faith in spite of what she sees because he always apologizes, reassuring her over and over that he still loves her. Last week was different. When Jim tried to make love to her after a fight and couldn't, he cried in her arms, apologizing profusely for his inability to perform, for his recent tantrums, and chalked it all up to working too many hours for her.

Nita steps out of the shower and dries herself off. She ties the straps of a black backless sundress around her neck and slips on her delicately laced black sandals with four-inch heels. She brushes her hair to a black sheen across her shoulders. She lightly colors her face before touching up her eyelashes and moistening her lips with gloss. She sprays herself with Jim's favorite perfume.

Nita looks at her watch. He should be home in a few minutes. She grabs her hand to stop it from shaking. *I wish I were as brave as Katherine Hepburn.* She takes one last look at herself in the mirror before returning to the kitchen.

She turns the heat down on the stove and sits in the chair by the window. Her heart quickens its pace every time she hears a car approaching. Thirty minutes later, she takes off her shoes. Jim still isn't home. Another thirty minutes pass as she shifts from pacing the floor to looking through the window. The silence is finally broken by the sound of the garage door opening. Nita primps in front of the mirror and rushes into the kitchen to continue the meal preparation.

Jim walks into the house as the grandfather clock chimes eight times. "Hi, honey," she says as she leans over to kiss him.

He tips his lips toward her just enough for them to lightly brush against hers. He doesn't say anything about the aroma of his favorite dish or the fabulous way she looks, and she is too nervous to notice. "I'm going to change my clothes," he announces before disappearing down the hallway.

Nita lights the candle on the dining room table and transfers their dinner from the pans in the kitchen to the serving dishes on the dining room table. "Dinner's ready, Jim."

"I'll be there in a minute," she hears his voice travel up the bedroom hallway.

She sits at the table, waiting a few more minutes before calling out, "Dinner's getting cold, Jim."

"Sorry, I was getting dressed," Jim responds as he makes his appearance at the dining room table. He looks at Nita's hard work sitting in front of him on the dining room table. "This is very thoughtful of you, Nita."

"I know how much you like my Pollo Enchiladas en Mole. It's not as warm as I was hoping it would be." She starts to rise from the chair.

Jim holds his hand up and says, "No, no, that won't be necessary. I'm sure it'll be great the way it is."

Nita picks up his plate as he settles back into the chair and fills it for him.

"Thank you for the wonderful meal," he starts again. "And you look really nice, Nita." He clears his throat. "I'm sorry if I gave you the wrong impression about my coming home tonight." He sets a document in front of her.

The heading, Dissolution of Marriage, pops off the page. Nita is silent until two words, mental cruelty, stick like glue in her eyes. She looks up from the page and asks, "What's with the mental cruelty?"

"I can't get a divorce without your consent."

"You want *me* to take the blame!"

"You said you didn't want a divorce, and I do. This is the only way to get it."

"So you're going to lie about the kind of wife I've been to you."

"It doesn't really mean anything," Jim declares. "It's only a formality, a requirement of the law, not a reflection of anything you've done to me. There is no other way."

"Yes there is. You could take the mental cruelty rap."

"It won't work if I'm the one filing for divorce."

"I could file."

"But you don't want a divorce."

"I've been a good wife. I take care of our son, cook meals like this for you, and clean up after you. What else—"

"I didn't ask you do to this," Jim interrupts.

She shakes her head wildly. "You repay me with a mental cruelty charge."

"It's not as bad as it sounds."

"Like hell it isn't!" she screams.

"I can't satisfy you anymore."

"Then you take the rap. I'm not the one having an affair."

"I'm not seeing another woman," Jim insists.

"Well then, what are you doing?" The fire in Nita's eyes burns through him. "I know exactly what you're doing during your so-called third shift job. I've danced around this for months—your mood swings, the heavy drinking, and everything else—because I love you."

"I love you, too."

Nita waves the document in the air. "Then why are you doing this?"

"I can't live with you anymore."

"What does that mean?"

"It's too late."

"I'm tired of your double talk!" she screams. "I've tried to make you happy, but nothing I do works anymore. Now you're blaming me for your affair by suing me for mental cruelty."

"I'm not seeing another woman."

"Stop lying!" she shouts. "You call me up at work to tell me you're coming home. I take the afternoon off without pay to make—"

"I didn't ask you to do this."

"I rush around, preparing your favorite dinner, and you come home an hour late with divorce papers that accuse me of mental cruelty!" she screams.

"Listen to the way you are carrying on, Nita. It's no wonder I opted for mental cruelty."

Jim's words simultaneously shock her and egg her on. "Okay, Jim. You win. Do you want to see what mental cruelty looks like?" Nita picks up his plate of Pollo Enchilada en Mole and dumps it over his head. She scoops a heaping spoonful of refried beans out of the serving dish and mashes them on his head. "Your mentally cruel wife isn't finished yet!" Nita yells as she throws the entire dish of rice at him. She washes her labor from his face with a blender full of Margaritas.

Nita sets the empty blender on the table and watches him wipe the liquid from his eyes. "Here you go," she bellows, tossing the white linen napkin she has wiped her mouth on at him. "You can clean up this mess for a change," she mutters. She leaves him with the banging of the door as he sits at the dining room table, wiping her carefully prepared dinner from his thick black hair.

The Closet

Judy turns away in disbelief from the man who has been sleeping with her husband. She doesn't know the man Jeffrey is eulogizing as her husband of twenty years. She wants to remember Pete the way he was when he was with her. When they met, he was a really cool saxophone player who bailed her out after she lost her money to an arcade game vendor on a band trip to the Wisconsin State Fair. Today, October 9, 2004, he is a deceased man who gave her two wonderful children. Everything else in between has been a long, jostling carnival ride.

As Judy sits between her children at Pete's funeral, she is faced with a reality Pete chose not to share with her. She thought the only lie he told was the same lie she told to build a façade of married life around his closet. Now she finds out his lies extended to secrets he kept from her and exposed to the world through a reality she didn't know. He was not discreet. He was parading his life with Jeffrey around to his gay friends in public.

Jeffrey tells family and friends sitting in the pews of *St. Mary's Catholic Church* that he met Pete at the first student-organized Vietnam War demonstration in Madison, Wisconsin. Pete told her that he didn't want to go with her on May 2, 1964, the day of her parents' twenty-fifth wedding anniversary party because he didn't like large crowds. She shrinks down in the pew, hoping that her friends, colleagues, and fellow researchers don't figure out that he met Jeffrey before they were married. It was the day that the Ku Klux Klansmen abducted the two black teenagers whose bodies were discovered two months later as authorities searched for three missing civil rights workers in the case known as *Mississippi Burning*.

Judy swallows hard to digest the reality that Pete was involved with Jeffrey while they were engaged. She recalls the introductions on the dive boat trip in Grand Cayman where Pete led her to believe Jeffrey was a stranger. She remembers the tautness of the sheets on Pete's side of the bed the morning after he disappeared from their honeymoon suite. She knows now that Pete spent their wedding night with Jeffrey.

As Judy grasps the reality of Jeffrey's description of Pete's activism, she is proud that he was involved in the anti-war movement. She remembers that he and Jeffrey went to Washington two years ago before the start of the Iraqi War to make a case against it to Congress. She didn't know that they were also involved in a Vietnam War protest with activist groups who surrounded the White House and marched to the Washington Monument in November, 1965, four months after her wedding night. She brings Kim and Jerry's hand in her lap as Jeffrey describes their presence at a Chicago march led by Martin Luther King. She squeezes their hands tightly, hoping he wouldn't mention the date of the march—March 25, 1967, because she was still in the hospital the day after the twins were born.

She is angry that Pete lied to her about his participation in anti-war demonstrations; the ones he encouraged her not to attend because they were dangerous. He told her when they started dating that he didn't want to think about, discuss, or go to any event associated with Vietnam because of his injury during his tour of duty. Even today, at his funeral, Judy doesn't know the nature of his injury or how it occurred. The scar tissue on his upper back is an indication that the injury was serious. The date it occurred suggests it had something to do with U.S. secret operations in Laos prior to the U.S. troop buildup in Vietnam.

Judy didn't mind avoiding Vietnam protests because there were too many other issues surfacing at the time that needed attention. Political activism was rapidly building in the early 1960s, and she wanted to be in the middle of it. The women's movement had been reawakened by the publication of Betty Friedan's *Feminine Mystique,* and Dr. King's March for Jobs and Freedom ending with his *I Have a Dream* speech on the steps of the Lincoln Memorial was enough to know where to put her energy during her graduate work at the University of Chicago.

Judy and Pete started dating in January of 1963, after they ran into each other in the lobby at the Edgewater Beach Hotel in Chicago where Martin Luther King had delivered *A Challenge to Justice and Love* at the National Conference on Race and Religion, commemorating the 100th anniversary of the Emancipation Proclamation. She remembers the call to action of the humble opening speaker, Albert Gregory Cardinal Meyer, Archbishop of Chicago, who inspired Judy to focus her dissertation research on racial inequality.

Judy smiles as Jeffrey describes the elaborate meals Pete used to make. She remembers the well-organized, fully stocked kitchen in his apartment where he prepared meals for her every Tuesday and Friday while they were dating. After they married, he insisted on making a nutritious dinner for her every night while she poured over her dissertation research. He also insisted that they go out to jazz and blues clubs every Saturday night where they discussed news, movies, music, theater—everything but her dissertation topic.

Pete opened his medical practice when the twins were two years old. It was a good time because Judy had just accepted a tenure track appointment at Northwestern University. Even though they immersed themselves in their careers while Judy's mother took care of the twins, they spent plenty of time with their children.

More than anything else, Pete has been a good father. Because of his father's distance and his mother's self-absorption, he wanted predictability for and engagement with his children. Judy remembers the schedule Pete developed to balance their roles as professionals and parents. Every Sunday, they had dinner at noon and spent the afternoon together. They took Kim and Jerry to places like Riverview or Santa's Village in the summer. In the winter, they toured the Breweries in Milwaukee, the Merchandise Mart in Chicago, and even the dirty steel mills in Gary, Indiana. He wanted his children to see the real world, not just the side of life exposed to tourists. He opted out of the golf course on Wednesday afternoons in order to have time alone with the twins. Thursday night was the only night he worked because it was Judy's exclusive time with Kim and Jerry.

She knew exactly what to expect from Pete until the confusion that hung in the air with the Carol's words at the airport, *Get used to it, honey*, invaded their life. She remembers the relief that washed through her as she and Pete left Jeffrey and Carol in Grand Cayman and headed for Jamaica for three days. After they made love for the first time, Judy lay awake in the dark, listening to Pete's heavy breathing and wondering if this was all there is to sex. There wasn't any foreplay or intimate conversation afterward, only a messy act that took a matter of seconds. The only thing it did for her was make her more cognizant of the distance that lay between with them on the nights Pete turned to her.

As Kim and Jerry leave the pew to carry the gifts to the altar, Judy thanks God that she hung in there for the first two years. Pete was as distant to her as he was close to their children. Things got better for her after they were born. Pete rarely asked and Judy didn't offer. It worked out better that way. Without the impending doom of the sexual act ahead of them, they began to enjoy their time in bed as conversation about Kim and Jerry replaced sex as their intimate nighttime activity.

As Judy turns around to watch the twins carry the gifts to the altar, she notices a young man sitting in the pew a few rows back. She blinks her eyes several times as she recognizes him as Nita's husband. She recalls the eulogy. Pete knew him. He was on the other end of the gay hotline at the clinic when this young man called in. She found out about his work at the health clinic when she went there with him in May after Carol called with the news. She finds out today that he had been providing volunteer medical services for the treatment of sexually transmitted diseases to the gay and lesbian community since 1974. *Where do the lies end and the truth begin?*

Judy follows the long pole that carries the bill she tossed into the offering basket back to the usher standing in the aisle. The smell of cigar smoke on his suit reminds her of the smell lingering on Pete's shirt the year his mother died. She closes her eyes and tries to shake away the nightmare of 1971, the year Pete's confusion intensified. She wants to forget the many nights she came home from work after picking the twins up from her mother's house to the same nightmare at home.

· · · · ·

Burning tomato sauce is caked on the stove. A partially sliced loaf of Italian bread is lying on the cutting board with the knife wedged halfway into the loaf. A dish of pine nuts, a bottle of olive oil, and a few cloves of garlic are sitting next to the blender. Dried basil leaves are strewn across the counter. The cooked Italian sausage in the frying pan is soaking in grease, the water for the pasta has boiled away, and Pete is nowhere to be seen.

Judy turns the burners off as the twins rush into the den looking for Daddy. "We're home, Pete," she announces as she walks through each room of their home. When she reaches the bedroom, the door is locked.

"Don't come in here," Pete shouts a warning from the other side of the door.

"What's wrong?" she asks.

He responds with gibberish.

"Come on, Pete. Open the door," Judy demands while pounding on the door.

"Mommy," Kim runs down the hallway with tears in her eyes.

"It's all right honey," Judy reassures her four-year-old daughter as she picks her up and strokes her hair. "Where's Jerry?"

Kim points toward the den as a television show echoes down the hallway. "Are you and Daddy playing hide and seek?" she asks.

Judy feigns a smile and nods at her daughter. "That's right, honey."

Kim smiles back. "Can I play, too?"

"Not today, honey. This game is for mommies and daddies," Judy says as she carries Kim back to the den and sets her on her feet. She turns the television volume down and switches to channel eleven. "Why don't you watch Sesame Street with your brother?"

"Okay, Mommy," Kim says as she sits next to Jerry.

Judy stands at the door of the den until the Kim settles in on the couch next to her brother. She walks down the hall to get a screwdriver from the utility closet. When she opens the bedroom door, she finds Pete sitting in the corner with his head in his lap.

"Pete," she says as she rushes over to him.

"Get out of here," Pete yells as his arms flail at her. "I didn't mean it." His voice softens with the repetitive nature of the mantra. When Judy sits on the floor next to him, he falls into her arms and sobs deeply as she comforts him. He looks in Judy's eyes and says, "It was dark. I didn't see it coming," before returning his tearful eyes to her shoulder.

"What didn't you see coming? Tell me what has happened, Pete."

Then as suddenly as he started crying, he stops. "What do you mean, what happened?" he asks Judy calmly.

"You said you didn't see it coming. Was someone here?"

He gets up off the floor and brushes himself off. "Don't be silly."

Judy can smell cigar smoke on his shirt. "Who was here?"

"No one," Pete whimpers.

"Why are you so upset?"

"Because I ruined our dinner," Pete cries.

Judy comforts him. "You're tired. You've had a really long day. I think you should rest a bit while I finish preparing the dinner you made for us." She waits until he is lying on the bed before she says, "I'll leave the door open and call you when dinner is ready."

When she returns to the bedroom, she finds Pete sound asleep. Judy closes the door and feeds the twins. They are in the den when he comes down the hallway. He sits on the couch and watches Judy play "Chutes and Ladders" with Kim and Jerry.

The nightmare returns after the twins are safely tucked in bed and sound asleep. Pete comes in the bathroom as Judy is getting ready for bed and hands her a bottle of perfume. "I bought this for you today," he announces.

"Thank you," Judy says with a smile.

"Will you wear it tonight?"

"Sure." She pulls the cap off and sprays it around her head.

"My mother used to put it on her neck," Pete explains as he moves the hand holding the bottle to her neck.

She takes a step back and asks, "Is this the perfume your mother used to wear?"

Pete nods.

"If this is your idea of a joke, forget it." She sets the bottle on the counter and walks out of the bathroom.

He follows her in the bedroom with the perfume bottle. "Please, Judy. Do it for me," he pleads.

"I'm not wearing your mother's perfume," she whispers sharply.

"Come on, Judy."

"Don't ask me again," Judy warns.

"Don't leave me," his voice rasps deeply as he throws his arms around her and sobs.

Judy doesn't know what to do to console him so she takes his hand and leads him to the bed. When he crawls in between the sheet, she covers him up with an afghan that belonged to his mother and returns to the bathroom to finish getting ready for bed. After checking on the twins, she gets in bed with him and falls asleep to the rhythm of his snoring.

• • • • •

Judy gets a whiff of the cigar smoke on the man bringing the offering basket to the altar. She recalls that some variation of the nightmare lingered for more than a year. Sometimes he woke up in the middle of the night to have sex with her. As soon as he penetrated, he would leap out of bed in a tirade. "I can't make you happy," he'd shout at himself. If Judy suggested that he touch her in certain ways, he barked at her, "Don't you like what I do?"

Judy turns her eyes away from the cigar smoking man as he walks back down the aisle past Pete's coffin. She remembers living in a constant state of panic that year. She didn't know what would set him off or how long the craziness would last. She was afraid to confront him with her suspicion that the episodes were related to his war injury, for fear that he would spiral out of control. She keeps her sanity by writing her first book about the Civil Rights movement during those crazy nights.

Judy remembers how relieved she was when Jeffrey and Carol moved to Chicago. Within a week after they returned, Pete's crazy episodes ceased. She didn't object when Pete wanted to go out with Jeffrey and Carol on Friday nights, even though she didn't like either of them very much. She was so grateful for the calm. After a few months, she found all kinds of excuses to stay home with the twins or work on her research so she wouldn't have to see them.

When Pete and Jeffrey got season tickets to the Bulls games, she and Carol were off the hook. Their time together at professional sports events extended into the summer and fall with the purchase of Cubs and Bears season tickets. Judy was relieved. Pete's craziness had disappeared along with his sexual interest in her, and her life returned to normal.

Tears well up in her eyes as she realizes the best part of Pete was never with her. He has always belonged to Jeffrey. The only part of him that belonged to her was his confusion. She accepted it because she was his wife. She made it through the psychic battle that followed her divorce because of her decision to be his wife despite his sexual orientation. She has been his faithful friend to the end because she cares for him. People think she is crazy, but she has no choice. How can she spend all these years by his side, going through all they did, without holding him close in her heart? But what did she gain by giving her life to a man who didn't want her?

Spinning through her life the way she has also reminds her of how much of herself she has lost. She can't get back any of these years. She can't erase the imprint he put on her heart. The lump in her throat is still coated with all the venom she has had to swallow. The alluring warmth of the façade they built around his closet still shrouds her shattered image. Even now, the thorns and thistles of his wilderness stick her with another secret she can't forget.

When she lays her arms on the back of the pew and around Kim and Jerry, she can feel Paul's concern gently squeezing her arms. She doesn't turn around to the pew behind her. She doesn't want him to see her tears. She is grateful that they have found each other again after a fifteen year absence. She wishes she could brush off the burrs of her saga with Pete and abandon all her slaughtered living to a heart that's ready to give her something back. Fortunately, Paul's heart has enough love in it to stay with her despite her circumstances.

When Judy tries to capture an image of what her life would have been like without Pete, she is surprised that Paul isn't in the picture. All she sees is her children sitting on both sides of her. Pete was proud of their children. He sat next to Judy at every one of Kim's piano concerts. They cheered Jerry through his little league games. They were together when Jerry received his medical degree and Kim graduated from Harvard Law School. Kim stood between Pete and Judy as she walked down the aisle. Two years later, they paced the floor of the hospital together waiting for their first grandchild to be born.

How can I wish for a different life, even after all that Pete has taken from me? He is the reason for these two precious gifts sitting here with me at his funeral. Judy smiles through her tears, knowing how much of Pete will be carried into her future as both a celebration of and a shroud over their married life together.

Coming Out

2009

I'm Listening

"What did you say?"

"I said I ran into Jeffrey yesterday, and he told me everything," Jerry tells his mother.

Judy steps into the hallway outside of her suite at the Drake Hotel and closes the door.

"Is Paul in there?" Kim asks.

"Yes, he is."

"Does he know?"

"Why don't you go downstairs and get something to eat? We'll talk after that."

"Don't shut us out, Mom," Kim pleads as she reaches out and gives Judy a hug.

"I'm not shutting you out, honey." She looks over Kim's shoulder at her son. "I wasn't prepared for this. That's all." She steps back from Kim and forces a smile on her children. "Why don't you go downstairs and get us something to eat. I need to talk to Paul—"

"I'm not hungry," Kim protests.

"This is ridiculous!" Jerry exclaims.

"—in private," Judy insists as she glares at her children. "I'll tell you what. Let's talk over dinner in my suite at"—she looks at her watch—"five thirty."

"Five thirty," Kim repeats.

"Yes, it'll be five thirty before you know it. By the time the restaurant prepares our dinner and ..." Judy searches for something that will keep them busy for an hour. "Why don't you get a bottle of wine at the liquor store around the corner on Oak Street?"

When they don't move, she says, "Go on. You don't want to get caught in the Saturday night rush."

"What would you like to eat?" Jerry asks.

"You pick." She opens the door to her suite. "I'll be right here when you get back."

As Judy leans her head on the door she closes on her children, Paul asks, "What was that all about?"

"They know."

Paul takes Judy's hand and leads her to the chair in the living room suite. "Sit down. I'll make you some tea."

"I should have left their father when they were babies," Judy scolds herself as Paul sets a cup of hot tea on the end table next to her.

"You don't have much sympathy for how you have dealt with some very difficult circumstances," Paul points out.

"There's no room for sympathy when you have to hold your family together."

Paul sits on the arm of the chair where Judy is sitting.

"And my children," Judy adds.

"You won't do them any good if you don't take care of your needs," Paul warns. He takes the saucer off the top of the cup and hands the hot tea to her.

Judy takes a sip and replies, "I'm too busy to need anything."

"What you mean is everyone crowds out your needs."

"What I mean is I'm too tired to know what I need."

Paul slides the chair at the desk toward Judy and sits in front of her. "Tired of what?" he asks.

"I'm too tired to talk."

"It can't hurt to talk," Paul replies.

"I tell my children that all the time," Judy chuckles. "And they say, 'What good will it do?' Well, they're right. Talking won't bring back all I lost in my sham of a marriage." Judy shakes her head in disgust. "I'm tired of taking care of whatever needs to be done to get through the next crisis."

"There are a lot of people who are willing to help you if you let them."

"Name one."

"Me."

"You can't give me what I need."

"No, I can't," Paul says with his eyes in his lap, "but Kim and Jerry—"

"I can take care of my kids," Judy snaps.

"You make it very hard for others to help you, Jude." Paul takes her hands and adds, "Sooner or later, you're going to have to let someone give back to you."

"I've been doing everything on my own for so long that I don't know any other way," Judy mutters.

"You'll learn."

Judy shakes her head back and forth. "I don't want to be a burden."

"You, a burden?" Paul exclaims.

"That's what you say now."

"No one is a burden to anyone who loves them, Jude."

"Are you handling me, Paul?"

"Only if you don't tell me what you need," Paul warns.

"I don't know what I need," Judy declares, "but I can tell you what I don't need. I don't need the absurdity of loving someone who is so confused about who they are that they don't have anything to give back to me."

"I'm glad to hear that, Jude." Paul smiles at Judy. "Let me ask the question differently. Can you tell me what makes you happy?"

"Being with my kids," she replies instinctively before adding, "And you."

"What about you?"

"I don't know, except that I want to live the rest of my life without any more lies."

"Great idea, my love," Paul pats her knee. "You can start with your kids."

• • • • •

"Why don't we have our dinner on the patio," Judy suggests.

"We got you a filet, Mom. Medium rare," Kim explains as she takes their dinner out of the bag.

"The way you like it," Jerry adds.

"With garlic mashed potatoes and creamed spinach—"

"—a bottle of wine and this," Jerry pulls small bottle of Kalhúa out of the bag and presents it to his mother.

Judy looks in the empty bag. "Where's the Cherry Garcia ice cream?"

"Kim convinced the front desk to put it in the freezer."

"The bellboy will bring it up later," Kim explains.

"I hope they don't give it to someone else." Judy wraps her arm around Jerry's neck and pulls his head toward her chest. Then she smiles at Kim and says, "I'm lucky to have both of you. Come on. Let's eat." She picks up her plate and wine glass and goes out to the patio.

"You look like a gloomy Gus," Judy ruffles her son's hair as they sit down.

Jerry turns his eyes to the table. "I'm so sorry, Mom."

"For what?"

"I didn't try to understand what it was like for you. I only saw Dad's lifestyle as my problem."

Judy pats his hand. "Eat your dinner before it gets cold."

"No!" Jerry exclaims. "Not until I say what I want to say to you."

Kim's eyes shoot a warning at him.

Judy sets down her fork. "Okay, honey. I'm listening."

Jerry takes a long drink from his water glass before he starts. "Kim reminded me this morning how much honor you brought to families like ours by helping them understand the experience of living in and coming out of a loved one's closet. And what did I do? I gave you all kinds of hell."

"It's not your fault, honey," Judy tells her son. "It's mine. I violated your trust by living the façade of a hetero—"

"Jerry is direct," Kim interjects, not wanting her mother to blame herself. "I avoid what I can't accept. Do you remember when I refused to talk about dad's life style? You persisted for months—"

"My campaign to break you of your silence," Judy recalls.

"—before I mustered up the courage to say fathers who struggle with their masculinity cannot affirm femininity anymore than they can affirm masculinity," Kim recalls.

Jerry recites. "And Mom said, now we're getting somewhere."

"My beliefs have changed since then because of Mom," Kim reminds her brother.

"Why did it take me so long to accept Dad's lifestyle?"

"No one moves at the same pace. Some accept it in weeks while others take—"

"Years," Jerry says.

"I think it runs in the family, honey," Judy replies. "Your father took years to accept it, years to tell me, and even more years to tell you. I don't have an excuse. I know silence doesn't honor, and yet I didn't tell you anything."

"You have nothing to regret, Mom," Jerry says. "You held the family together as we stumbled through each new problem and came to respect Dad's relationship with Jeffrey."

"Don't get sappy on me," Judy teases her son. "Eat. Your dinner is getting cold."

"I'm almost done, Mom." Jerry lifts his wine glass and says, "To the best mom in the world."

And Kim says, "I second that, Mom."

Breaking News

"I'm glad you called, Jude. I'll see you at ten," Soledad says before hanging up the phone. Her head is spinning with speculation. *What did she tell Paul? What are they doing at seven thirty on a Monday morning driving back from Chicago to Evanston? Why are her kids with them? Oh, why didn't she just tell me over the phone?*

She takes her e-ticket from the printer and reviews her schedule. The cab will pick her up at one for her 2:40 p.m. flight. She'll be in Providence by six. *It's silly to worry about Judy. People don't convey good news over the phone, but bad news... The phone call I received Thursday night was really bad news.*

· · · · ·

She is on her way out the door, terribly late for Judy's book warming party, when she hears the voice of her ex-brother-in-law, Kenny, on the other end of the line. He clears his throat and gets right to the point. "Dad died yesterday."

"Oh," is the only word Soledad can utter. She plops into the chair next to the door and asks, "What happened?"

"The doctor has been treating him for a bad cold, but persistent headaches brought him to the hospital yesterday. He lost consciousness about an hour after he checked in. It was pneumococcal meningitis. Brain tissue swelling cut off the oxygen supply."

"That's awful." Soledad reaches over to turn the light back on.

"We had to sign papers, you know, to take him off of life support. We were all there when he passed."

"That's awful," she repeats, focusing her attention on the pendulum of the clock on the mantle swaying back and forth in a steady, rhythmic movement.

The uncomfortable silence pushes the words from the back of Kenny's throat to his lips. "I know we haven't seen each other in..."

"Twelve years," Soledad murmurs.

"Robert, I mean Bob, wants you to know ... He wants you come to the funeral. We all want you to come. Dad would've wanted it," Kenny rambles on.

Soledad closes her eyes and murmurs, "Of course, I'll be there."

"The wake is Monday night from five-to-nine at Peterson's Funeral Home in Providence. The funeral is at 10 a.m. on Tuesday at the church. The name escapes me. It's the one where you and Bob were married." Soledad hears Kenny cough. "Sorry. You can stay with Susan and me."

"I have friends," Soledad snaps a lie at him. "I mean, thank you Kenny, but I'll stay with my friends."

They fall into an awkward silence. Kenny says the first thing that comes to mind, a polite question one would ask any old acquaintance one hasn't seen in a longtime. "So how have you been, Soledad?"

"I'm fine." Soledad fires back more polite chitchat. "How's Barb?"

"She's fine. Her girls are twelve and fourteen. The youngest was born right after you and Robert, I mean Bob, divorced." Kenny clears his throat and returns to the safety of polite questions. "Are you still working at the *Sun Times?*"

"I am with *The Tribune,*" she corrects. "Are you still at RISD?"

"Not anymore. An art studio in Boston picked up my work about ten years ago. Bob moved there with, um ..."

"I don't know how long I'll be able to stay in Providence," Soledad announces. Impatient with her own reluctance to hang up, she says, "I'm late for an appointment. I'm glad you called, Kenny. I wish it could have been under better circumstances."

"Soledad?"

She puts the phone back on her ear. "Yes."

"He won't be at the funeral alone."

"I know. I'll see you Monday. Goodbye." She pushes the off button before Kenny can say anything else.

"Bob," Soledad whispers. She grins and sneers, loving and loathing the sound of his name. Her heart is wildly pumping as a familiar knife slashes its way through the glacial crevasse that has severed her marriage to Bob from the rest of her life. She holds her breath, hoping to stop her heart from pumping blood across the twelve-year-old divide.

She leaps out of the chair and stands in front of the balcony doors overlooking her garden. Heavy snowflakes glisten in the night air. She watches them fall into a soft, white blanket settling in between the blades of grass still poking through the early winter cover. She turns to the closet where their shared life has been lying under cover for twelve years. Her fist clutches the handle of the closet door that opens to three rows of boxes neatly stacked across the floor. She steps back and sits on the bed as her mind spins its way through the contents of the boxes and comes to rest on the last photo album, the last year of their marriage when she began the impossible task of forgetting.

The chime of the mantle clock strikes seven. She returns with her phone to the foyer and slides her coat on as she waits for the voice mail greeting to end. "I'm running late, Jude. Keep the wine chilled."

She shivers when she opens the door, inviting the late autumn air to enter her lungs. The blast of cold air is like a vacuum sucking the memory back across the crevasse and into the grave she maintains in her heart, away from all those who wish it dead, so she can forget all over again, even if only for a little while longer.

Wake Up Guys

"How's Soledad?"

Jay groans. "I haven't heard from her in two weeks."

Paul looks puzzled as he asks, "What happened?"

"Who knows?" Jay shrugs. "Just when I thought things were going well, poof, she's gone." He looks out the café window. "It's too cold to be November," he murmurs. He turns back to Paul and says, "She really gets under my skin, but I'm too ticked off to care. She won't take my calls or answer the door. I don't know if she is sick, injured, out of town, mad at me, or just plain doesn't want to see me anymore," Jay explains. "To top it off, she left a message on Friday that she is out of town and wants to talk when she gets back."

Jay and Paul exchange greetings with Larry and Steve as they join them for coffee.

"Would you like me to find out if she's okay?" Paul asks.

"Yes. No. Yes. Listen to me. I'm just as bad as she is." He stuffs his arms in his coat sleeves and rapidly pulls the belt tightly around his waist. "I'm sorry, Paul. I forgot to ask you about your weekend at the Drake?"

"I'll tell you later, unless you're in court."

"Never on Monday," Jay replies before walking out of the café into a blast of cold air.

"She's a tough one to read," Steve comments.

"I didn't know you knew Soledad," Paul says.

"She used to have coffee with us," Steve explains. "She'd tell really cool stories about her world travels, but we weren't really sure how much truth there was in them."

"It didn't matter to me whether or not her stories were true. She spawned life into our morning conversations until," Larry pines, "she disappeared."

"Because I asked her out," Steve explains. "It didn't go anywhere. When I suggested we get together, she'd say, 'that would be nice.' When it came to setting a date, she always had some excuse. I stopped by her place just like Jay did. She didn't answer the bell for me either. I finally mailed her a note that said, 'I hope this card has a better chance of reaching you than I did.'"

"Clever," Larry comments.

"I thought so too," Steve gloats. "It worked. She called. We talked about getting together, but it never happened. I finally gave up on her."

"She still comes in from time to time," Larry explains, "but it always ends the same way. She disappears."

"Just when we think she's gone for good," Steve adds, "she walks into the café."

"Soledad means well," Larry insists, "even with her comings and goings."

"I don't believe it." Steve slaps his forehead. "She got to you too."

"We went out a few times."

"Are you nuts?" Steve exclaims.

Larry turns to Paul. "She told me she didn't want to date an almost divorced man, so we became friends. We'd talk for hours about my divorce, right there at her favorite table by the window …" Larry's voice drifts off in memory.

"Only because you had the hots for her," Steve reminds him.

"Yeah, Steve," Larry agrees, "I was in love with Soledad. I probably still would be, if she'd have me."

"She'll never have anybody in her life," Steve predicts, "because she cares more about things than people."

"Why would you say that?" Paul asks.

"She had a party at her condo a few years back," Steve explains, "and someone knocked a glass gondola off the fireplace mantle. She made such a big deal about it that the person who broke it sent her a check. Soledad felt so bad about getting the check that she sent it back with an explanation that the glass gondola was irreplaceable, as if that was supposed to make the person who broke it feel better. She cares more about things than people."

"She's tricky, but she cares," Larry defends Soledad. "She had some orphans over on Christmas Eve last year. She made a turkey dinner and had presents for them under her tree."

"You can't believe everything she says," Steve cautions.

"She's not the one who told me," Larry snaps at Steve. "I found out from a friend at the shelter that Soledad took fourteen kids to her condo. The shelter wanted to limit the number to ten, but Soledad wouldn't hear of it. She didn't want anyone to be left out. So Steve, I think you owe Soledad an apology."

"Judy told me Soledad's parents died when she was eight," Paul jumps in.

"In a car accident," Larry adds. "I think she was raised by her aunt."

"Maybe that's why she has so much trouble with relationships," Paul comments.

"She told me she's never been in love," Steve says.

"There must have been someone," Larry speculates, "because of the way she set me straight when I was so hard on my ex. It's impossible for someone who knows as much as she does about relationships to never have been in love."

"I wonder who broke her heart," Paul ponders.

"She doesn't have a heart to be broken," Steve retorts.

Stick It in Your Ear

"Rick saw Nita go into Douglas' office," Laura tells Betty. "The door was closed for a long time. When they came out, it looked as if Nita had been crying."

"Maybe Douglas dumped her," Betty speculates.

"I don't think so. He gave her a hug in the parking lot."

Betty mockingly bats her eyelashes at Laura. "She has no shame."

"He followed her car down the campus lane, and they both turned right at the light." Laura leans toward Betty and whispers, "If he was on his way home, he would have turned left."

"She's doing Douglas," Betty asserts.

"She did the same thing to Eric Higgins when she took his class," Laura continues. "You know him, the Chair of Computer Science."

"Would you do it with the chair? Would you do him anywhere?" Betty mocks.

"I heard they're getting a divorce," Laura whispers as she eyes the table of women sitting behind Betty.

"She's doing Douglas and Eric doesn't like it." Betty sneers, pulling her sweater tightly around her torso and thrusting her size D breasts toward Laura. "She wears her sweaters so tight that her nipples show through. Her skirts are so far up her thighs that her ass hangs out." She jiggles her behind on the chair and spits out a laugh. "I wonder how many professors have grabbed it?"

"Do you remember that day she strutted past the Ph.D. office?" Laura reminds Betty. "One of the Ph.D. students leaned so far out of his chair that he took it to the floor with him. She just stood there, smiling at him, you know, as if she knows she's hot."

Betty blows a laugh through her nose. "She's a communication major with an emphasis on body language. I'll bet she did the whole bunch of them right there in the Ph.D. office."

"She's at a conference with Douglas right now. She even wrote a chapter with him in Judy's book. It's about," Laura looks around the cafeteria before whispering, "sexual promiscuity."

"A topic she knows intimately. I wonder how many professors she has wrapped her legs around." Betty throws her head back in a laugh and finds Ana standing behind them.

"We weren't talking about your daughter," Laura sputters.

"Look at you, sitting here so innocent when we all know you're nothing but a coward," Ana accuses Laura. "You don't even have the guts to admit you said what all of us at that table heard you say," she nods to the table where a group of secretaries is sitting.

Betty tries to get up from the table, but Ana blocks her way. "You're not leaving until you hear what I have to say."

"I don't have to listen to you."

"Oh yes you do, miss smarty pants."

"No—"

"I'm telling you to sit down and shut up," Ana insists. "You better sit down too," she says to Laura.

After they both sit down, Ana says, "I'm only going to say this once. I don't give a damn what you think of my daughter, because you'll never have even an ounce of the character she has. I don't care how shocked, offended, or appalled you are by what you seem to think you know about her. But I am warning you right here, right now, in front of all these witnesses, that if I ever hear you talk about Nita or anyone else in the way you have today, in my presence or in the presence of anyone else, I swear I will report you to the affirmative action office and do whatever I need to do to make sure you no longer have a position here. Is that clear?"

Laura nods.

Ana glares at Betty and asks, "What about you?"

Betty fidgets in her chair as Ana hovers over the table, waiting for her to respond. "I'm not leaving until we're clear," Ana insists. She looks at her watch and adds, "I have more time than you."

When Betty finally nods, Ana says, "I'm glad we understand each other. Now if you'll excuse me, I have some work to do."

We're in It Too

"What have we done to our daughter?"

"All I know, Ana, is what you told me. She went to her advisor—your boss—for advice on what to do with her personal life."

"It's our fault she didn't come to us."

"We're not ruining her life. She is!" Carlos yells. He flips on the TV. "There's something wrong with our daughter."

Ana turns it off. "There isn't anything wrong with wanting to divorce a man who doesn't care about her."

Carlos clenches his fist together. "I'm not defending him, Ana. There are thousands of men who would have been better for her. That's the problem. She's making foolish choices about her life."

"You're damn right she is. Can't you see that she married a man twice her age a year after her divorce because she needed someone to help her through Jim's coming out? And what did we do? We ignored her. If we had been paying attention, we could have stopped her."

"Where did you get that idea?"

"From Judy," Ana replies while following Carlos into the kitchen.

"Well, what do you know," Carlos comments sarcastically. "Our daughter goes to a stranger for advice and my wife believes her."

"Stop it, Carlos. Nita drove around half the night before waiting in the university parking lot so she could talk to me when I came in this morning. Judy arrived at the office before I did. What are you doing?"

"I'm making a sandwich," Carlos explains as he takes one container after another out of the refrigerator.

"Sit down, honey." Ana takes the loaf of bread from his hand. "I'll do that for you."

"I can't sit down. What did Nita say to her?"

"She told Judy that Eric wrote a letter to Douglas, telling him that Nita was dropping his class, and signed her name to it. He sent a copy to the registrar's office, and they dropped her from the class. Now she can't get back into the only class she needs to take to graduate."

Carlos opens the refrigerator. "Why would he do that?"

"She says he won't let her be her own person."

"I can't imagine Nita being anything but her own person."

"He thinks she's having an affair with her film professor." Ana slices a few pieces of bread and asks Carlos, "What kind of sandwich do you want?"

"I really don't want a sandwich," he mumbles as he returns the items to the refrigerator.

"What do you want, honey?"

"I want my daughter to be okay!" Carlos exclaims.

"She thinks you care more about Eric than you do about her."

"Where did she get that idea?"

"From you."

Carlos stuffs his hands in his pants pockets. "That's absurd."

A trail of Ana's words, "You're walking away from me the same way you've been walking away from Nita ever since she divorced Jim," echoes through the hallway as she follows him into the living room.

Carlos turns toward Ana and shouts, "Don't tell me I don't care about our daughter! I can't see her pain. I only see what she is doing to herself, and all I seem to be able to do is stand by and watch her ruin her life."

"She's in trouble," Ana reminds Carlos.

Carlos plops down in the chair. "What do you expect me to do, read her mind? She doesn't tell us anything anymore."

"—because we stopped listening!" Ana exclaims. She sits in the chair next to him, swiveling it around to him so she can look him in the eye. "We told her to try harder to save her marriage to a gay man."

"We didn't know."

"We didn't want to know. We haven't let her talk about Jim leaving her for a man. Every time she brings up his name, you find an excuse to leave the room. I'm just as guilty. I tell her to forget about it. We've pushed our daughter so far away from us that she doesn't tell us anything anymore."

"Where do you come up with these things?"

"You didn't talk to her. You scolded her for not wanting to tell us why her marriage fell apart," Ana reminds Carlos. "Nita told us she didn't want to talk about that vile, repulsive liar who called himself her husband. Then she stormed out the door and refused to come over until we stopped nagging her."

"That was before we knew," Carlos defends himself.

"We didn't talk to her the night she rented *Day Trippers*," Ana continues.

"What's that?"

"It's the movie about a woman who suspects her husband is having an affair that Nita brought over a few months after her divorce."

"Oh yeah," Carlos utters as a familiar stab pierces his stomach. "I didn't say anything even after Nikki confirmed my suspicion."

"That was a long time ago, Ana."

"We're still doing it, Carlos," Ana explains. "Remember when Nita begged me to read her film critique last Friday night. I refused while you hid at the top of the stairs."

"What's so important about knowing Jim is the way he is?"

"You can't say it. Can you?"

"Say what?"

"You can't say Jim is gay."

"Yes, I can."

"Then say it."

"Jim is ..." Carlos hesitates. "He is." He shakes his head. "This is ridiculous."

"If you can't say the word *gay,* then how can you help our daughter?"

"I can't," Carlos admits as he walks away from Ana.

"You act as if she should be ashamed of her marriage to Jim."

Carlos turns around on the landing. "I never said—"

"Stop," Ana's voice follows Carlos up the stairs. She is on his heels when he goes into the bedroom and sits on the bed. "Every mistake Nita has made in the last five years started when she stopped coming to us for help."

"She came to us during the divorce," Carlos recalls.

"Uh uh," Ana disagrees. "Did you know that Jim used the letter of the law to spend the night before the divorce at their house simply because he didn't want to fight rush hour traffic to get to the courthouse in the morning?"

"The letter of the law?" Carlos repeats.

"The law says it's his house until the divorce is over," Ana explains. "He said he had a right to stay there. Our daughter and grandson spent the night in a hotel instead of coming here."

"I'm not sure he's right." Carlos jumps up and paces the floor. "We can't help Nita if she doesn't tell us what's going on."

"I don't recall waiting for the kids to come to us when they were in trouble. All the signals have been there, but we have chosen to ignore them because we are uncomfortable with Jim being gay. We have abandoned our daughter, Carlos, when she needs us the most."

"I don't understand this generation of men," Carlos admits. "I don't know how to help our daughter."

"We have to find a way," Ana insists.

Carlos' eyes drop to the floor as he admits, "It's not in a father's nature to talk to his daughter about these kinds of things."

"Why not?"

"I'm supposed to protect my daughter from what I know any straight man wants from her. How can I… any man would… he didn't want her," Carlos stammers. "How am I supposed to protect Nita from that? I only know how to get rid of the kind of guy who only wants one thing."

"The kind of guy like Eric," Ana reminds him.

"You made your point, Ana," Carlos fumes as he leaps off of the bed and paces the floor again. "I am a terrible father."

"You are not a terrible father. Sit down, Carlos," Ana insists. When he settles onto the edge of the bed, she rubs her hand across his back to comfort him. "Maybe you were defending Nita's attractiveness to men instead of protecting her from them."

"That's the most absurd thing I ever heard," Carlos scowls.

"Maybe," Ana concedes, "but neither of us tried to stop Nita from marrying a man who doesn't want anything from her except sex."

"I should have stopped her from marrying that jerk," Carlos sputters.

"Don't get all riled up again," Ana warns. "You'll feel better after you talk to Nita."

"I don't know what I should say?"

"She needs to know you are on her side," Ana encourages him. "Tell her you want to help but don't yell at her."

"Should I tell her I know about Jim?"

Ana groans. "You haven't told her you know that Jim is gay!"

"No," he admits as he plops down on the bed. "I don't know how to help Nita. I'm in over my head," he stammers. He rolls over on his back and their eyes connect. "Promise you won't laugh at me, Ana."

"I won't, honey."

"I talked with someone about Nita yesterday."

"A therapist?" Ana asks in disbelief.

"Of course not, Ana," Carlos replies. He props his back up against the decorative pillows on the headboard and stretches out his legs out on the bed. "I've been worried about Nita for a while, especially after the way she stormed out of the house Friday night."

"It was silly of me to refuse to read her paper," Ana mutters to herself as she stretches out next to Carlos.

"I talked to my friend, Andy, the detective, because I wanted to know what Jim was, you know, doing while they were married."

"What did he say?"

"He told me that Jim can't help being who he is. I asked him why he is so sympathetic toward a man who dishonored my daughter. Jim sues Nita for mental cruelty when he's the one—" Carlos leaps off the bed and resumes his pacing across the room.

"You're getting yourself all riled up again," Ana states the obvious. "Jim didn't do it because he's gay. He did it because he's not a nice person."

"Hogwash!" Carlos exclaims. His voice escalates with every word he speaks. "He marries our daughter even though he knows who he is. He doesn't portray himself as the person he really is. He gets down on his knee and proposes to her. He doesn't think about who he is before he comes to us with a promise to take care of our daughter. He makes a false promise to Nita at the altar of our church and continues his cheating lies during their marriage. And our church expects our daughter to jump through hoops in order rid herself of him and go on with her life."

"Stop it, Carlos. It doesn't matter anymore why Jim did what he did. We have to help our daughter. We've been wrong to expect Nita get over this so quickly. How can she go on with her life if she can't trust anyone anymore, including us? I agree that he betrayed her in every imaginable way, but we've been sitting here in silence—"

"—because we're mad as hell at him!" Carlos exclaims. "He promised to love and honor my daughter, but I see no honor in betrayal." He flops on the bed face first and buries his head in the pillow.

"Relax, Carlos." Ana positions herself next to him. He lays his head in her lap as she massages his head and talks to him softly. "You're spinning around in circles. I agree that all of the hurt and confusion Nita has had to deal with could have been avoided if Jim had been honest with her from the beginning, but I wonder who you are really mad at, honey."

"We made it worse by being silent," he mutters.

"Shhh. Just listen and breathe deeply with me."

After they take a few deep breaths together, he says. "That felt good, honey."

"Are you okay?"

Carlos nods. He opens his eyes and looks up at Ana. "How can I help Nita when I'm ashamed of what happened to her?"

What's the Scoop

"It's going to be an early winter," Judy mutters as she stares out the window. Her eyes follow a snowflake falling from the gray sky as it melts to a teardrop on the sill outside Soledad's den. "My life would be different if only…" her voice drifts off as Soledad sets a large mug in front of her on the coffee table.

"What is this?"

"It's a warm pick-me-up of apple cider and spices." Soledad sits down next to Judy with a cup of espresso. "I wonder if it is as cold in Providence as it is here."

Judy blows away the steam rising from her mug. "I told Paul everything," she says softly.

"I see," Soledad says as she slides the box of Kleenex across the coffee table to Judy. "You should have told him a long time ago."

"How could I when I found out yesterday afternoon," Judy replies.

Soledad's words, "What did you find out yesterday afternoon?" are expelled into the air at the same time as Judy's question, "What should I have told Paul a long time ago?" reaches her ears.

"I don't like the way you've been toying with Paul," Soledad tells Judy.

"Toying with Paul?" Judy repeats.

"You shouldn't be leading him on when…" Soledad pauses, "you're a lesbian."

Judy laughs loudly for a bit before she says, "You got it wrong, Sole. I was the wife of a gay man," Judy explains.

"The wife," Soledad echoes in dismay.

Judy shakes her head up and down several times until it sinks in.

"Well, what do you know, you're not gay," Soledad says softly. She walks over to the fireplace and scolds herself, "What kind of friend am I, making all kinds of assumptions about you?"

"I did the same thing to you," Judy reminds her.

"But you were right."

"You still have time to change all that."

Soledad turns her back on Judy as the angst builds. She focuses on her desire to leap into the fire. "There was someone," she murmurs. Her silent breathing can be seen in the deep, steady movement of her back.

"He must have broken your heart," Judy speculates.

The back of Soledad's head bobs up and down. She spins around quickly and expels the words, "There is no story, Jude. I'm going to Providence for the funeral of my ex-father-in-law."

"You were married!" Judy exclaims.

Soledad shakes her head deeply. "I was married for fourteen years." She turns toward the fireplace again. Her eyes are drawn to the painting mounted above the fireplace. She remembers what Theo said to her when he sketched out the idea for the painting at the hotel in Platja d'Aro. Her words, "I'll never get used to how mysterious she is," catch in her throat as a lone teardrop plops on her shoe. She coughs. "He's the same as your ex-husband, Jude."

"Oh!" Judy exclaims while staring at Soledad's back.

Soledad takes several deep breaths before spinning around to face Judy. Her voice cracks as she explains, "Twelve years ago, Bob started liking men more than me." She throws her arms up and gives Judy an exaggerated shrug. "I caught them together."

"Ouch," Judy says.

"We were happy. I trusted him implicitly. Now I don't know if I'll ever trust anyone. He's ruined it for me with men. How can I believe any man will turn out to be who he says he is?"

"Did he deserve your trust?"

"Yes. I think so. I mean I thought he did, but he turned out to be someone else. So how can I? I don't know." Soledad stops. "I've backed myself into a corner because of it. If we had a bad marriage, it would make sense. But none of it makes any sense to me. How do you make sense of all the things we did as husband and wife and how happy we were together when he ended up preferring men? If I hang on to what I know we had when we were married, I have to make sense of a straight person turning gay."

"It doesn't make sense, Sole. There are a lot of things in life that don't make sense. If you keep looking for answers, you'll drive yourself crazy."

"I can't help it. I don't know how someone can be so strongly one way one minute and turn out to be so strongly another way the next. I can only conclude that men aren't capable of being honest about who they are, because they don't really know who they are."

"You're trying to put something illogical into a logical framework and use it to draw conclusions about men," Judy explains. "It's perfectly understandable, but it won't help you."

"Can you tell the difference between straight men and men who pretend to be straight?"

"I never said I was good at it." Judy shrugs. "Sometimes we can only have faith."

"What's that?" Soledad grunts.

"It's a belief in something that you can't explain. Do you have faith in your marriage?"

"I believe in my marriage even though I can't explain what happened at the end of it. I used to talk about my life with Bob. Why shouldn't I? I was proud of it," Soledad's voice resonates passionately through the room. "But there hasn't been any respect for my marriage or empathy for what I went through, only a belief in the untruths people need to believe about what went on between Bob and me."

Soledad takes a glass from the cupboard and fills it with water before continuing. "One day, I just stopped talking about it. It was easier to let people create their own reality about my love life than it was to tell them the truth. I didn't correct these misperceptions because no one would believe me."

"I believe you." Judy pats the couch. "Sit down, Sole. You're making me nervous." When she does, Judy asks, "How do you keep track of what you tell people?"

"It's easy, as long as everyone in the same circle believes the same story and my circles of friends don't overlap." She laughs out loud as she continues. "I created pasts that I couldn't have imagined living. I've been divorced from a straight man, lived with a lawyer, left my husband for another man, and never been in love. Believe it or not, I was even a widow for a while. It sounds crazy Jude, but it's better than having to digest the lies people want me to believe about my life with Bob."

"I did the same thing in a different way."

Soledad pivots her body toward Judy and asks, "You were happily married?"

"Au contraire, Sole," Judy corrects her as she wrinkles her nose. "My marriage was awful. I was ashamed of being so naïve. I told myself I would have known if I had insisted on having sex before I married him. I created a façade of a straight marriage around his closet to convince myself that I was happy, but I was miserable. I blamed myself for it. I wasn't trying hard enough. He would have been a better lover if I had liked sex. Because I wouldn't let myself believe the truth, I became what I wanted to believe I was supposed to be.

"The difference between our situations is that you let people create stories about the life you had during your marriage because you were protecting the truth from people who couldn't accept it. I, on the other hand, pretended to have the kind of marriage I was supposed to have and be the kind of wife I was supposed to be because I was the one who couldn't accept the truth about my marriage."

"What is the truth, Jude?" Soledad asks.

"Pete was conflicted, and it wore me out." Judy sets the mug on the coffee table. "I was unhappy for so long that I didn't even know what it was like to be happy. The longer I lived the sham, the more of myself I had to bury. Before long, there wasn't anything left of me. One day, a man came along and saved me."

"Paul," Soledad asks.

Judy smiles through her tiredness. "You should have seen him thirty years ago, Sole. He knocked my socks off in every imaginable way. I let him go to protect my kids. It didn't take long to realize my sham of a marriage had been keeping me from finding someone who could love me the way I wanted to be loved. I divorced him a few years later, when the twins were in college."

"Do you still see your ex?"

"I did because of the twins, but he died five years ago."

"The funeral," Soledad sighs. "Maybe seeing Bob will help."

"When was the last time you saw him?" Judy asks, happy for the diversion.

"It was at a friend's surprise birthday party a year after my divorce. I ran away from it because I couldn't take my father-in-law's effort to get Bob and I back together wrapped around the birthday party of a good friend who is now married to my ex-brother-in-law." Soledad laughs. "My life is a soap opera."

"Mine is too." Judy laughs along with Soledad.

"Bob won't be alone at the funeral, Jude," Soledad adds.

"What are you going to do?"

"Go to the funeral."

Judy looks at her watch. "When do you leave?"

"Don't go, Jude. It's only eleven. My cab won't be here until one. I've been so wrapped up in my situation that I haven't given you much of a chance to tell me what you came here to tell me."

Judy inhales a long breath. "Your story makes mine easier to tell. Pete was confused about his sexuality. He tried to be the kind of man that he was supposed to be. It tormented him that he couldn't. I tolerated it even though I didn't understand it because that was what married people were supposed to do at the time."

"Living with a sexually confused husband wore me out. There was no room for me, Sole. I didn't have time to think about what I needed. One day, I woke up with a desperate need to make sense of my life. I didn't know where to start. I didn't know anyone who had a gay husband. The only person who knew and understood was

Paul, but he was gone because I let him go. When I looked him up after my divorce, he was married."

"How awful," Soledad empathizes.

"I was miserable," Judy continues. "I had to do something. I searched for articles, books, movies, anything that would help me make sense of my life with Pete. I found all kinds of things about the homosexual experience and the coming out process for gay spouses, but no attention was given to our experience or what we needed to get through the psychic confusion that goes with having been married to a gay man. So I created my own research agenda."

"...and Paul," Soledad prods.

"Five years ago, I was lucky to find him again. I had told him everything about my miserable marriage during our year long affair, but he didn't know what had transpired after he returned to UCLA. I was afraid to tell him I had been exposed." Judy takes a drink out of her empty mug. "Pete and I didn't know we needed to take precautions. AIDS didn't come on the scene until the 1980s, long after the disease had done its damage."

Soledad puts her hand over her mouth and gasps.

"I was diagnosed in May of 2004, right before you moved here. Pete died in the fall. I was put on a drug treatment regime to slow my T cell destruction. I was doing fine until last Thursday when the doctor told me my days were numbered."

"Oh, Jude!" Soledad cries.

Judy runs her finger around the rim of the mug in her lap. "I told the twins this weekend when they paid me a surprise visit at the Drake Hotel."

"What about Paul?"

"Paul knows Pete died of AIDS. I told him five years ago that I've been infected. He didn't know the end is in sight until Friday night after he asked me to marry him. It has been hard..." Judy's voice trails off.

"You love him," Soledad declares.

"You bet I do. We keep the physical thing light or Paul will—" Judy stops. "Have you been tested?"

"I have. I'm clean."

Judy closes her eyes and squeezes her forehead. "What is in this cider, truth serum?"

Soledad takes the empty mug from Judy and sets in on the counter. "This is incredible, Jude. We have known each other for five years and neither one of us knew the other has a gay ex-husband."

After Judy wraps herself in her coat, Soledad stretches her arms around Judy and pulls her to her chest. "What am I going to do without you?"

"Not so fast," Judy warns. "I'm not going anywhere until you come back and tell me what happens at the funeral."

Burying the Coffin

All Soledad is capable of doing as she approaches the man standing in front of her ex-father-in-law's coffin is smile. There are so many things she wants to say to her ex-brother-in-law, but the words are tangled up in the altercation she had with him at her cousin's wedding reception. Her discomfort reveals itself in the way she folds her hands in front of her thighs as they silently acknowledge each other. Her fingers are tightly intertwined in a clenching grip, wringing the life out of the discomfort that she so readily shifts back and forth from one foot to the other. The sparkle in her sapphire eyes reflects anticipation, a longing to release the life she has kept so close to her chest.

Soledad's soft-spoken words, "He looks so peaceful, Kenny," break the silent uneasiness that has separated them for the last twelve years. Her eyes dart back and forth between her father-in-law's body and the man who is walking toward the coffin with Bob.

"Thank you for coming, Soledad," Bob greets her politely. Her eyes elude the stare of the man standing a few steps back from Bob as she tells him how sorry she is about his father's passing. Kenny waits with the man as Soledad and Bob turn toward the coffin and speak to one another in a tone of voice used in a library. When they turn back around, Bob says, "I'd like you to meet William."

Soledad relocks her hands into a protective shield and nods to William. "It's nice to meet you."

"Same here," William returns her polite greeting. "I've heard so much about you from Robert."

"Sole!" Barb exclaims as she walks up behind them. "I'm so glad you came." She locks Soledad into a long hug, giving Bob and William a chance to escape.

Soledad smiles warmly at Barb and recalls, "The last time you hugged me like that there was a baby between us."

"She's right there, next to Janie." Barb beams as she points to her daughter across the room.

"Janie looks so much like you," Soledad says. "The younger one is—"

"Her name is Soledad," Kenny interjects.

Soledad's face lights up as Barb nods. Barb motions to the funeral director standing off to the side as she addresses Soledad. "You came so late that we haven't had time to catch up. Come with us to the Hill for dinner."

"Oh no, I can't," Soledad protests.

"It's already arranged," Barb insists.

Bob's words, "It would be terribly difficult to change the reservation," precluded the protest Soledad was about to make.

"Susan left for the restaurant a few minutes ago. I'll go with you," Kenny offers.

"Okay," Soledad agrees apprehensively. "I'll wait by the door."

Barb takes her hand and says, "Dad would have wanted you here with us."

As Soledad stands in front of her ex-father-in-law's coffin, she finds comfort in being with the people who used to be her family. She blinks a teardrop out of the corner of her eye that mirrors the one trickling down the side of Bob's face. In that instant, everything between them is the way it used to be. And then they let go.

When Soledad slides into the car, Kenny finally has the nerve to say what he's been waiting to say for the last twelve years.

"I am sorry. I was a heel at your cousin's wedding. If I had known," Kenny confesses, "I wouldn't have leapt out of the chair and…"

"It was nothing, Kenny," she says flatly.

He didn't like the nonchalant way she dismissed his contribution to the end of their marriage, so he said, "It meant something to me."

"It wasn't your fault."

The blandness of her assurance didn't stop Kenny. "I've struggled with this for years."

"*You've* struggled," she repeats.

"We all did," he replies.

"You *all* struggled," she repeats.

"When Bob told us you were getting a divorce, we were shocked," Kenny proclaims.

"*You* were shocked," Soledad repeats.

"Yes," Kenny replies. "When Dad tried to convince him not to divorce you, he ran into Bob's circular logic. Why didn't you tell us, Sole?"

"It wasn't my place, Kenny," Soledad defends her silence.

"We didn't know anything about it at the time of the divorce. Bob told us, eventually, in his own way."

"I heard," Soledad mutters as she recalls the gossip at Susan's birthday party.

"He came to see me a few months before your cousin's wedding," Kenny explains. "He was toying with the idea of leaving you. He told me your job was getting in the way of having kids. If I had known at the time what I know now, I wouldn't have talked him out of—"

"He told you I didn't want to have a child?" Soledad interrupts.

"I'm not sure. He may have said he wanted to have a kid, or I may have assumed you didn't want one. I was making all kinds of assumptions at the time. I thought he was protecting you."

"From what?" she asks.

Kenny's words, "From how we would respond to whatever you had done to him," feel like a slap that reels Soledad's head around. She gives him a disapproving glare.

"I know it's not a very good excuse, Sole," Kenny defends his family, "but we didn't know. I was crushed when I found out the truth. I had wrongly accused you of ruining everything based on what I saw the night of your cousin's wedding. Will you ever be able to forgive me?"

Soledad's nod encourages him to say more.

"We lost you, Sole," he explains. "It happened so fast. One

minute you were happy, and the next you were gone. Little did we know…" his voice drifts off.

"For the record, we both wanted a child," Soledad proclaims. "We had been trying for a few months before I found out Bob was gay."

"You would have been a good mother."

"Where is this place?" Soledad adds in a tone of voice she uses when she doesn't want to talk about something.

"We have to go all the way to Atwell Avenue," he tells her.

Soledad turns her eyes to the road and asks, "Why didn't you tell me this before?"

"I wanted to," Kenny replies. "At one point, I drove up to Boston so I could talk to you. After all the damage I had done, I—"

"You didn't do the damage."

"I was afraid of what you might say to me. When we found out the truth, I was angry with Bob for not telling us. It would've saved all of us a lot of grief if he had told us from the beginning. Mostly, I was ashamed of all the false impressions I had of you."

She stops at a traffic light and points to the corner restaurant. "Is that the place?"

"It is, Sole." He returns to his explanation, knowing what little time they have left to be alone. "We knew when Robert brought William home, but we didn't want to believe it. It's strange that not one of us, even to this day, has ever talked about it. And Dad will go to his grave tomorrow believing what he wanted to believe, that Bob has a roommate, not a lover."

"I thought I was the only one who had a hard time with this."

They drive around Federal Hill looking for a street parking space, reflecting on their conversation. Soledad breaks the silence. "Do you have any idea how many times I wished my marriage would get the respect it deserves?"

"We respect it."

"You do because you were there. Imagine what it's been like trying to explain this to someone who didn't know us. I'm not even sure I can trust that the happiness I thought we had was real."

"It was real, Sole. I wish I hadn't been one of the people who made it so hard for you."

"You aren't, Kenny. There's one," she interrupts her thought and stops next to a parked car. She stretches her arm out on the back of the seat, looking out the back window to park the car.

"I wish I knew what happened," Kenny utters. "It's harder to understand now than it was back then."

When the car is snugly tucked into the parking space, Soledad opens the glove box and takes out a package with five pieces of broken glass inside. "Can you fix it?"

Kenny opens the box and assesses the damaged gondola. "It's in pretty bad shape. It'll be easier to make a new one for you," Kenny suggests as he hands the box back to Soledad.

Soledad nods.

"What happened to it?"

"Someone knocked it off my fireplace mantle a few years ago." She wraps the broken pieces of the gondola in the wrinkled tissue and puts it back in the glove box. Then she puts her hand on the door and changes into her protective demeanor as quickly as the engine stops.

It is like old times in the restaurant, except that Soledad is at one end of a long table with Kenny, Susan, Barb and her husband while Bob and William are at the other end with his elderly aunt and uncle. Barb's girls sit in the center of the table between them.

"Do you remember our holiday in Vienna when you got locked in that park after the Mozart Symphony?" Barb reminds Soledad.

"That was a long time ago," Soledad says. "I'm less adventurous than I used to be."

"As I recall, you had one of those big birthdays last month," Kenny teases.

"I did," Soledad whispers loudly, "but don't tell anyone here."

"Next Wednesday is my birthday," William breaks in to the conversation.

Soledad looks down toward the other end of the table. "Happy birthday," she says politely. "How old will you be?"

"I'll be sixty."

Soledad turns her head back toward Barb, Kenny, and Susan and mutters, "He left me for an older man." Laughter roared from her end of the table.

"Robert is giving you a dirty look," Barb informs Soledad.

"I don't give a damn." Soledad chuckles, proud of her flippant courage, of the way she made her point with sarcasm while reminding Bob of how much she was hurt. Poor William is the instrument of cupid's arrow aimed at Bob to slap the sting out of his betrayal. She smiles anyway, knowing that she has returned the deed to Bob's closet to its rightful owner and relieved herself of the burden she has been dragging around for the last twelve years. She has let him know she has him on the edge of his seat; right where he had her the night of her cousin's wedding.

It's His Life

Nita sits in the front seat of the car with her father, observing the gay men congregating in the park along the Chicago lakefront on an early December night. She takes note of the expensive cars lined up in a long row of parking spaces in front of the boulders that separate the lake from shore. Men of all ages are scattered throughout the park. Some are sitting together on the park benches, sharing their day's experiences with one another in the same way her family does at the dinner table. Others are strolling along the path toward the dunes. They come here to get away from their families. They come here to meet their gay lovers.

"How did you find this place, Dad?"

"This park was under surveillance when you were married to Jim. A friend of mine is the detective who ran the undercover operation. He told me he was surprised when," Carlos clears his throat, "he got to know these men. He discovered, contrary to his expectation, that these men aren't criminals. Most of them are upstanding, respected citizens of the community, you know, doctors, lawyers, politicians, business executives, and the like. Many of them are married. They come here because they need to be discreet. They don't want anyone in their families to find out, you know ..."

"I know," Nita says. Her eyes follow a male couple coming back from the dunes toward the bench. They walk past a man sitting on a park bench all by himself. He is crying.

"It's perfectly safe here," Carlos repeats, more as reassurance to himself than to Nita. "I asked my friend, the detective, to check his records to see if," he clears his throat, "Jim might have been one of the men who came here during that time. He doesn't remember meeting Jim, but he is listed on the report as someone who came here when you were married."

"So this is where he used to go," Nita comments.

Carlos fidgets in his seat as a car pulls up next to them. A man in a blue pinstriped suit jumps out of his BMW and runs over to the man who is crying on the bench. His sulky demeanor quickly changes to a smile as his partner gives him an amorous hug.

"How could I make it work under these circumstances?" she mumbles.

"This has been hard on you." Carlos begins to scold himself. "I've been a terrible father, turning my back on my daughter when you need me most."

"It's okay Dad."

"No it isn't, Nita. I should have paid more attention to what was happening to you."

"Everything I have touched since Jim left has turned to poison."

"Your life is not poison, honey." He turns his entire body toward her. "I don't want you to worry anymore. Your mother and I will do our best to help you with," he points to the park, "whatever this is. Things will be much better after you divorce Eric."

"You approve of another divorce?" Nita asks with surprise.

"You bet I do." He takes a piece of paper out of his pocket and hands it to Nita. "I asked my friend in the DA's office for the names of a few good divorce attorneys. I'll help you find someone to represent you."

Nita points to the first name on the list and says, "I can't afford this guy."

"I'm paying for it."

"Dad—"

"You don't want to hurt your old man's feelings, do you? Now after work tomorrow, your mother and I will go home with you so you can get your things. I'll tell Eric you won't be back. I'm sure Nikki or Ned will watch José if you ask them. We want you to come back home until this is over." He smiles at her. "It'll be nice to have you and my grandson at the breakfast table with us."

Nita reaches over and hugs Carlos. "I love you, Dad."

He smiles at her. "Did I ever tell you what a beautiful woman you are?"

"No, but I'm glad you did today."

Carlos turns his focus back to the park. "What else do you need from your father?"

Nita chuckles at her father clinging on to the steering wheel. "I need you to get me the hell out of here."

"My sentiments exactly," Carlos says without hesitating to start the engine.

"Can you take me to Dairy Queen for a hot fudge sundae?"

Carlos ruffles her hair and says, "Anything for my girl."

Where Did You Go

"I wanted to tell you at Susan's birthday party," Bob explains as they stand in the living room of her ex-father-in-law's cottage on Prudence Island. "I don't blame you for leaving, the way my Dad was pushing me at you."

"He was protecting himself from what he didn't want to see," Soledad defends him. "He wanted us to be together."

"We were good together," Bob says softly.

Soledad nods. "Tell me what happened, if you still remember."

"I remember everything." He holds up a picture of them on their sailboat and says, "This was Dad's favorite picture of us. After our divorce, I wanted him to put it away. I couldn't get him to part with it. Now I can't part with it. I proposed to you right there," he points to the cockpit, "near a rocky outcrop along the Bold Coast. Right there was the first time we ..."

Soledad smiles at Bob. "And then it was over."

"You didn't deserve any of it."

"No, I didn't."

"I was angry with you at the time."

"You were angry with me?"

"I didn't know what was happening to me at the time. In my entire life, I had not slept with a man until the end of our marriage. You probably have a hard time believing ..." he pauses.

"I believe you," Soledad interrupts.

"I didn't want anything to change between us. But then ..." Bob's voice wanders off with his thoughts.

"I love the bay, even when it's gray," Soledad murmurs as she stares through the window at the estuary.

"I want you to have this," Bob hands Soledad the picture.

"I thought you said you couldn't part with it."

"It's the original. I made a copy for me."

Soledad takes the picture and holds it to her breast. "Thank you."

Bob grabs Soledad's coat draped over the chair and offers it to her. "Let's take a walk."

Soledad starts laughing as he slides a red fox fur coat around his shoulders.

"Are you laughing at my coat?"

"It looks silly on you," she giggles.

"No it doesn't!" Bob exclaims.

"I'm sorry," Soledad says when she gets her snickering under control. She turns her eyes to the bay and breathes in the sea air. They walk toward the water in silence. When they reach the road she says, "I miss this place."

"Do you miss me?" Bob teases her.

"That's not funny," Soledad articulates the words clearly. She examines her ex-father-in-law's favorite picture. "It's hard not to miss what was so good…" She pauses to looks at Bob in his red fox fur coat. "But you are not the same person as this man in the sailboat."

"I know," Bob concurs. He hands her an envelope. "Dad wanted you have this. There's enough in there to charter a sailboat in the Caribbean for a few weeks with your friends."

Soledad brushes her hand across the envelope and whispers, "How did he know?"

"I told him it was one of our, I mean, your dreams."

"Thank you," Soledad looks at the gray water. There isn't a single sailboat in sight on this early December morning. "When did it change?" she asks.

They held the bay in their eyes as they walked toward the edge of the water. "It happened on our thirteenth wedding anniversary while you were working in Moscow. I was lonely. I didn't even know him. It was the reason I didn't show up for our anniversary celebration in Venice. I thought it had something to do with you at the time."

She stops and asks, "What did I do?"

"You didn't do anything. I was guilty. I had never done anything like that before. I just wanted to forget it. I didn't see anyone else until I met that electrician four months before your cousin's wedding," Bob continues the story. "You know who I'm talking about, that subcontractor I hired for a mansion renovation in Newport."

Soledad nods. "Why," she asks.

"I was drawn to him like a magnet. I tried to find things he could do on the job just so I could be with him. Then it happened. I was as miserable as an addict who hates his addiction but can't stay away from it. I called it off the week before your cousin's wedding. I didn't want you to go to Moscow because I was afraid I'd turn back to him. I had the strange idea that none of it would have happened if you hadn't been away."

"You thought I was the one who ruined our marriage?"

He pivots toward her and looks directly in her eyes. "Don't ever think that, Sole. I never thought you ruined anything. It was me. I just didn't know it at the time. I didn't know if I was gay or straight. All I knew is it was over for us."

Soledad kicks the pebbles out from under her feet. They walk in silence down to the end of the beach where the path takes them back to the road. It isn't until they reach the road that Bob returns to his story. "I didn't know for sure if I was gay even after we divorced. I dated both men and women for a while. By the time I met William, it was clear that I was gay and wasn't going back."

"He seems like a nice man," Soledad whispers.

"I'm as happy with him as I was with you when we were married."

"I'm not sorry for what we had, even though most people think I should be."

"I've had trouble with that too."

"It's not a fair comparison, Bob. You know what happened because it happened to you. Yet I'm the one who gets all the questions."

He gives her a puzzled look. "You do?"

"Sure. Most people think it is too personal to ask you about your coming out, but I'm considered fair game. I don't know what happened to you. I only know what I lost."

"We both lost it."

"I lost more. You were not betrayed by me, but I was—"

"I didn't mean to betray you."

"I know you didn't. Your coming out has had a big effect on me."

Bob stops in front of the ferry dock. "What has it done to you?"

Soledad hesitates to tell Bob her thoughts. *I wonder if I'll ever stop worrying about something in a man that will take him away from me.* She holds up the envelope and says. "I wish I could thank your dad for this. Goodbye, Bob," she adds as she reaches out to shake his hand before turning from him and walking up the ramp to the ferry.

As she watches Bob and the island that were so much a part of their life shrink into the horizon, she fondles the envelope that holds her passage to a different sea. A light breeze pushes Soledad's hair off her face as she glides with the wind back to shore. She notices the only two sailboats left in the Narragansett Bay on this gray late fall day are sailing at full mast in opposite directions.

She kisses the envelope and puts it in her purse. Her head is spinning through all the men she has discarded since her divorce. She pauses for a moment on Theo and listens to the wind bring his voice to her like music floating across the water. The wind moistens her eyes as she remembers the last thing Theo said to her. *I wait because someday your heart will break free.*

She leans on the rail and hums the song of her last day at sea. Theo was at the helm, listening to her chant the music in her heart as they reached out to the Mediterranean Sea. Theo's voice echoes across the water with words he spoke to her on the day she left. *I don't want to bring him back to you, but I want you to come back.* Soledad sighs as the wind whistles her refrain. *Come back to me. My heart is free. I'm sorry, dear Theo. I didn't let you wait.*

She steps out of the wind and opens her cell phone. She searches the call log for the number she erased from her phone book. She waits for an answer. The voice on the other end of the line brings a smile to her face.

"Hi," she says before listening to his long response. "Yes, you can pick me up. Do you have a pen?" Her smile widens as she replies, "I'd love to have dinner with you tonight." She pauses. "I'm on United flight 452 from Providence that arrives at O'Hare at four forty-five." She laughs. "I can't wait to see you, Jay."

What Have I Done

Judy stares out the large glass window of the coffee shop. Her thoughts are as heavy as the snowflakes that come to rest on the windshields of the parked cars lined up in front of the café. She watches a woman bundling her winter coat up around her neck as she walks past the window.

"Here you are, my dear." Douglas sets a large mug of steaming hot coffee in front of her and says, "They made it just the way you like it."

She points to the pile of research papers on the table. "Over one hundred research papers and six books, and people are just as intolerant as they were twenty years ago."

"People are far more accepting today than they were back then."

"People are more politically correct," Judy corrects him. "It's not the same as acceptance."

"You sound like a bitter woman."

"I haven't made a bit of difference," Judy's voice slowly fades away as she flips through the book she wrote five years ago.

"You've made a difference to me."

"You're a good friend, Douglas."

"You have no idea how much you have done, Judy…" He pauses to hold up the research papers on the table before continuing, "Or how many people have benefited from your dedication to this research. I couldn't have worked things out with my ex without your advice. She did what you suggested, stepping back from her feelings and seeing how her lifestyle has affected my kids and me. Because of you, we get along better as a family, far better than we would have without you."

"One family doesn't change anything."

"Change only happens through one family at a time.

"It isn't enough," Judy says softly as she takes a sip of coffee.

"It's never enough when you care, but it's a damn good start."

"I'm retiring because I'm tired of caring."

"It's not a good idea to make a decision like this when you're so discouraged."

"My mind is made up. Other than Nita's thesis, it's pretty much over for me. She cares more about my work than anyone else, but she has a husband who ..." Judy pauses. "Let's just say he's leading her to pursue other endeavors."

"I don't like him either," Douglas shakes his head.

"He came to see me a few years back. He wanted me to take Nita off what he called my homosexual project."

"You can't expect a jerk like that to appreciate our perspective."

"No one cares about our perspective."

"You don't wear negativity very well," Douglas tells her.

"I'm in a sour mood today," Judy frowns. "When I showed my new manuscript to my department colleagues last week, it bounced around the table as if it was poison."

"No one touched it?" Douglas asks.

"Someone flipped through it politely. Someone else read the first paragraph, but only one of my colleagues offered to read it."

"At least one person cares. It's more than most academics can say about the papers we publish."

"It's what has kept me going all these years."

"You don't have to retire," Douglas explains.

Judy puts her head in her hands and smiles through her tiredness. "Paul and I are getting married."

"Married," Douglas exclaims with a chuckle. "Why did you let me ramble on about your retirement like that?"

"We're getting married Christmas Day in Rhodes, Greece, and taking a Greek Isle cruise with our children."

"What does Paul say about taking your children on your honeymoon?"

"He's all for it. At our age, honeymoons aren't all they are cracked up to be. We're touring the African continent for the next year. We want to see as much of the world as possible."

"I'm going to miss you."

"Stop pouting and do me a favor. Work with Nita on her thesis. I'm afraid I won't be much help to her on a different continent."

Douglas grins. "It'll be a pleasure."

"She's getting a divorce," Judy whispers.

"It's the best news I've heard all day. She doesn't belong with a burnt-out old fart like Eric."

Judy shakes her finger at Douglas. "She doesn't need another boyfriend."

Let Me Be

"Judy would be proud of you," Douglas tells Nita the day before her graduation from Northwestern University.

"I'm officially divorced," Nita announces. "In the fall, I'll be in graduate school, thanks to Judy." She pauses. "I found a place in Hyde Park, close enough to get help with José from my family and far enough away to get a fresh start."

"Can I come to your place?"

Nita lays her hand on top of his and says, "You'll be one of the first."

Douglas turns his hand over and wraps his fingers around hers. "I was hoping I could take you to one of the restaurants in Hyde Park."

Nita takes her hand back. "Douglas—I can't."

"I'm forty. I must be within ten years of your age," Douglas adds.

"Nine," Nita corrects him. "It's hard to believe I'm twice divorced at thirty-one."

"It's not your fault."

"Legitimate reasons don't turn bad choices into good ones."

"Nita, I think we could be—"

She interrupts Douglas with a question. "Can I share the dream I had last night with you?"

"Sure."

"I'm a race car driver, speeding through a construction site so fast that everything around me is a blur. My eyes are peeled to the road in front of me as the car sputters to a stop. When I look back to check it out, I am shocked to find out that the entire back end of the car is missing. I can't go anywhere because I am so focused on getting past the construction that I don't know what happened."

She looks down into her lap. "As much as I want to get to know you in a new way, Douglas, I can't be with anyone right now. If I don't take time to fix what I left behind, I'll end up in the same place all over again."

A Brand New Sail

In every parting, there is a moment when the beloved is already gone. Jay is with Soledad when the phone rings. It is Paul, calling from Kenya.

Soledad hangs up the phone with tears in her eyes. She leads Jay to the den. "Sit right here," she tells him, patting the back of the sofa. "I want to show you something."

She opens the closet door that houses nothing but fourteen boxes. She lifts the box from the top row and sets it on the floor. She carefully cuts long layers of tape that have kept her life with Bob comfortably buried in the dark confines of the boxes in front of her. She removes the cover and brushes her fingers several times across the dusty cover of a photo album. She takes it out of the box and sits next to Jay on the couch. "I have a story to tell you."

She opens the album to a picture of a couple floating along the Venetian Canal in a gondola. "We went to Venice on our honeymoon. Since I had a writing gig in Moscow on our thirteenth wedding anniversary, I made arrangements to stay at the hotel we were at on our honeymoon. Bob never showed."

"Oh," Jay says as he squeezes her hand.

"I gave the room key to a young couple waiting in the lobby for a room and took the night train back to Moscow. Bob fell into the arms of a man simply because I wasn't at home with him on our anniversary. I don't want anyone to need me that badly," Soledad adds as she closes the album.

"Maybe you need someone who needs you in a different way," Jay suggests, "someone who is comfortable enough in their own skin."

Soledad snaps her fingers. "It was over just like that. The man who used to be my husband was replaced by a man who is gay."

"I understand," Jay replies. "My wife became a different person after she had an affair."

"That's not a fair comparison." Soledad cringes. "Imagine how you would feel if you lost a five-year-old child, and I compared it to the death of an eighty-year-old parent."

"Your point is well taken," Jay agrees. "I don't have any idea what it has been like for you, but I do know people with similar situations. Everyone one of them said it was the worst thing that ever happened to them."

"It was for me," she agrees. She puts the album on the shelf next to the others. "That's it."

After Soledad settles in on the couch next to Jay, he says, "I want to tell you something, but I don't want to scare you away again."

"I'm ready," Soledad encourages him as she braces herself.

"I think there's something really good going on between us."

Soledad smiles at Jay. "I do too."

Jay sighs with relief. "I'm falling in love with you, Sole," he begins. "You are an incredibly woman with lots and lots of layers that I want to know. I've only touched some of the layers. Others I don't know about yet. Are you willing to take a chance on me?"

"I'd like to."

"But ..." he coaxes her on.

"It's impossible to reconcile the difference between the man I married and the one I saw at the funeral." Soledad pauses to look at Theo's painting of the woman above her fireplace. "I need to take one day at a time."

"One day at a time," Jay repeats. "Okay. What would you like to do tomorrow?"

Soledad glances at the envelope on the mantle beneath her ex-father-in-law's favorite picture of her. On the coffee table is the new glass gondola Kenny sent to her last week. She picks it up and holds it to the light. Its shape and reflection is very different than the one he made for her after her divorce from Bob. The woman in the middle is reaching her hand toward the man in front of her and letting go of the hand of the man behind her. Soledad smiles and says, "Let's go sailing."

Afterword

By Amity Pierce Buxton, Ph.D.

Like me, you might feel slightly dizzy having lived vicariously, backwards and forwards and from many perspectives, the lives of three women whose husbands turned out to be gay. Denial, disbelief, deception, diversions, and distractions—generated out of disorientation, confusion, and self-blame—color each story. Their pain is woven into a tapestry of individuals, couples, and families alongside their husbands' apparent lack of awareness of the degree to which their disclosure impacted their wives and children. Stitched throughout are anger between parents and children, secrets kept for protection, out of fear of reality, and blindness to one's own feelings. As we first follow the women interacting with current and past partners, children, and parents, there is a disconnect between memory and circumstance.

Gradually, despite what they say or do, we glimpse what is really going on and the unique history unfolding within each relationship. Yet, even the reality of meeting an ex-husband's lover or the finality of being infected with AIDS barely cracks the surreal pretense the women created out of the shards of everything they thought they had, knew, or believed. It is this shattering and the cause of it that lies at the core of the tumultuous experience portrayed so well in this novel.

The story told in *Left in His Closet*, however, is not fiction. Feeling that one is functioning in an unreal world is the real-life experience of any woman or man whose spouse comes out or is found out to be gay or lesbian. Based on my own experience and thousands of stories I've heard from straight spouses, their partners, and their children since I began to study the phenomenon in 1986, this book captures the interior and exterior worlds of most spouses whose partners disclose being gay or lesbian. There are a lot of us. Up to two million have been or are married to a gay man or a lesbian, some of whom have come out, some who will, and others who will stay closeted. We can be found in every racial, ethnic, economic-social, educational, occupational, and religious group.

As the women's stories illustrate, common issues for straight spouses revolve around their sexuality, the marriage, parenting and children, and their own identity, integrity, and belief system. These areas of concern plagued their gay and lesbian partners too, before they share their secret with their spouses. Once they do, these concerns become less pressing. However sad they may feel about the impact their sexual orientation has on the family, and however fearful they are about losing social status if their secret is known outside the family circle, they feel liberated to some degree.

In contrast, their spouses are stunned and disbelieving, though some feel relieved to know the truth. Only then can they slowly face the facts and implications of the sexual mismatch, often feeling sexually starved, short-changed, and inadequate, wondering if any man or woman would desire them now. Confused about what the relationship really was, realizing it was based in part on a lie; they worry about its future. They are concerned about how the revelation will affect their children, not to mention effects of a possible divorce. Their identity uncertain, they feel worthless, without self-esteem or confidence. Their moral compass broken by the deception, they feel powerless, controlled by their partners' secret. With assumptions about gender, marriage and their future shattered, they feel purposeless. Nothing has meaning. Pain, fear, and anger run pell-mell through their coping until they dare face, acknowledge, and accept the new reality.

At this point, most let go of the past, and by working through their grief, begin to heal, to reconfigure their identity, integrity, and belief system, and to transform their lives. The process is one of fits and starts because of the complexity of the issues and life events. It may take years to resolve issues, especially if they get caught in a whirlpool of conflicting emotion. Reaching the transformation stage typically takes from three to six years. In the majority of cases, the couples divorce.

The women's stories in *Left in His Closet* also mirror how family and societal contexts affect the spouses' coping. Unlike their gay mates who find a bevy of relevant literature and support, there is little for them. If they dare tell family, friends, or professionals, including therapists and clergy, most receive scant help, attention, or understanding. If an outsider finds out, or a spouse shares the secret with someone, the reaction is often one of stigmatization or disbelief, accompanied by questions as to why they married a gay person or how come they didn't figure it out. Clergy may talk only about the immorality of being gay. Even therapists miss the mark, approaching the crisis with tools designed for heterosexual relationships and traditional family problems.

I founded the Straight Spouse Network in 1991 to provide support and education for the many wives and husbands who retreated into isolation after not finding outsiders who understood their crisis. Many stop asking for help. Coping alone, they avoid criticism or embarrassment about a situation that does not fit traditional expectations. There, they can protect their mates from discrimination at work or in the community, and their children from peer rejection or weakening of the child-parent bond. In their isolation, many don't find out about the worldwide support and individual contacts provided through the Straight Spouse Network. Each thinks she or he is the only person in this situation, since mixed-orientation marriages are invisible, or if made public, are quickly re-closeted like those of Reverend Ted Haggard and former Senator Larry Craig. Because of this invisibility, many spouses live a life of pretence.

Without a ready-made toolbox to deal with this personal crisis or family and friends with the key to open the straight-spouse door, they can't cope constructively. To fill this gap, I wrote *The Other Side of the Closet: the Coming-Out Crisis for Straight Spouses and Families* at the request of the Gay Fathers of San Francisco, who wanted to

understand why their wives were angry so they could open communication with them enough to be allowed to see their children.
Recognizing the need to help all outsiders comprehend challenges
straight spouses face, I expanded the subject to include not only
spouses of gay men, but also those of lesbian and bisexual partners;
gay, lesbian, and bisexual spouses, and their children. I also broadened its purpose to present research findings about sexual orientation and my own research on the full range of mixed-orientation
marriages for as wide an audience as possible.

Left in His Closet is another noteworthy book for a broad audience that depicts the personal turmoil of straight spouses trying to
cope with the many-layered effects of a life of pretense as the gay
spouse retreats to the closet. Like Soledad, Nita, and Judy, they
hide their own pain and confusion and pretend to be alive and well,
busy, and active. Their closets provide the safety that perpetrates
the deception and secrets that slow or prevent the re-creation of a
good life. Secrets, especially those kept from oneself, are unhealthy,
and their toxicity is catching.

The women's encounters with various people throughout the
book highlight the tension between real life experience and these
social expectations. Most importantly, their efforts to move beyond
the mental, emotional, and spiritual suffering exposes the domino
effect of discriminatory attitudes very often manifested as exces-
sive questioning or silence about their marriages to gay men and
lesbians. One could say, in fact, that straight spouses of gay and
lesbian partners are victims of victims of discrimination against
homosexuals.

Viewed together, the stories of pretense and pain captured in
this book are a prism though which to view conflicting views about
sexual orientation and marriage in the larger society; conflicts that
cry for resolution. Its pages open a window into the dissonance
between on-the-ground social changes and concepts of gender,
sexual orientation, marriage, and family that have been in place
for years. On the one hand are increasing scientific findings about

sexual orientation, more widespread acceptance of gay and lesbian persons, and growing attention to the quality of relationships as distinct from structure of relationships that have led to new behaviors and mores over the past forty years. On the other hand are the ongoing social patterns systems and institutions based on what is a predominantly heterosexist and codified society, where legislation at the federal level and in more than half the states prevent gay men and lesbians from legally marrying and conservative faith communities continue to counsel their gay and lesbian congregants to marry someone of the opposite sex.

Until we as a society take a candid look at mixed-orientation marriages as a microcosm of the conflict between social change based on increased knowledge and traditional paradigms about sexual orientation and marriage, couples like the ones portrayed in this novel will continue to marry and build closets of pretense. Despite strides in equality for women in general and for gay men and lesbians in particular, long-held role assignments for each of the two sexes and concepts of marriage remain strong. The forces on both sides of this conversation are formidable. Yet I believe we are at a transition point, able to move toward recognizing the pain of everyone in a family in which one of the spouses is gay or lesbian and then to acknowledge that these tragedies result from entrenched assumptions that need to be reexamined in the light of scientific research and real life experience.

Reading *Left in His Closet* can open such a dialogue by demonstrating that the same either/or thinking that permeates much of Western thinking—black or white, rich or poor, Republican or Democrat, gay or straight—also makes it difficult for people to comprehend the experience of women and men after their spouse reveals that they are homosexual. By engendering a deeper understanding of the experience of straight spouses caught in the crosshairs of antigay attitudes and silencing norms of the larger society, it might lead to dialogue and action, both public and private, toward achieving equality across the spectrum of sexuality and marriage as we enter the second decade of this new century.

Readers Guide to

Left in His Closet

By: Mary A. Krome, Ph.D.

Cast of Characters

Judy Clark: sixty-six-year-old Professor of Sociology, married in 1965, divorced in 1985

> Children: Kim and Jerry, born in 1967
>
> Judy's Companion: Paul
>
> Gay Ex-husband: Pete, now with his lover Jeffrey
>
> Parents: Edna and George

Soledad: fifty-year-old journalist and song writer, married in 1983, divorced in 1997

> Ex-in-laws: Barb, Kenny, and Kenny's wife, Susan
>
> Gay Ex-husband: Bob, now with his lover William
>
> Soledad's Companions: Jay, Theo, Bill.

Nita: thirty-one-year-old student, married twice

> Family: Ana and Carlos, parents; Jose, son; Nikki and Ned, siblings
>
> Gay Ex-husband: Jim, married 1998, divorced, 2003
>
> Second Husband: Eric Higgins, married 2004
>
> Film Professor: Douglas

Discussion Questions

The novel opens with the introduction of three women from the perspective of a brother-in-law, father, and son. How is the relationship of these three men to Soledad, Nita, and Judy affected by the discovery of their brother, son-in-law, and father's sexual orientation?

Discussion questions for Nita

Nita tries to engage her parents in a discussion of her marriage to a gay man. What is keeping Ana from reading her daughter's film critique? Why is Carlos hiding at the top of the stairs?

What reasons, other than the lack of support of her parents, does Nita have for marrying a man twice her age a little more than a year after her divorce from Jim?

Nita withdraws her son from preschool after seeing the priest about an annulment. Do you think the marriage covenant broken or never existed?

Nita finds herself uncontrollably drawn to sexual encounters with the opposite sex. Do you agree with Betty that Nita is a whore? How do you explain her sexual interest in men?

When Jim comes home to Nita with divorce papers, why does he blame her for mental cruelty instead of telling her that he was gay? In what other ways does Jim betray her?

Do you think he does it because he is gay or because he is a cruel person?

When Nita's parents finally recognize her problems are caused, in part, by their lack of support, Carlos asks Ana, *How can I help her when I'm ashamed of what happened to her?* Why is he ashamed?

In Nita's interview with Douglas, he tells her of his experience as an ex-spouse of a lesbian. What are the similarities and difference between his experience and that of the three women in the book?

Discussion questions for Soledad

Both Soledad and Nita are faced with family members who want them to try harder to save their marriage. Do you agree with Soledad's decision not to tell her sister-in-law, Barb, the reason for her divorce?

At Susan's birthday, Soledad is confronted by her ex-father-in-law's *hope of bringing her back into the story in order to change the facts* and the gossip of her friends about their recent discovery of Bob's sexual orientation. In what ways do the people closest to her add to her burden of *making sense of her life with Bob without all the relevant facts?*

Soledad runs into an old family friend, Susan, at a beach front bar in Barcelona and is annoyed when Susan, asks "What makes a guy gay?" Why do you think Susan is questioning Soledad about Bob's sexual orientation instead of asking Bob?

Throughout the book, Soledad suggests that Bob was a good husband in every sense of the word. Do you agree with her ex-boyfriend, Bill, when he tells her at the Water Fire that she is fooling herself?

When Soledad is in the Alaskan wilderness, she makes up a story about her life with Bob. Why do you think she told Nick and Abby that she was responsible for the breakup of her relationship with Bob?

When Theo discovers that Soledad's husband isn't dead, she tells him, *"I'm not sorry you thought Bob was dead. I wish you still did."* What advantages are there for Soledad in having others believe her ex-husband is dead?

Soledad gets a call from ex-brother-in-law, Kenny, about the death of her ex-father-in-law. How would you feel about going to the funeral? How would you feel about meeting Bob's gay partner, William?

Discussion quetions for Judy

Judy's research focuses on families of gay people, yet Soledad believes that her research is about gay and lesbian issues. Why do you think that Soledad believes Judy is a lesbian?

Throughout the book, Jerry suggests that Judy's research is making a spectacle of their family life. Do you agree with Jerry that someone's homosexual lifestyle is a private matter that should remain private? What value, if any, is there in Judy's research for her children?

During dinner in Grand Cayman, Kim presents her mother with her spectrum of sexuality theory. Do you think it is possible for an event, like puberty or a mid-life crisis, to alter someone's sexuality orientation?

Jerry is upset with Judy when he discovers twenty years after the divorce that his father is gay. Do you think he is angry because his father is gay or because his mother kept it from him for twenty years?

When Judy and Pete discuss their children's reaction to his impending marriage to Jeffrey, Judy tells Pete that *Jerry is not ready to accept his life with Jeffrey without feeling he is betraying her.* Do you think that accepting a gay parent's lifestyle is a betrayal to the straight parent?

When is the best time to tell a child that they have a gay parent? What issues do you have to consider when you tell them?

Judy's year long affair with Paul helps her realize how much of herself she has given up in order to keep Pete's lifestyle a secret. What factors, other than her children, may have caused her to let Paul go and return to her sham of a marriage?

Judy and Soledad have shared many stories about their lives during their five year friendship, but have kept the circumstances of their marriage and divorce from each other. Similarly, Nita's brother doesn't know that Nita's ex-husband is gay. What is it about having a gay ex-husband that causes these women to keep their married life in the closet?

A participant at the Grand Cayman conference states, *You're well on your way through the lack of support stage.* What can you do to be more supportive to family and friends who have had this experience?

How has your perspective of what straight spouses go through and need when their partner announces they are gay changed after reading this book?

Acknowledgements

I had no idea the journey that lay ahead of me when I began writing *Left in His Closet* or the many people I would encounter who gave me encouragement, advice, compassion, support, and friendship.

This novel was inspired more by what is absent from rather than what has been written about the topic. Judging from libraries and bookstore shelves, it seems as if the focus of fiction and non-fiction has been on issues related to the gay and lesbian experience including: identity struggles during the coming out, stigma attached to their sexual orientation, practical concerns about their gay lifestyle, and the recent moral and political debate about same-sex partnerships. Little, however, has been written about the parallel experience of straight spouses when their gay partners come out of the closet.

There was one book, *The Other Side of the Closet,* that spoke to me a long time ago of the straight spouse experience. The leadership and courage of its author and founder of *The Straight Spouse Network,* Amity Pierce Buxton, in providing a realistic portrayal of the experience was an inspiration to me at a very difficult time in my life. I am immensely grateful to her for her seminal work and writing the afterword to this novel.

Inspiration for this book also came from the misperceptions people have of the experience for partners of gays and lesbians who come out of the closet. Most do not recognize that straight partners also struggle with similar identity issues, practical concerns, and reactions of family and friends as they try to make sense of their relationship with their gay spouse. Many people do not view the experience as a severing of deep emotional bonds, beliefs about reality, sexual relationships, and close family ties that straight spouses developed during their marriage. Still others are unaware of the inadequate support for addressing the confusion and raw emotion that arise as we are drawn into a political and moral debate about a controversial reality of our time.

Most importantly, inspiration for this book came from my common bond with straight partners of men and women who lived in and came out of the closet. They are the true heroes of this book. My heartfelt appreciation is graciously extended to the many men and women who shared their stories with me over the years. Their names are not mentioned here because many of them still wish to keep their personal situation private.

There were many others who made indispensible contributions as I wrote for months into the wee hours of the morning. The enthusiasm my friend and children's book author, Florence Parry Heide, has about writing incited me to begin this novel. Mimi Yang, Brigitte Crepin, Steven Tegu, Brent McClintock, and Donna Howell served as sounding boards for my ideas. Charlene Blockinger, Sharon Peters, Sandy Hub, Joe Garcia, and Jeff Berkson gave me feedback on early drafts of the manuscript. Robert Rosen gave me helpful tips on the publishing process. Many other people I met on this journey gave me confidence in the mass appeal of this book. My friends at the Unicorn Café, colleagues at Carthage College, Rich and Peg Baron, Carl Krome, and the Cassity family gave me much needed solitude and support while reaching out to check on my progress.

I am thankful to Donna Chumley for recognizing the value of this story and to my editor, Angela Faulkner, for her keen eye, thoughtful comments, and enthusiasm about the story. I would also like to extend my heartfelt thanks to Edward Arents and Judy Gillmore for proofreading the final manuscript.

Most importantly is my deep gratitude for the values that have been passed on to me by my parents. My father, Edmund Krome, lived in the spirit of cherishing the good in every person even if he didn't agree with them. I learned from my mother, Lorraine Krome, the importance of continuously challenging the prevailing opinions of those around us. There is no better gift to pass on from generation to generation than extending our love to all of God's creatures by questioning our biases.

About the Author

Dr. Mary Krome received her Ph.D. from the University of Virginia in 2003, an M.M. from Northwestern University's J. L. Kellogg Graduate School of Business in 1990, and a B.A. magna cum laude from Loyola University of Chicago. Her award-winning research focuses on leveraging diversity through intergroup relations and processes that address identity, behavioral, and perspective differences. She was awarded the George Harvey Award for Outstanding Dissertation Thesis on Diversity, sponsored by the SEI Center for Advanced Studies in Management at the University of Pennsylvania's Wharton Graduate School of Business in 2003. She was commissioned a Kentucky Colonel in 1989 for her work with science educators. Last year, her newspaper column in the Kenosha News and her election series on the economy led to interviews on WGTD, an NPR affiliate, and Wisconsin Eye. She founded the Worldwide Advanced Education Association that develops learning partnerships and training opportunities between universities and professional organizations. She is a member of the Society for Cross-Cultural Research, International Association of Conflict Management, Society for Personality and Social Psychology, Society of Business Ethics, Academy of Management, Academy of International Business, National Organization of Women Business Owners, and the Straight Spouse Network. She has written a book of poetry and is working on her second novel.